TWILIGHT MANOR

(The Village)

by

Charles A. Beckett

Order this book online at www.trafford.com
or email orders@trafford.com

Most Trafford titles are also available at major online book retailers.

Note for Librarians: A cataloguing record for this book is available from Library and Archives Canada at www.collectionscanada.ca/amicus/index-e.html

Printed in Victoria, BC, Canada.

ISBN: 978-1-4269-0577-3 (sc)
ISBN: 978-1-4269-0578-0 (dj)

Our mission is to efficiently provide the world's finest, most comprehensive book publishing service, enabling every author to experience success. To find out how to publish your book, your way, and have it available worldwide, visit us online at www.trafford.com

Trafford rev. 8/4/2009

www.trafford.com

North America & international
toll-free: 1 888 232 4444 (USA & Canada)
phone: 250 383 6864 • fax: 250 383 6804

Also by Charles A. Beckett

Push the Rain Away (2007)

With love and gratitude to my children--Steve, who with hardware and patience brought me into the computer age; Al, who was my technical right hand during the publishing process; and Sandy, who was there for me when I needed someone to be there for me. Together they made it possible for me to move seamlessly and gracefully into my twilight years. Without them this book would not have been published.

Chapter One

LIFE

EMMY SAT AT her kitchen table staring unseeingly at the half empty tea cup before her. She was deep in thought about life, which she felt had passed her by. In her youth, she had been a promising dancer. Her mother had seen to it that she had lessons--contemporary, acrobatic, and even a year or so of ballet. She had never cared for ballet--too structured and too much discipline involved. And besides, it made her toes hurt. She preferred the more free style dancing as glamorized by Fred Astaire and Ginger Rogers in their movies. They had been her role models, especially Ginger, whom she tried to emulate--with limited success. She especially marveled at Rogers' ability to gracefully match each move of Astaire's, step for step--in reverse.

While in college, Emmy had accepted invitations to several fraternity house parties when she heard they had music and dancing. She soon discovered that some of the frat boys' interpretation of what the word dancing meant differed from hers. But, she continued to go anyway. She was tall, slender, poised, and, with her flawless complexion, classic features, and blonde hair pulled back into a ponytail, she was well aware that she could be seen as a worthy trophy for some frat boy's reputation. Although most of the young men were basically nice when forced to be, they still had reputations to uphold in front of their peers. But, Emmy quickly learned to deflect their crude advances with humor and intelligence. And, the parties did give her an opportunity to dance to some good music, sometimes played by a live band the fraternity had hired. But, once the word got around that all she was interested in was dancing, she was seldom invited to any more social events.

Emmy's life had been a happy one. Shortly into her junior year of college, her roommate, Susie Straussman, told her the New York City Music Hall Rockettes were going to have open auditions for dancers. It had long been a dream of Susie's to become a Rockette, and now she saw a chance to fulfill that dream. Susie persuaded Emmy to try out too, and she reluctantly accompanied her to the audition. Although Susie was not selected, Emmy was. She worked long, hard hours mastering the rhythm, routines, choreography, and discipline required to remain in the reserve dancers group. After a year, she was promoted to the performing line, where she became a primary member of the chorus. To Emmy, life was good and the future seemed to hold unlimited possibilities.

While on a trip to Albany with another dancer, their car was broadsided by a commercial vehicle when it ran a red light. The other girl sustained only minor injuries, but Emmy's left leg was broken in two places. The initial diagnosis was that it would have to be amputated above the knee. Emmy rejected this medical opinion and when told she would probably die if surgery was not performed, she said, "Well, then, I guess I'll just have to die, but I refuse to let you take my leg." Another orthopedic specialist was called in for consultation. After reviewing the X-rays, and a lengthy examination, he told Emmy he would attempt to repair her leg, but could make no promises--that chances for success were, at best, only about twenty percent. Without hesitation, Emmy, forcing a smile, replied, "I'll accept those odds."

Surgery was scheduled and the operation was performed. The surgical team worked four hours in their attempt to repair her mangled limb. The lead surgeon implanted two long steel rods in her thigh, removing much of the bone they replaced. When Emmy awoke in the recovery room, she was greeted by the face of a man dressed in green, smiling down at her. Her heart pounded. Could she feel her leg? She wasn't sure. And she was too weak to raise her head to look. Calmly, the doctor told her that her leg had been saved, but with bone removal, it would be an inch shorter than the other one. She was momentarily elated, and then realized that her dancing career was over. Her perfect life had just made an abrupt and unexpected U-turn.

When released from the hospital, Emmy returned to her parent's home, depressed and insecure about the future. To help rid her mind of negative thoughts, her mother convinced her she should return to college and complete her degree requirements. Although she had almost constant pain in her repaired leg, she threw herself into her studies, taking courses she still needed to earn a bachelor's degree in social science. In addition, she took elective classes in music--voice and piano, excelling in both, which gave her a degree of confidence about the future.

Once Emmy became a college graduate, the question again arose as to what she was going to do with the rest of her life. As an interim, she put a notice on a supermarket bulletin board offering piano lessons in her--that is--her parent's home. Several weeks passed before she received her first telephone call--from the mother of a twelve year old girl--inquiring about lessons. She had her first student. If nothing else, her stay in the hospital and six months of painful physical therapy had taught her patience, which helped her tolerate the obvious lack of interest and talent shown by the girl. Through word of mouth, Emmy obtained three more students for twice weekly lessons, not enough money to move into her own apartment, but it was a beginning. She still had too much idle time on her hands to prevent her from occasionally falling into moods of depression. To take her mind off her personal problems, she volunteered as a telephone contact representative in the family waiting room at the hospital where she had been a patient. She was good with people, and, with her own hospital experiences, was able to empathize with the families and friends of surgical patients.

Three months later, the hospital business office needed to fill a vacancy. Emmy had become popular with the hospital administrative staff and medical personnel. As a result, she was offered a part time clerical position in the office while they recruited for an accountant. It would be a paid position. Emmy quickly accepted. A month later, after the new employee had been hired, Emmy was retained in a full time position, to help her get settled in.

While working at the hospital during the day, Emmy continued to give piano lessons evenings and on weekends. She no longer thought much about her medical misfortune, instead concentrating her attentions on her dual careers. The music lessons continued to take up more of her time. Even with two sources of income, she still was not making enough money to move out of her parent's home. One day, during her lunch break at the hospital, Emmy noticed an ad in a newspaper for a part time assistant instructor at a dance school. She called and made an appointment for an interview. The interview went well, but Emmy felt obligated to explain her leg problem. Reluctantly, she admitted, "I'd like the job, but I need to tell you that I have a bad leg and wear an orthopedic lift in one shoe--and there are just some physical things I can't do."

The studio owner nodded and smiled. "I appreciate you telling me, but I'm not hiring you for your feet. I'm more interested in your head. I can demonstrate the steps to the students and do the choreography, but I need someone who can explain the movements, position students in their stances, and encourage them in their performance. I noticed on your resume that in addition to your background in dance, you also play the piano. That's another talent I can use. I believe you're the right person for the job. All I need to know is if you want it, and if you can work from six to nine PM three days a week, and eight hours on Saturday."

Emmy was elated. "I want the job. And the hours are fine. When would you like me to start?"

"Is tomorrow too soon?"

"No. That's fine. I'll see you tomorrow at six. Oh--and thank you!"

Emmy left the studio with a sense of relief. She would be able to mesh her two jobs without any overlap or conflict. And the extra money would come in handy to build a nest egg for the future. Best of all, now she could give up her piano teaching, which she had never much cared for anyway. The world was looking bright again. She remembered a saying of Alexander Graham Bell's, "When one door closes, another one opens." She vowed never again to look back at any door that closed for her, but to concentrate on the future and potentially opening doors.

With her busy work schedule, Emmy had little time for a social life, or even an opportunity for meeting someone. There was, however, one man who was showing some interest in her and stopped to chat whenever their paths crossed. He was an X-ray technician at the hospital. Like her, he had a friendly personality and an easy smile; and he didn't seem to notice her limp, or, if he did, he didn't mention it. He invited Emmy out to dinner and she accepted, although somewhat hesitantly. With their different work schedules, they were not able to spend much time together, but their friendship showed signs of blossoming into a romance. This frightened her somewhat. What would any man want with a crippled thirty eight year old woman, whose only experience with men was a brief and stressful relationship in college? Fortunately, before this question needed to be answered, a floor nurse Emmy occasionally had lunch with informed her that her new friend was well known among the nursing staff as a womanizer. Worse, he was a married womanizer. Emmy felt another door close. She found it difficult to trust any man after that--not that she had much opportunity, at the time, to form a relationship with anyone else. She continued to immerse herself in her work, and gave little thought to the opposite sex. Although, she had to admit that she would have liked to become a wife and mother. But, as she approached forty, in her opinion, time was robbing her of both those opportunities.

The years passed. The dance studio closed and the hospital eliminated her position in an economic scale down. Two more doors had closed--with no potential opening ones in sight.

Then, unexpectedly, another door did open. A law suit she had brought against the company whose truck caused her injury had languished in the courts so long that Emmy had forgotten about it. Then, to her surprise, she received a telephone call from the lawyer who had initially handled her case on a contingency basis. He had good news. The courts had awarded her a sizeable settlement--more money than she could earn in a lifetime. She was speechless and her heart felt like it would leap from her body. After the legal details of the financial arrangement were completed, she moved from her parent's home into an apartment downtown. Finally, she was on her own. Her future was still uncertain, but at least, financially, it was secured.

Chapter 2

A NEW LIFE

FOR SOME TIME, Emmy had been unhappy with her living arrangements. Her second floor apartment faced a major city street, with its unwelcome noise from fire engine and ambulance sirens, and the steady drone of bus, truck and automobile tires on the pavement below. Even on nice days, she was forced to keep her windows closed to keep out the smell of diesel fume emissions from a seemingly endless stream of buses. These intrusions to her peace were made even worse by the bright lights from the never sleeping boulevard, which forced their way through the slats of her window's blinds. Many nights, when all else failed her in efforts to sleep, she resorted to a sleep mask and ear plugs. Traffic had continued to become heavier and parking availability around her building scarcer. She had looked at other apartments. They had been either too large, too noisy, or, because of her inherited frugal nature, more than she was willing to pay. Not being one to make hasty decisions, she reluctantly decided to continue to tolerate her current living conditions.

Emmy fixed herself a second cup of tea and began thumbing through the newspaper as was her regular morning ritual. Her attention was drawn to a small ad in the corner of a page of the classified section.

"Unhappy with urban living? Fifty five or better? The Village at Twilight Manor may be right for you. A rural retirement community for active seniors. Nestled in a meadowland seven miles from the picturesque town of Braxton Falls. Scenic view of a mountain range in the distance. For more information call 1-800-Twilite."

For some unknown reason, she decided to save the ad, cutting it out and attaching it to her refrigerator door with a decorative magnet. There it remained, until three weeks.later, when Emmy received a form letter from the apartment management. Beginning the following month, her rent was to be increased fifteen percent to cover increased costs of operating and maintaining the building. This news provoked her to action. Removing the curling, almost forgotten ad from the refrigerator, she dialed the number listed. She was greeted by a pleasant voice saying, "Twilight Manor Village." Emmy was surprised to find she was connected to a real person, instead of an electronic device spitting out a list of numbered menu options from which to make a selection.

"Hello? Yes," Emmy said hesitantly. "I recently noticed your ad in the Daily Globe and would like some information about your facility."

"Certainly. It would be my pleasure," the pleasant voice assured her. "Do you have any specific questions or would you prefer I explain our features in general terms?"

"In general, please," Emmy replied.

"Certainly. As you already know from our ad, we are located in a country-like setting near the town of Braxton Falls. Basically, we offer three floor plans--alcove apartments, one bedroom apartments and two bedroom deluxe apartments. Some of our amenities include a fitness center, indoor pool, hot tub, nine hole golf course with putting green, tennis courts, complimentary laundry facilities, cable TV . . ." The pleasant voice took a breath, then continued, "library, styling salon, reserved parking, and scheduled transportation to and from town for those who prefer not to maintain a car. Lunch and dinner are served daily in our comfortable, well appointed dining room--and breakfast is available in our cheery breakfast nook. We also provide optional weekly maid and linen service." Another breath. "And, all utilities are covered, except for your telephone. Do you have any questions, or is there anything else I can tell you?" the pleasant voice asked.

"I can't think of anything, uh, at the moment," Emmy said, her brow knitting in an unsuccessful attempt to conjure something up.

"I would be pleased to send you some detailed literature," the pleasant voice offered.

"Yes. Please!" Emmy gave her name and address.

"I'll send that out to you right away. Thank you for your interest. Have a pleasant day," the pleasant voice replied in a convincingly sincere tone.

"Thank you," Emmy said, and hung up the phone, wondering if she had been too impulsive. But, she decided, she had not, since merely asking for information did not obligate her to any action.

Two days later, a large, colorful envelope arrived, bearing the Twilight Manor return address. Emmy hurriedly opened it. Inside was a glossy, tri-fold brochure with pictures of some smiling people, obviously enjoying recreational activities--tennis, golf and dancing. Inside the fold was pictured an attractive silver haired couple, hand-in-hand, gazing lovingly at each other, while walking down a serpentine pathway toward a white gazebo near an azure blue lake. A separate, single page flyer provided diagrams of the various floor plans, prices and related information. Emmy was pleased to learn that Twilight Manor had no buy-in costs or contractual requirements. Residents paid monthly and were free to leave at anytime, after one month's advance notice. The monthly rates at Twilight Manor were not much more than she would be paying for her present apartment after the rent increase.

And Emmy had practically no amenities where she now lived, other than an aging and poorly maintained rooftop swimming pool, which she never used.

Since her accident, Emmy had gradually grown more reclusive and not given to making impulsive decisions--or, for that matter, any decisions, if she could avoid it. This was just the opposite of her philosophy of life before the accident. She had been adventuresome in her "live forever" youth. Her motto had been "nothing ventured, nothing gained." But, those days were long behind her. She had gradually retreated into a safer and less optimistic attitude toward life as a result of self-consciousness about what she felt was her awkward way of walking and her occasional unsteadiness. She felt that people were staring at her and judging her to be less than a complete person. However, it was rare that anyone even noticed her slightly limping gait or occasional stumble.

In spite of her cautious nature, she rationalized that there was nothing stopping her from investigating a possible change in lifestyle. What did she have now? She lived alone. Her only living relative was her sister Lorraine Stratton Patric, who, during their childhood had condensed Emmy's name, Mary Elizabeth, into her initials. Lorraine lived in Boston with her husband, Philip, and their daughter, Christine—better known as Chris--who attended Boston University.

Emmy's sister was her junior by two years. Growing up, they had been close. But, once Lorraine married, moved to Massachusetts and started a family, the two seldom saw each other, except for rare visits Emmy made east during holidays. They did, however, keep in touch regularly by telephone.

Emmy had no male friends, having discouraged and avoided suitors after the accident, ashamed of what she considered her mutilated body, which consisted merely of two vertical scars on the thigh of her damaged leg and a one inch reduction in its length. Outside of her sister's family, there was only Sally, a former co-worker from her hospital days, whom she considered more an acquaintance than a friend. At best, they met once or twice a month for lunch. Financially, Emmy had no concerns. She had always lived conservatively, accumulating a modest amount of savings during her years as a dancer, music teacher and hospital worker. Although her small nest egg had dwindled over time, it had later been nicely augmented by a generous insurance settlement from the corporation judged responsible for her accident.

Emmy's instincts convinced her that the timing was right. She had turned fifty six the previous month, and had no responsibilities or commitments to anyone or anything. Her time was her own. Without hesitation, she picked up the phone and once again dialed Twilight Manor's number. Her call was again answered by the same pleasant voice she had talked to previously. Emmy made arrangements to visit the community for a tour and weekend stay over. This was definitely untypical of her, she kept telling herself. But, a small part of her former independent spirit of adventure remained deep within her and occasionally surfaced when least expected. This was one of those occasions.

The next day, Emmy awoke alert and eager. The morning was sunny and clear. "A good day for a drive," she voiced. She showered, dressed, and put on her face--as she called it--although she had never worn much makeup, except during her Rockette dancing days. She did not need makeup, just a touch of lipstick for color. Her pale skin still was flawless, except for a hint of crow's feet beginning to form at the outer edges of her eyes, and one or two barely visible spider web thin lines across her high forehead. Her encroaching gray hair blended so well with her natural blondness, it was practically unnoticeable.

She had her usual breakfast--a cup of tea, toast and orange marmalade. Whenever she had been teased about her light eating habits, she would laughingly counter with, "I have to watch my girlish figure, you know."

Emmy had always been naturally thin and had never had weight problems, no matter what or how much she ate. She had been the envy of her former co-workers and girlfriends, who seemed constantly to be on one diet or another. And, her willowy, but shapely figure had not been overlooked by quite a few young men during her college days. Her weight had only increased seven pounds since she quit dancing. She was unaware of what a strikingly attractive woman she was. When anyone complimented her on her figure or her looks, she would thank them, but immediately dismiss the comments as simply flattery--or worse, pity.

With a feeling of nervous anticipation, Emmy pointed her sky blue Volkswagen Beetle west, toward a new, and hopefully, successful adventure.

"We'll see," she said. Having lived alone so long, she had gotten in the habit of talking to herself, or as she referred to it, "thinking out loud."

Her little car rolled smoothly over the well paved road surface. She sang along with the radio, her trained alto voice in tune with the music. Once on the highway, the fact she had a long drive ahead of her did not faze her in the slightest. The sun was shining, the air was fresh and the sky was clear. This was a new day, and unsuspected by her at the time, was about to become the beginning of a new life.

Approaching a roadside sign that read "Braxton Falls 7 miles," she knew she was almost to her destination. She soon entered and quickly exited the town of small stores and clapboard houses. Not long afterward, she turned right, onto blacktopped Junction TT. She followed it to and through a once red, but now faded and paint peeling, covered one lane bridge spanning a dry creek bed. At the top of the next rise, she saw it--a large, square fortress looking structure. Coming closer, she could see that it was a two story stone and brick building. Approaching a sign reading simply "Office," she pulled her car into a visitor parking space and turned off the engine. Exhaling, she said, "Well, here I am. Now what?"

Chapter 3

MYSTERY OF HISTORY

THE VILLAGE OF Twilight Manor had not always been a community for active seniors. It was originally built and served for an unknown period of time as a convent--the cloistered home of the Little Sisters of Mercy religious order. It had been constructed on the high point of a forty acre rolling meadow and adjacent woods as a square stone and brick building, surrounding an open courtyard in the fashion of a college quadrangle. Townsfolk referred to it as "the square donut." Records relating to the property and its inhabitants had been lost in a county courthouse fire many years ago. There were no existing records of when the imposing structure was built, how long the sisters had inhabited it, why it had been located where it was, when and why it had been abandoned, or where the original occupants had gone--leaving it to deteriorate in its emptiness. The only history available was oral recollections of the few remaining residents of nearby Braxton Falls old enough to still have vague memories of its existence, or who had had stories passed down to them about the location's life as a convent. Much or most of this history was questionable--at best. Stories seemed to change, depending on who was telling them and the current state of the tellers' fading memories. Apparently, the convent had preceded the incorporation of Braxton Falls by many years, during a time when the area around it was dotted by small farms. During the Great Depression, most local tillers of the soil had been forced to give up their land for economic reasons.

One theory as to why residents of the order left their home was that they had gone to minister to victims of a plague in the east and had never returned, possibly succumbing to the disease, themselves. Another popular story was that, being so remote, the convent attracted very few new novitiates, causing the order to eventually die out from natural attrition. Still another version was that a two year drought in the area produced grape crop failure. Since the producing and selling of wine was believed to have been the main source of income for the order, the sisters could no longer afford to live isolated from the outside world. One teller even claimed there was an unmarked graveyard on the property--although none had ever been found. In all probability, no one had ever bothered to look for it. Another storyteller claimed the nuns had not only been known for their production of quality wine, but also for the uniform and sturdy arbors on which the grapes had been grown. No one seemed to know or remember the label under which the wine produced, if there was one, had been marketed. Although there had been no grape arbors found, it may simply have been, again, that no one had taken the time or trouble to look for them. There was, however, some minimal evidence to support the wine theory, inasmuch as a wine cellar had been discovered in the sub-level of one of the wings of the building by the developers of Twilight Manor. During renovation of the building, the cellar was left intact and remains to this day beneath an apartment in C wing, and is used for general storage. Depending on the weather, some residents of the Village claim to be able to detect a faint aroma of wine wafting up from the inside stairway that leads to the entrance of the cellar. As the living histories died, their stories passed with them and were quickly replaced by speculation and rumors. One of the more sensational rumors which circulated was that in the 1920s or 30s, a well known prohibition era bootlegger and his gang had used the building as a hideout and storage site for their products. They were eventually discovered, and in the ensuing gun battle with law enforcement officers, all of the gang members were either killed or captured and sent to prison. No verification of this story could be found in any newspapers of the time. Another rumor--as could be expected--was that the facility was built by space aliens who had found the adjoining meadow an ideal landing site for their flying saucers, with the woods providing effective concealment for their spacecraft. As time passed, stories as to the mysterious disappearance--without a trace--of the nuns from their Eden continued to become even more imaginative, even resulting in a parlor game of sorts by the residents, which they named "Nun Left." There had even arisen a theory that supernatural forces had come to play in the disappearance of the sisters, and that they had been beamed up by the aliens to their spaceship and taken away. One history minded resident even compared the members of the order's disappearance to those of the Aztecs from Machu Piccu in Peru, the Anasazi Indians from the cliff dwellings of Colorado and New Mexico, and the pilgrims from Jamestown. The more conservative theories advanced were that members of the order probably left for financial or physical reasons. Or, perhaps, the Church had simply moved the nuns to a more convenient, less rural area. If nothing else, the rumors gave those residents of the Village, who were so inclined, something to ponder during their pondering moments. And, of course, there was a stalwart group who refused to become involved in the debate at all, claiming it was all just silly speculation and what difference did it make, anyway? Their attitude was that Twilight Manor is what it is, and who cares what it was!

One curious resident of Braxton Falls, prior to the development of the site as Twilight Manor, searched the grounds and surrounding area with a portable metal detector. He was rewarded with nothing more than a few modern era coins, buttons, hair pins and a variety of other small, metal objects.

The actual number of years the premises remained unoccupied is still open to question. During its absence of residents, the site of the former convent remained an idyllic country setting, with its lush landscape and small lake that rose and fell subject to the generosity or stinginess of Mother Nature. To the near east lies an orchard of sturdy oak trees and a variety of other smaller, leafy interlopers. In the distance, to the northeast, a shadowy mountain range is visible on the horizon. Town locals dubbed this sight Ghost Mountain, as a result of its otherworldly pale grayness.

Junction TT runs off of county highway 342 to the convent--and ends there. After disappearance of the nuns, the location was discovered by the young people of Braxton Falls and other nearby small towns. It became attractive to them as a place for their courting rituals--until the Highway Patrol began routinely visiting it.

The area's evolvement from a convent to the Village of Twilight Manor came about partly by accident and partly by circumstance. Two out of state tourists, Ray and Faye Kimmerman, who were visiting Braxton Falls during its annual flea market festival, on leaving town, took a wrong turn, finding themselves on Junction TT, heading toward the former convent. Arriving within sight of the silhouetted structure, Ray, a building contractor, remarked to his wife that this would be an ideal location for commercial development. Faye, the more practical of the two, told him that in her opinion, the quiet, out of the way location was too far from any large population centers to do well as a shopping mall, office or industrial complex. She suggested, instead, that its secluded and peaceful setting would be better suited to a place for active, older people to retire and enjoy their golden years, away from the overdeveloped senior citizen communities so common in the south and far west. She was quick to add that from the look of neglect of the building and the wild growth of vegetation that surrounded it, the building had obviously sat vacant for a considerable period of time. She felt the property, if for sale, would probably be reasonably priced. She also reminded her husband that, in a few years, they would likely be looking for a place to retire, in a similar setting. Respecting his wife's instincts and reasoning, Ray, after returning to highway 342, turned west, back toward Braxton Falls, instead of east toward home.

Upon arriving back in town, Ray looked up real estate agents in a local telephone directory and began calling them until he found one who seemed familiar with the property. The realtor told him that the building and forty acres of surrounding countryside had been abandoned for at least twenty five years--which was how long he had lived in the area. There had never been any serious interest expressed--in Braxton Falls or any of the other nearby small towns in the area--in buying the building and acreage since no one had ever come up with any workable ideas for putting the property to practical use.

The realtor told the couple about the courthouse fire and the property's deed and all other legal and financial records relating to it having been destroyed. Braxton Falls, the nearest town, had unhappily assumed ownership by default of what was considered an albatross around its neck, since the property was neither saleable nor tax producing. When told the entire site was available for back taxes, Ray and Kaye paid a hurried visit to the town hall and talked to the assessor. Upon being told how reasonable the back taxes were, Ray had only one question, "Where do I sign?" After the legal details had been taken care of, the Timmerman's became the new owners of the old convent building and its grounds.

When residents of Baxter Falls got word of the purchase of the old convent property by some crazy eastern big city fella, their consensus was that this had been a mistake waiting to happen. However, to Ray and Faye, it had been an opportunity too good to pass up. So, a wrong turn and the germ of an idea resulted in the present Village of Twilight Manor. To some skeptics, finding the ideal location for Twilight Manor had just been a matter of a lucky coincidence. The Timmerman's belief was that coincidence was merely fate in disguise. Several years later, Ray sold his construction business and he and Faye became full time residents and managers of the property they had bought and developed into a tranquil and successful retirement community.

Chapter 4

RESIDENTS

TWILIGHT MANOR IS more than a community of seasoned citizens. It is a composite of its residents, who range in age from fifty five to ninety three. It is a welcome retreat from the frantic pace and demands of the outside world. Whatever its true history, the Village is an ideal place to enjoy one's middle and golden years. A quiet sense of peace and serenity pervades the complex. The oldest resident is a spry woman just turned ninety three. She is a retired school teacher. In her younger days, she and her now deceased husband traveled the length and breadth of America and Canada, and much of the world beyond. A personal joke between them had been that one day they would venture to the South Pole. Their explanation for not doing so was that they had to work for a living and did not have the time. Mildred O'Neill Mitchell, or "Mom," as she is affectionately known to the other residents, still possesses a sharp mind and clear recollections of her earlier years. She captivates her younger audiences with tales of travel adventures she and her husband experienced. Though widowed for thirty seven years, when she speaks of her husband, their love for each other and their lives together, the years fade from her weathered face as it softens and brightens. Like Mom, each of the other residents are living histories of this century and the one recently passed, with interesting stories to tell--some sweet, some bitter, others a mixture of both.

Women comprise the majority of the Village's population. Many are widows, some burying more than one husband due to age, infirmity or fruitless wars. Others have been divorced, and a fair number had never entered the sanctity of matrimony. Just less than thirty percent of the population consists of married couples. The remainder of the population is comprised of single or widowed men. But, one thing all members of the community share in common is that once they had been young, productive members of a society that, in their minds, had seemed to change all too quickly and become increasingly complex and challenging. Most miss the good old days, although truth be told, when pressed, many would admit that those times were probably not quite as good as remembered. A blessing of aging for some residents is that, with selective memories, the good times continue to grow in clarity and many of the bad ones have mercifully faded into obscurity. And, a few residents remember events that never happened--their memories becoming the masters of reality. To many, in their youth, life had seemed everlasting. With age, they have become aware of how much it still has to offer, what is still left to be done, and how limited the time is in which to do it. Some of them use the initialism TM not only as shorthand for Twilight Manor--but also for Time Remaining. Others choose simply to enjoy each new day as it comes, and find peace and contentment in listening to the singing of birds, viewing sunrises and sunsets, the strength of their religious beliefs, the beauty of the countryside, and being surrounded by friends who share common interests and histories.

Of the housing choices at the Village, many married couples prefer two bedroom apartments. In their later years, they have come to better appreciate the privacy of a room and a bed of their own--especially if one partner has a tendency to snore, monopolize bedcovers, or flail around in his or her sleep. Others simply enjoy the luxury of being able to read, listen to the radio or watch television late into the night without disturbing their less nocturnal partner.

Overall, the community provides a happy, stress free environment. The apartments are brightly decorated, well lit and provide two options for outside viewing. One option is a view of the well manicured inner quadrangle, with its bright flowers, well manicured hedges and other shrubbery, a pleasant patio area, and a Japanese rock garden--complete with waterfall. The other option provides a view of rolling green hills and meadows, dotted by groves of trees, clustered together like small armies of tall soldiers standing proudly at attention, their branches swaying rhythmically during windy days.

The Village has something for everyone. And, except for one resident, Mr. X, everyone actively takes advantage of one or more of the facility's wide variety of offerings.

Chapter 5

DOMINIC (MR. X)

DOMINIC XAVIER GRAYSTONE reluctantly opened one eye and was greeted by a sliver of sunlight penetrating it. He had obviously neglected to properly close the mini blinds on the window of his bedroom the night before. He was not a morning person and resented the unwelcome intrusion of daylight. He sat up slowly and heavily put his feet on the floor, trying to decide whether to arise further or let gravity pull him back down onto the bed. His bladder made the decision for him.

This was no life for a man of his stature, he reasoned, as he stumbled barefoot in the direction of the bathroom. Why, he had been a star on the silver screen in his time. Well, maybe not a star in the conventional definition of the word, but he had been a highly respected actor in films. Well, maybe not, he grudgingly admitted to himself, but he was a talented and capable journeyman character actor and had shared the screen with many highly respected Hollywood leading men. Oh, sure, he usually had got beaten up, or worse, at the hands of the main characters--but he died well. No one could dispute that.

As a young stuntman for Monolith Picture Studios, he had worked steadily until being seriously injured in a fall from an unfriendly horse. As he prepared to take his planned departure, his foot had become tangled in a stirrup and he was dragged on the ground until the horse tired of pulling his weight. Two crushed vertebrae and a pinched nerve in his back ended his stunt performing days. After he was released from the hospital, a sympathetic director hired him to fill a small roll in a picture he was making--one line of dialog in a gangster film. He remembered the line well. "Oh! You shot me!" It was difficult to admit to himself that his best acting seemed to have been built around his ability to die convincingly. His rugged Italian looks, coupled with a sinister scowl and broken nose, a souvenir another stunt man had given him when he forgot to duck, made him a natural for playing gangsters or other villainous types. His looks had type cast him early in his acting career.

Dominic had paid to see every movie he was in, to critique his acting, no matter how brief the part. And it was always a thrill to see his name in the cast credits, as they scrolled toward the end, where Frank Gray, his professional name, appeared--even though probably nobody knew that Frank Gray was really Dominic Graystone. The studio had changed it, as he was informed that ethnic names were not in vogue at the time. "What about Rudolph Valentino?" he had asked, a bit indignantly. He was told that there was always an exception to the rule, and that he was no Valentino. Secretly, he had fantasized that one day a moviegoer would recognize him from a film and ask for his autograph, but this was yet to happen. And, no one at Twilight Manor had recognized his name or his face. This was understandable. He rarely enjoyed a close-up shot and often the camera filmed him from the back or side, and many of his scenes, especially in film noirs, were darkly lit. His crowning achievement in motion pictures had been playing a liveried chauffer and sidekick to society detective Rance Merriwether, in the Mattingly Murder Mystery movie. He had even received a comment from the assistant director, "Well, at least the uniform fits you." He had considered that a compliment. His main responsibility to the role was to look tough and emote such memorable lines as, "There they go, boss," "What time do you want me to come back for you?" and, "Yes sir, Mr. Merriwether". He had more camera time on this picture than most of his others, since he appeared in every scene in which Merriwether needed to be driven somewhere. He had difficulty memorizing lines, so his dialog was mostly short and infrequent, and he spoke it in clipped east coast tones. He was usually chosen for roles more for his unique facial features and awkward mannerisms than for his talent, which he would never admit was minimal. Another director had once remarked that Dominic's voice reminded him of a young George Burns. He also had taken that for a compliment. But, in his favor, he had always been dedicated to his art. He was usually paid scale, and was never able to live the life style of mainstream character actors. But, it was a living and it paid the bills. Of his movie memorabilia, he was most proud of a colorful old lobby card for "Farewell my Lovely." He had kept it in a steamer trunk all these years. It showed him with hands raised and a startled look on his face, with Robert Mitchum, as private detective Philip Marlowe, pointing a pistol at him. He remembered that scene clearly and fondly. It had only required seven takes. By the time the director yelled "Cut. Print!" Dominic had a headache from the clicker board that preceded each take and his arms ached from holding them over his head. On the set he had even made a friend of sorts with a young actor about his age named Sylvester Stallone. Dominic often wondered whatever became of him. Fond memories, all. In the small print at the bottom of the card, if one looked closely enough, there was his name--not preceded by "co-starring," "with," or "also with," but simply "Frank Gray."

Dominic remembered that as a youngster someone had asked him how a fine Italian boy like him had a name like Graystone.

His father had been American, but his dear departed mother had been born and grew up in Sicily. Until her dying day, she hadn't managed to master the English language, but she was always able to make herself understood to him and his father, who had met and married her while he was stationed in Stressa, Italy with the United States Army after the war. His parents made an odd couple. His mother had been dark, short and round, with deep, piercing brown eyes. She wore her hair in a tightly wound bun at the back of her head. His father had been fair, tall and angular, with a large head, a low brow and pale blue eyes. Whenever he looked at his image in a mirror, which was usually only when shaving, Dominic decided that he had his father's head and his mother's dark eyes, chin and shortness of height. He had no idea from whom he had inherited his unusual mouth.

Dominic wondered what his parents had seen in each other. His mother probably had been pretty when she was young, although he didn't remember seeing any photographs of her in her youth. But, they had seemed happy together, from what Dominic could remember. They seldom argued, though his mother had had an easily ignitable temper. On the rare occasions his parents did have a disagreement, his mother's voice would rise to a soprano pitch that filled the room and beyond-- and her arms would flail around her head, doing a fair imitation of a symphony conductor waving his baton. She would spew out a barrage of words in excited Italian that neither he nor his father could understand. It probably was for the best, and possibly kept arguments from escalating.

While shaving, Dominic closely studied his face. With his heavy beard stubble, he looked even more sinister. Maybe he would stop shaving, he thought. It was a bother, anyway. He agreed with the mirror that he had a strong face, just ugly enough to be attractively interesting. His heavy lidded eyes always made him look as though he was plotting something evil—or about to doze off. He had a good mouth, but when he smiled, somehow it seemed to curl into a sneer. He had good teeth, although the upper ones had been straightened and capped at the insistence of a former director. But, he hadn't minded. The studio had been good to him. It was due to them that he was able to live at Twilight Manor. They paid his room and board and Actor's Equity provided him with a modest pension. It was enough to get by on, although he sometimes had to budget his money closely to make it last until the next month's check arrived. So, he couldn't complain--although he enjoyed any opportunity to do so. But, these days he had no one to complain to, since he didn't mix with the other residents who, unknown to him, referred to him as Mr. X.

Dominic had not made friends during his residency at Twilight Manor. Most of the residents were women and married couples. Oh, they were all nice enough to him, and smiled and said hello when he passed them in the hall or dining area. But, he had never been comfortable around women or strangers. He did not quite know what to say to them after "Hi," accompanied by his lopsided smile. And, he was no good at small talk and had cultivated very few social graces. Basically, he was a loner and a bumbler. This he readily admitted to himself. He was better at man talk. He missed his old cronies at the studio. Since most of his movie scenes only lasted from a few seconds to a few minutes, he had plenty of idle time to sit and chat with the other stuntmen and crew members. It was a challenge to see who could out lie and out brag the others about their virile and exciting lives and accomplishments. His group of comrades had referred to themselves as "The Liar's Club," of which he had become a member in good standing--although more as a listener than a talker.

After Dom, which was what his old friends at the studio had called him, finished his bathroom chores, he stumbled slowly into the living room and sank into his easy chair by the window. He felt that this would be a day like every other day, and muttered, "Oh, how the mighty have fallen." Where had he heard that? Was it a line from a movie he was in or had he read it somewhere?

He enjoyed reading, preferably novels with unhappy endings. He seemed to always be looking for things to depress him. Once he became depressed, he was happy. He was willing to admit to himself that he had never been mighty, but he clung to the belief that he had always approached his jobs as both stuntman and actor in a highly professional and dedicated manner. What he lacked in talent, he more than made up for in enthusiasm. He enjoyed his memories. He much preferred them to the realities of his present life.

His thoughts turned to what he would do today. Twilight Manor offered a wide variety of activities. They had a nice pool, but he didn't swim. There was a well equipped gym, but he was afraid he would look foolish in exercise clothes. Yoga and Tai Chi classes were offered, but when he walked by the fitness room, it was obvious that it was all women, and he would feel self conscious, being the only man. Besides, from his brief observations, the women were obviously a lot more limber than he was, even the one who looked like she was a hundred years old. The outside putting green tempted him, but he had never played golf and did not want to look awkward. The library didn't have a selection of the types of books he liked. They weren't depressing enough. The brochure he had received when he first arrived claimed to feature "A little night music, a touch of romance. Dances are one of the many activities on the social calendar at Twilight Manor." Obviously, that wasn't written with him in mind since he felt he had two left feet. His main activities were thinking about the days when he was young, and watching television, especially the old movie channel. He kept hoping that one of his films would be shown. But, they never were. Sometimes, when the weather was just right, he would walk down the flagstone path to the postcard perfect gazebo and sit and reflect about life, past, present and future, while watching the antics of the geese and other feathered creatures in and around the lake. On one occasion, he had even taken some bread with him and enjoyed watching how eagerly they gobbled it up. He liked listening to the tree birds songs.

For some reason they made him happy. But, he fought hard not to be happy. It wasn't in his nature. If he became happy, then something surely would go wrong and rob him of his happiness.

Like many other things, Dominic would not admit that he was a lonely man. Most of his life he had spent by himself. He had never been in love, had a steady girlfriend or even come close to marriage. Oh, there was that cute little Rita Ralston in high school, but he could never muster up enough courage to talk to her, let alone ask her out. He had tried once, but became so flustered that his face turned red, he garbled his words and he could feel perspiration running down his back. She had given him a strange look and stood patiently, waiting for him to become coherent. But, embarrassed, he turned and quickly walked away, leaving her with a puzzled expression on her face. After that, whenever he passed her in the hallway or they shared a classroom, he would pretend not to notice her. His love life was behind him before it even began. He had given up on the fairer sex at an early age, and buried himself in his work, such as it was. However, there was that bit player who had flirted with him with her big, doe-like eyes, and had seduced him once in the back of the costume room. But, any further expectations were doused when he learned that she came on to all the men on the set, from the stars to the floodlight operators and grips, and she had the reputation of being a tramp. She was obviously not someone for him to get involved with. So, now, here he was, approaching the twilight of his years in a place called Twilight Manor, surrounded by a group of people he didn't know, or want to know. His back began to hurt, and he painfully shifted his weight to another, less uncomfortable position.

Chapter 6

TUESDAY

As Emmy sipped her morning tea, a newspaper spread out in front of her, she read about what had gone on in the outside world since yesterday. Then, she remembered that this was Tai Chi day and looked up at the clock on the kitchen wall. She had plenty of time. It was still an hour before the mid morning class, which met every Tuesday. The afternoon classes met on Thursdays. This arrangement seemed to meet the needs and schedules of most of those who were interested in taking part in the relaxing exercise and meditation get-togethers. Several members of the Village, all women, were regulars at both sessions. Emmy preferred the morning session, as it seemed to set the tone for the rest of her day. Although classes only lasted an hour, they seemed shorter. During their first class, the teacher had explained to the students what Tai Chi was and the role it played in practitioners' lives. She said that the Chinese words literally mean Supreme Ultimate Boxing, which is a somewhat misleading translation. In Chinese, the words seem to conjure up a more exotic, gentle picture of the form. She emphasized that there is no boxing involved, although some of the moves imitate boxing punches and pushes into thin air, in a soft, non-threatening way. Emmy eagerly looked forward to each class. Other than the exercise, another benefit of the class was that it provided a social environment where class members could catch up on what was happening in each others lives, and best of all, discuss the latest Village gossip.

Emmy realized that she had better be paying attention to the time so that she would not be late for class. And she still had another mouth to feed before she left. A month or so earlier, she had noticed an adult gray cat outside her sliding patio door, staring in at her. It had looked scruffy and forlorn, and was rail thin. She wondered about its history. Was it an indoor cat that had gotten out of the house one day through a carelessly left open door and couldn't find its way back? Had its people moved and forgotten to take it with them? Had it jumped out of a car while its people traveled to some faraway place? Or, had someone purposely dumped it in the little creek under the nearby bridge to get rid of it? If so, that was fortunate, as the creek seldom had more than a few inches of water in it--when it wasn't completely dry. The Village had a policy against four legged indoor pets, but surely no one could argue with her feeding a lost and lonely cat.

Emmy had always had a soft spot for animals, especially dogs and cats, with their gentle, pleading eyes and affectionate ways. Her grandparents had lived on a farm and had had several cats and a lop eared Heinz 57 variety dog. The cats were kept to keep the mice population in the barn and fields under control. The dog's job was to keep the cats out of the hen house. One year, in her youth, while spending her summer vacation from school at her grandparent's, she named all of their cats, but then couldn't remember what name she had given to which cat. So, she just called each one by whatever name came to mind at the moment. She enjoyed feeding them and playing hide-go-seek with them in the tall grass in the acreage back of the farm house. She and "Hound," the dog, would chase each other through the fields and nearby woods. Those were halcyon days. It had been a long time since she had been able to run. She missed those times.

There he was, waiting patiently on the lower step of the patio, looking up at her with those big, round, blue eyes. Emmy placed a bowl of half wet and half dry mixture of food in front of him. She checked the water bowl to see if it needed refilling--or freshened. It didn't. She sat quietly on the step and petted "Stray," the name she had given the cat, as he eagerly gobbled his food. She talked to him while he ate, telling him her plans for the day, about her Tai Chi class and that she needed to go to the market in town after lunch to buy him some more food--and to get some less important items for herself. She asked him what he was going to do after finishing his breakfast. Was anyone else feeding him, or would this his only meal of the day? Did he find mice or any other food in the surrounding countryside? Of course, he never confided the secrets of his solitary life away from her. She knew that cats were very secretive and weren't very good communicators, except when they wanted to be fed, petted or needed a warm lap to curl up on for a nap. She knew that you needed to accept them the way they were, as it was doubtful they would ever change just to please their humans.

Emmy had spent more time than planned talking to Stray, and hurried back to her bedroom to don her "Wonder Woman suit," as she referred to her Tai Chi attire. It consisted of a pair of loose, light gray sweatpants and an oversized matching T-shirt worn over a sports bra. She never wore shorts as she was self-conscious about the scars on her leg. She compensated for its shortness by doing the exercises on the toes and ball of her left foot. This made both legs appear approximately the same length and helped her maintain her equilibrium. Wearing the lift she usually wore in her shoe was not practical, as the class wore only socks or went bare footed on the padded floor. She self-deprecatingly referred to herself as "The Leaning Tower of Pisa," or "Hop-Along-Lizzy." No one in the class had ever mentioned her leg or her posture.

Actually, no one else had even noticed it. She was more aware of and sensitive to her condition than were others.

Emmy arrived at the exercise room five minutes late for class, which hadn't started yet. The other women were still enjoying a pre-class chat. There were seven of them there, including her. Five were regulars, plus a woman she hadn't met or seen before. Emmy introduced herself and by the time the class ended, she knew the woman's name, Sally Baird, her apartment number, C-7, and much of her personal history. They were to become arms length friends in the coming months.

While the class was doing the Five Elements, the form the teacher's calm voice was leading them through, Emmy's yet unfocused mind involuntarily turned to thoughts of Mr. X, as the other women referred to Dominic. He had never introduced himself to any of them and kept almost exclusively to himself. He was a strange man. He seemed to always be looking for something in the carpet, or on the parquet floors of the Village's hallways, and around the outdoor flagstone pathway. She wasn't sure, when she passed him on rare occasion and said hello, whether he replied with a responding hello, or just a grunt. Then her mind focused on the soothing voice of the Tai Chi master, and she continued to move slowly and gracefully through the rest of the form, in step with her classmates.

The warm shower felt good cascading down her body in rivulets. After Tai Chi class and a shower, Emmy usually felt at peace with the world and experienced a deep sense of calmness and well being. She patted herself dry and dressed in her usual casual attire, jeans and cotton, patterned T-shirt. She combed and pulled a rubber band over her pony tailed, still damp hair, which seemed to fall into place from memory as it dried. She mentally added two more items to her shopping list, to be purchased during her trip to Braxton Falls.

Chapter 7

BRAXTON FALLS

BRAXTON FALLS IS a picturesque town much like many typical small towns of an earlier era. The entire downtown area is listed on the National Register of Historic Places. Now, tourist trade provides the main source of income to the community. A major motion picture was made there some years earlier and the town still lives on people's memories of it. The young star of the film died at an early age and a cult following had grown up around him, his life, his movies and the locations where they were filmed. Once, the town had been a thriving commercial and agricultural center, shipping its cattle and farm produce to market by rail. The train station still stands and is now used as a tourist information center and gift shop. The tracks are no longer used and are overgrown with weeds--an occasional tree attempting to grow between the ties. Only a few small farms remain in the surrounding countryside, their produce now transported to market by truck. The downtown area includes a bank, two grocery stores, three sit-down restaurants, and two fast food chain franchises. There is a two floor hotel and a sprinkling of bed and breakfast inns. A one screen, 1930s art deco movie theater, the Odium, continues to show a different second-run film every week or two. Countless antique and gift shops are strung along Main Street, and there are enough churches and taverns to satisfy the particular needs and preferences of the majority of the population and visitors. Just beyond the city limits--two at one end and one at the other--stand three filling stations, two of which offer full service and automobile repair. The other one is self-service. The educational system consists of a public grade school and adjoining high school.

Bored and with little else to occupy his time or mind, Dominic had driven to Braxton Falls, mainly to charge his car's battery. He wasn't much to wander and his car often sat in the Village's parking lot for weeks without being moved. Most of his personal needs were met by the convenience store at Twilight Manor. It was a nice day. The sun was warm, the breeze was cool and the humidity was low-- a perfect combination of weather. Dominic was hard pressed to find anything to be depressed about. But, during his drive into town, he thought he heard an unusual noise in the engine compartment of this car. Was that a bearing going, or a rod knocking? He tuned his ear to the sounds. He began to worry that his engine would suffer a major failure and he would be faced with a huge repair bill, which he felt he could ill afford at this time. Surely, he rationalized, his Checker car, which had originally been a New York taxi, with barely two hundred thousand miles on the odometer when it broke, couldn't be having mechanical problems yet.

When he arrived in town, Dominic was pleased to see there were practically no tourists or townspeople on the streets. But then, Tuesday was normally a slow day for business, in general. He was happy about that and it mellowed his depression a bit. Depressed or not, he enjoyed walking down Main Street and window shopping. He liked old things and the antique shops had a variety of items he recognized from his youth, even faceted glass door knobs just like in his parent's house. Browsing through the shops was almost like growing up all over again. On a previous visit, he had even bought a tin Popeye figure carrying two large suitcases that he had noticed in an antique shop's window. When he wound up the figure with its metal key, the suitcases acted like legs, propelling Popeye forward. It was much like a toy he had received for Christmas when he was seven or eight years old. The toy had been an impulse purchase, and caused him to have to frugally budget his money for the rest of the month. He had paid sixty five dollars for something that had probably cost his parents no more than a dollar or two. He began to question his sanity. Remembering what he had paid for the toy began to depress him.

At the opposite end of the street, Dominic saw a lone figure coming toward him. He hoped it wasn't someone from the Village who would smile and cheerily say hello. He hated that. It always made him uncomfortable. As the figure came closer, he could make out that it was a woman--tall, slender, with light hair, pulled back. She walked with a seemingly graceful ease. Watching her almost made him forget his depression. As she came closer, he recognized her as a woman from the Village. The last thing he needed was a cheery hello. As she came even closer, he remembered seeing her in the dining room. She usually sat with two or three other women and he could swear that once she had looked directly at him. Maybe he was wrong. When she was still several feet from passing him, she suddenly appeared unsteady, stumbled and fell hard onto her hands and knees on the cracked concrete sidewalk. Dominic's heart jumped a beat. It was the last thing he had expected her to do. Random thoughts flooded his mind. What should he do--go to her assistance and see if she was alright, or walk by like he hadn't noticed her falling? Or, he reasoned, he could simply pretend he hadn't seen her and cross the street. He stopped thinking and instinctively rushed to her side and leaned down to her.

"You all right?"

"I'm OK," Emmy replied, obviously embarrassed. "I'm just a little clumsy today."

She had done more walking than usual, and her weak leg had suddenly given way under the weight of her step. Normally, when she came to town she used her cane to steady herself on the uneven pavement. This time she had left it in the car, as she felt it drew unwanted attention to her.

Emmy looked up into the pair of eyes staring down at her. They were dark and heavy lidded, but she could detect concern in them. Dominic was startled by the paleness of the eyes staring back up at him. Doubts were replaced by action and he offered his large hand down to her. She accepted it and was carefully and gently helped to her feet by two strong arms. Emmy leaned against him momentarily to regain her balance and composure. Her face was close to his. He noticed how nice she smelled and how pretty she was--in a delicate way. Then, old habits returned, and backing away from her, he quickly looked to the ground. This was as close as he had ever been to any woman other than his mother, and that one brief encounter with the young starlet.

"Sure you're OK?" he asked again, looking for confirmation.

"I'll be fine. Thank you," Emmy said in a shaky voice.

"OK, then." With that said, Dominic, head down, continued his walk up the street. He had an urge to look back to see if she was looking at him, but resisted it. Emmy looked toward him as she brushed herself off and straightened her shirt and tucked it back into her waistband. In the fall, she had torn a small hole in the knee of one leg of her jeans, and the palm of her left hand was bleeding. She wrapped it with a handkerchief. She didn't seem to be hurt anywhere else. Other than her hand and knee, the only other thing that was bruised was her ego from making a public spectacle of herself. She was glad there hadn't been anyone else close by to observe her mishap. Looking up the street at the shrinking figure of Dominic, Emmy noticed that he was bow legged. With his head down, and his rounded legs, he reminded her of a monkey. She uttered an involuntary laugh, then immediately felt guilty about her thought and having laughed at him. Who was she to criticize the flaws of other people? Then, she remembered his eyes and the compassion she was certain he would not have wanted anyone to see in them. "What a strange man," she said aloud. She had had this thought other times at the Village when she had seen him there, but this was the first time she had allowed herself to voice it.

Dominic was shaken by his experience on the sidewalk. This was the first time he had spoken to a female without stuttering and having difficulty finding words. He held the memory of how soft she had felt and how good she had smelled. It made him forget his depression for a few moments. He couldn't get her pale blue eyes, so full of life, out of his mind, although he made a valiant attempt by returning to worrying about what was wrong with his car.

Chapter 8

COMPANY COMING

EMMY SLAMMED HER car door and hop-stepped through the lobby and down the hall to her apartment, slamming that door behind her even harder. She was angry at herself for her clumsiness in town--especially at having to take her dive in front of Mr. X. He must have thought her a fool. Worse than the abrasion on her knee and her still bleeding hand, was the reminder that she was not like other people--other normal people. And Mr. X--of all people. He had appeared more embarrassed than she had. But, he did have kind eyes. They were seldom on display due to his heavy eyelids and his seeming to be perpetually examining his shoes. And his touch had been surprisingly gentle. Strange man.

In the confusion, she had forgotten to buy cat food for Stray. Oh, well, she thought philosophically, there's always tomorrow. She welcomed any excuse for driving to town. She enjoyed the peacefulness of the countryside, with its rolling road and the leafy canopy of trees forming an arch across it in two places. Most of all, she enjoyed going through the covered bridge which marked the halfway point to town. Although it was much in need of painting, it seemed sturdy enough, and it had a certain charm that made her feel secure. And the smell of its aged wood had a pleasant aroma that seemed to linger with her for awhile after exiting it. She vowed to use her cane next time. She just hoped that she wouldn't run into Mr. X again. She wasn't anxious to create a repeat situation.

Emmy enjoyed browsing through the antique mall and other vintage stores on Main Street. Her sister had given her a porcelain humming bird on a wooden stand for her last birthday. Since then, during her antiquing explorations, she made a habit of looking for other similar figurines. She had accumulated three more, a cardinal, a pair of goldfinches on a branch and a barn owl. The owl had cost more than the sum of the other two. But, she couldn't resist the sad look of the owl's eyes. She felt she had to have it. The shop keeper told her that it dated from the late 1800s. Someone had once told Emmy that if you had more than three of anything, it was a collection. She didn't know if that was true, but if it was, she now had a bird collection. The trio stood, side by side, on the mantel of her gas fireplace. She enjoyed looking at them. They made her somehow feel at one with nature.

Her knee had begun to throb, and on the palm of her hand was a red welt around where the skin had been broken. Gently removing her jeans, she saw a matching redness on her knee. She washed and cleaned both areas with rubbing alcohol and applied antibiotic cream to them. What hurt more than the sharp sting on her skin was that now she had a ragged hole in the knee of her best jeans. Taking a pair of white walking shorts from a drawer, she gingerly pulled them on. She enjoyed the freedom of short pants, but only dared wear them in the apartment, where no one else would see her. The telephone rang, interrupting her thoughts. "Who could that be?" she asked the mirror. She only engaged in talking to herself through inanimate objects when alone--for obvious reasons. "Why don't you answer it and find out," was what the mirror probably would have replied, had it been able to speak. "I think I will," she replied, in answer to the mirror's unspoken question.

"Hello?"

"Hi Emmy." It was her sister Lorraine.

"Sis! It's good to hear from you."

"It's been awhile since we talked. So, what have you been up to lately?"

"What have I been up to? Do you mean besides falling down and making a complete idiot of myself in front of a stranger? Not much."

"Feeling a bit sorry for ourselves, are we?" Lorraine learned long ago not to give in to the temptation to comfort Emmy when she was having health related problems--short of a major one.

"No. I'm sorry for my tone of voice. I'm just not too happy about my clumsiness."

"I thought that Kung Fu, Karate or whatever stuff you're doing was supposed to keep things like that from happening."

"Tai Chi! It helps, but I haven't gotten to the lesson that teaches you how to pay attention to what you're doing and watch where you're going, especially when you're walking on cracked pavement and cobblestones."

"Oh! Hope you didn't hurt yourself," Lorraine said, feeling that a consoling comment was appropriate under the circumstances.

"No. Just my pride." Then Emmy related the entire incident to her sister.

"Sounds like Prince Charming came along at just the right time."

"I'd hardly call him Prince Charming." Then Emmy changed the subject.

"So what's new with you, Sis?"

"Not much. Phil's been working long hours the past few months, and I decided it's time for him to take a break, so we're going to Egypt on vacation. We leave next Sunday."

"Is Chris going with you?"

"No. That's why I'm calling--besides it been too long since I talked to my big sister."

"Oh?" Emmy was waiting for the other shoe to drop.

"That was a suspicious sounding 'Oh.'" Anyway, Chris is on summer vacation from school, and doesn't want to go with us—and, she doesn't want to stay in our big house alone."

"And?"

"And, how would you like some company for a couple weeks?" There was a long pause before Emmy answered.

"Do you know how small my apartment is?"

"Chris doesn't take up much room. And, besides, I thought it would be good for the two of you to spend some time together. After all, you're her favorite aunt."

"I'm her only aunt."

"Well, you're still her favorite, regardless. It would do you both good. Like the old saying about the colliding of two bodies."

"I think that has something to do with astronomy or physics. And I don't know if I could survive the collision."

"Are you getting set in your ways in your old age?"

"I'm not old, and I'm certainly not set in my ways--not much anyway. I'm just thinking of how boring it would be for Chris."

"She's very mature for her age. And, next year she'll be a college graduate, with a degree in psychology. Maybe then, she can straighten out my big sister."

"Well, I'm definitely too old to be straightened out. Have you run this idea past Chris yet?"

"She's got her bags packed."

"You're kidding!"

"Well, sort of. We talked about it, and she thinks it's a grand idea. I'd let her tell you herself, but at the moment she out shopping for clothes for the trip."

"I knew having twin beds would backfire on me one day. There's an old saying, 'Never have a spare bed unless you want company.'"

"There you go. It's settled, then!"

"OK, you've beaten me down. But, if she comes back home complaining about what a miserable time she had with her old maid aunt, don't say I didn't warn you."

"Thanks, Em. She's got a road map and knows how to read it. She'll be in your driveway some time after noon Saturday."

"I don't have a driveway, just a parking lot."

"Close enough. Have her call me when she gets there so I'll know she didn't elope with some strange young man instead. We'll be jetting out the next day."

"Don't worry. The only young men here at the Village are at least fifty five. But, I haven't done a survey of the male population of Braxton Falls, yet."

"OK, Emmy. She's all yours."

"Thanks, Sis. Bring me back a pyramid."

Lorraine laughed. "I will. Love you, big sister. Talk to you when we get back."

"You, too. Bye." Emmy hung up, her face formed into a frown. Her thoughts began to scatter.

"What in the world am I going to do with a twenty--or is she twenty one--year old house guest for two weeks?" she queried the now silent telephone. Her throbbing knee and burning hand were forgotten for the moment. Knowing she would need to be going back to town in the next day or two to stock up on groceries, she sat down to make a list. The first item she put on it was cat food.

Chapter 9

CHRISTINE (AKA CHRIS)

CHRIS WAS EXCITED about going to visit her Aunt Em, as she called Emmy. And any excuse to shop for new clothes was welcome. She was carrying two full bags of mostly casual clothes she had bought at the mall, when she passed in front of the Lady Chic Boutique shop. There it was in the window--a tennis outfit--white shorts and matching white V-neck sweater blouse with red trim. Surely, they had tennis courts at Twilight Manor. As far as Chris knew, no respectable retirement community was without them. And surely, Aunt Em played tennis. She looked like a tennis player--tall, slender, with a tennis player's classic pony tail. At least, that was Chris's image of a tennis player. Then she remembered how sensitive her aunt was about her bad leg. So, she walked on past the boutique--shopping completed.

It was a solid twelve-plus hour drive to Twilight Manor if you observed the speed limit, which Chris rarely did. She planned on getting away from home by six or seven o'clock Saturday morning--providing she didn't oversleep. That should make her estimated arrival at Twilight Manor around nine or ten PM. She had never been an early riser, and had been successful in scheduling most of her college classes late morning or early afternoon. The only first hour class she had taken was as a freshman--Medieval History, at eight thirty. Although a B plus student, she had received a C grade for the course. But, she rationalized, who could concentrate on history at that hour of the morning? Her parents didn't quite see it from Chris's viewpoint. They told her that her lack of attention was because she didn't get enough sleep. Not only didn't she like arising early, she didn't like going to bed before midnight.

When Chris had told her parents she wasn't interested in going to Egypt with them, she neglected to mention that she had an alternative motive for not making the trip. She had been keeping company with Bradley van Hooten, a senior pre-med student. The two of them would have two weeks of the summer together without parental interference and restrictions on the comings and goings imposed by her father. He felt that since she still lived at home, she was expected to observe house rules. Unfortunately, when the spring semester ended, so did Brad. He went home to Urbana, Illinois for the summer. Since he was going to begin his first year of medical school at Washington University in the fall, he told Chris it was best they end their relationship. He said his heavy academic schedule would make it difficult for him to maintain a long distance romance. She suggested they could at least write to each other now and then, which he agreed to, as long as she didn't expect him to answer every one of her letters.

Brad was the only boy Chris had ever dated more than casually, or for any length of time. She had never given much thought to what would happen to their relationship once he graduated and moved away. For almost a year, they had lived in the moment, just sharing each other's company, and not worrying or talking about the future. She realized how immature and short sighted that had been, taking so many things for granted. But, she remembered something that Aunt Em had told her after her dancing career came to an abrupt end after her automobile accident. It was

Alexander Graham Bell's saying, "When one door closes, another one opens." Chris thought that all Bell had ever done was invent the telephone.

Aunt Em was an intelligent woman, but Chris felt sorry for her. Not only did she have a career she loved cut short in her prime, but, in addition, she never met the right man. To her credit, at least outwardly, her aunt had never seemed bitter about the trick fate had played on her. And Chris rationalized that her aunt was still young enough to find romance in her life--if she wanted it. Chris's mother had told her that there had been at least two men in her aunt's life who were serious about her, but she would never let herself get too close to either of them emotionally because of her sensitivity to what she termed her "game leg." When a relationship looked as though it might become serious, she would back away and end it, much to her suitor's confusion and disappointment.

Although her aunt didn't look it, Chris figured her to be at least in her mid fifties, since she knew the policy of most senior community's was that residents had to be at least fifty five. Chris's mother had told her that today's fifties and sixties were yesterday's thirties and forties. People lived longer now. She found it hard to believe that in the 1950s the average life expectancy was only in the low sixties. And, now it was almost eighty--with an increasing number of the population reaching the century mark. So, if that was true, her Aunt Em was still a young woman. However, Chris never thought of her parents as having once been young. After all, they were her parents and how could a grown woman of almost twenty one have young parents? Maybe the university should offer a course in Parent Psychology. She laughed inwardly at the idea.

So, deep in thought, Chris found herself in the shopping center's parking lot, inserting a key into the ignition of her 1976 white Mustang. She had only a vague recollection of leaving the mall. She shifted her thinking from her aunt to preparations for Saturday morning's trip. She had made an appointment for Friday to take her car in to have its roadability checked--oil changed, tire pressure gauged--and whatever other mysterious things mechanics do to people's cars to ensure they run right. She had filled her gas tank earlier that day, so she needn't worry about that. The day after tomorrow, she would be off on her high adventure into the countryside to visit her aunt. She was looking forward to it. The closer it came to time to leave, the less she thought about Brad. She kept reminding herself that she needed to keep thinking about open doors. She would let life take her where it would. She and Aunt Em would have a fun two weeks. No classes, no studying, no men to put up with--just her and her aunt, enjoying each other's company. At least, she hoped that's how it would be. Her mother had told her that she had talked to her sister and that Emmy was looking forward to Chris's arrival.

Saturday morning arrived quicker than expected. Chris awoke with the sun in her face. She had overslept. It was already twenty minutes past seven. She had planned to leave by seven. She took a quick shower, hurried into her clothes and carried her suitcase and garment bag downstairs. It was fortunate that she had packed the night before. Now all she needed to do before leaving was throw her night clothes and toilet articles into her bag. She smelled coffee and stuck her head into the kitchen. Her mother was at the stove and her father sat at the kitchen table engrossed in the sports page of the morning newspaper. Her mother, having heard water running in the upstairs bathroom, was making pancakes and had poured Chris a cup of coffee. Her parents had always had trouble getting her to eat breakfast. Her father had once remarked to her that starting a day off without breakfast was like beginning a trip with an empty gas tank. In both instances, he had emphasized that you were running on fumes. Chris wasn't quite sure she fully understood the analogy, but trusted her father that there must be some moral in it. She quickly drank her coffee--burning her tongue in the process.

Without sitting down, she spread grape jelly on her pancake, folded it taco style, and with an expected degree of sloppiness, quickly began eating it. This forced her mother to say, "Child, you keep eating like that, you're going to have stomach trouble by the time you're twenty five." Chris laughed. She had been hearing that for as long as she could remember. Her mother urged her to sit down and let her food digest--but Chris said she didn't have time.

Quickly kissing her mother and father, Chris said, "Well, I'm off. Have a good vacation in Egypt. See you in two weeks." With that said, she was out the door, with part of the folded over pancake protruding from her mouth, and a bag in each hand. It was a warm, sunny morning--an ideal day for traveling. Birds serenaded her imminent departure. She bounced into her car's contoured seat and backed quickly out of the driveway, tires squealing. Putting the gearshift lever in drive, she headed down the street with, "Get 'em up, Musty!" her pet name for the car. It was almost nine o'clock. Traffic was usually light on Saturday mornings. Today was no exception. She was starting out two hours later than she had planned. Fortunately, she encountered only one short road construction delay, and her car galloped smoothly and rapidly over the tarmac. Many hours later, as fatigue was setting in, she saw the Baxter Falls sign and reduced her speed to almost the 25 miles per hour posted speed limit. She was on the last leg of her trip to Twilight Manor. A few minutes after leaving Baxter Falls, she came to Junction TT and turned onto its blacktopped single lane surface. She soon passed through a paint starved covered bridge, which she compared to a long garage with doors at both ends--and breathed a sigh of relief. The sun had long since disappeared below the horizon.

"We're almost there, Musty!" Chris said. Then, she heard a noise, followed by a flapping sound. "Oh, oh. That can't be good," she said. Her car pulled to the center of the narrow road. She adjusted her steering and coasted to the right, onto the wide, dirt shoulder. She knew without looking that she had had a blow out. Getting out of the car to inspect the damage, she found the left front tire completely flat. She popped open the car's trunk, removing the tire, jack and lug wrench. The wheel cover had gone scurrying across the road into a dark cornfield, so she didn't need to remove it. She made a mental note to retrieve it after she got the tire changed.

Musty had not had a flat tire in the almost two years she owned it. But, as a college freshman, Chris had changed a tire on her father's car one night when she had borrowed it without his knowledge. However, unlike her father's car, Musty did not want to give up its wheel's lug nuts. They seemed to be welded in place. "Now what?" she wondered aloud. She hadn't seen another car since turning off the main highway several miles back. "Just my luck," she muttered. "So near, yet so far." Frustrated, she kicked the flat tire. This act gave her no satisfaction or relief--only a big toe that now throbbed.

In the distance, Chris noticed a pair of headlights coming toward her from behind. As they came nearer, she stood at the side of the road behind Musty and waved her arms frantically. A dark, square looking vehicle pulled up behind her car. A silhouetted figure emerged from it and came slowly toward her in the darkness. When he was close enough to see his face, she was startled--and somewhat frightened. In the reflection of the car's headlights, she could dimly make out his features. He had a tangle of thick, dark hair, small eyes, a crooked nose, and an oddly shaped mouth. She was torn between asking him for help and running into the cornfield to escape. She decided to stand her ground. There was really no other option than to talk to this strange looking man.

"Trouble?" The voice was soft and gentle, belying the face and body.

"I've got a flat tire and can't get the lug nuts loose," she replied nervously.

Without a word, the man examined the damaged tire. He bent down and firmly picked up the tire wrench in his huge hand. Chris involuntarily shuddered at this act, and took a step backward from him, looking over her shoulder at the cornfield behind her for reassurance. Silently, he knelt beside the faulty tire, attaching the wrench to a stubborn lug nut. He gave a grunt, and Chris heard a squeaking noise. She heard another squeaking noise, and then three more. He had managed to break loose all five lug nuts.

"Where's your spare?" the soft voice asked matter-of-factly, without looking up. She pointed to where it leaned darkly against the side of her car. In what seemed like only moments, he had jacked up the car, removed the lug nuts, changed the tire, put the damaged one and the tools neatly back into the trunk, and closed the lid. Chris jumped at the sound the trunk lid being closed.

"Should be OK now," the man said.

"Thank you," Chris said, appreciatively. But, almost before the sound of her words had faded away, the strange looking man was back in his car and continuing his shadowy journey down the road--to who knows where.

"What a strange--but nice man," Chris thought, half audibly. "He certainly was a man of few words." In the excitement, she had completely forgotten about the errant wheel cover, now hidden somewhere in the dark cornfield. She decided she would worry about finding it tomorrow, during daylight.

Getting back into her car, she noticed that her trip odometer indicated she was probably only a few miles from Twilight Manor. "It was nice of that man to help me, but if he hadn't come along, I probably could have walked the rest of the way," she said to the night. This made her feel a little less helpless in her dilemma. The car's clock made Chris aware that, due to her oversleeping and tire problem, she was running almost three hours late. It was just past midnight. She wondered whether her aunt was worrying about her, or if she had given up and gone to bed.

Emmy looked at her watch. Her niece should have arrived hours ago. She paced the floor. She considered calling her sister to see if perhaps Chris had gotten a late start. She had a reputation for not being very punctual. Or, maybe she had changed her mind, and wasn't coming. All sorts of scenarios danced through

Emmy's head. Or, maybe, she thought, her watch was wrong. She looked at the kitchen clock, which confirmed the accuracy of the time.

Slow footsteps could be heard in the hallway. They stopped at Emmy's door. There came a light knock. Opening the door, Emmy saw Chris's tired but smiling face and outstretched arms. "I'm home!" she said, imitating a greeting she had seen on some television program. She gave Emmy a hug. "It's me, your long lost niece, Aunt Em."

"Thank Heaven. I was getting worried sick about you."

"No need. You know me. The bad penny. Never shows up when expected and is hard to get rid of." They shared a relieved laugh.

"It's good to see you. Did you have a good trip?"

"It was great, until a few miles back, when I had a flat tire.

"Oh, my!"

"My words, exactly. Well, not exactly! I had a few others, too. But, a strange man came to the rescue and changed the tire for me."

"A strange man?"

"Uh-huh. He reminded me of a gangster from an old movie I saw a long time ago on television."

"Really?" Emmy had a thought, but quickly dismissed it. That would be too much of a coincidence. "What did he look like?"

"Oh, I don't know, it was pretty dark. Medium height. Stocky build. Lots of hair. Soft voice. The most disturbing thing about him was his eyes, at least what I could see of them. They reminded me of a sleepy owl."

"Really?" That was all Emmy could think of to say.

"Really! He wasn't much for small talk. Fixed my tire and left. He seemed to be in a hurry. But, a nice man."

"Really?" Emmy was still at a loss for words. However, in her mind, she somehow knew it had to have been Mr. X. What an odd coincidence, she thought. Finally, she regained her composure and said, “Here, let me help you in with your bags. We’ll put them in the bedroom and I’ll help you unpack later.”

Chris looked around the small, tidy apartment. “I like what you’ve done with the place. It has a warm, cozy feel. And I like your birds. Are you a collector?”

“Kind of, I guess--half by accident. I enjoy looking at them. When did you last eat?”

“About five hours ago, when I stopped for gas. I had a hamburger, a piece of pie and some ice tea.”

“You must be starved. Sit down, and I’ll fix you a roast beef sandwich and a glass of milk, if that’s OK.”

“Perfect!”

The pair talked about the trip, Twilight Manor and what they had been doing since they had last seen each other. Neither of them could believe how quickly the time had passed. Emmy was looking at a grown up young woman, and Chris was seeing a strikingly attractive middle aged lady. They continued to talk and reminisce into the midmorning hours.

Chapter 10

BILLY MEETS MR. X

BILLY INCH'S NAME belied his stature. He was a rangy, six foot two inch tall young man of twenty three, and the youngest person in the Village. He was the building and maintenance assistant, under the tutelage and watchful eye of Pop Bates, chief building and maintenance engineer. Everyone at Twilight Manor liked Billy. He wore a perpetual smile and had an insatiable curiosity about all things maintenance and mechanical. He was readily identifiable, even when he could not be seen, by the sound of his whistling while he worked. He had even been given the nickname "Happy" by one Villager, as in one of Snow White's seven benefactors. He was even heard to do his rendition of the "Whistle While You Work" tune while busily engaged in his chores. After two years of working under Pop, there wasn't any building problem which could occur that he could not take care of--except possibly for the aging boilers in the sub-basement, which Pop prided himself in keeping in running order. Otherwise, Billy had become a first class maintenance and repair man.

One of the more senior residents of the Village would call Billy with a made up problem whenever her arthritis acted up. She claimed that his ready smile, whistling and the jokes and stories he told gave her more relief from her pain than the pills her doctor prescribed for her. Billy was aware of her ploys and patiently humored her, telling her that anytime she had a problem to give him a call. In fact, with his outgoing nature and positive attitude, it was only natural that he lifted the spirits of most of those with whom he came into contact. If happiness is not a sprint, but a marathon, Billy could always be relied on to be out in front of the pack. His jokes were older than he was, but the Villagers never seemed to tire of hearing them. The previous year, when an elderly resident had to transition to a nursing home, Billy found a copy of Captain Billy's Whiz Bang joke book in a closet while painting her apartment for a new tenant. It wasn't long before he had memorized all the jokes, and told them whenever opportunity presented itself.

Besides being handy with his hands, Billy had a good mind--even though he hadn't done very well in school. Not that he was unable to learn, but his interests seemed generally to be outside the traditional classroom. Instead of paying attention to his teachers, he would doodle and draw schematics of plumbing systems or electrical circuits, or design carpentry projects. Even in his pre-teen years, he had been good with his hands. He had a natural curiosity about how things worked, much to the misfortune of his father's pocket watch and his mother's toaster. It wasn't long before his talents for fixing things caught up with his curiosity about them. No matter how complicated a problem was or whether he had seen the object to be repaired before, if it was repairable, he was usually able to put it back in working order. After a less than spectacular freshman year, and failing an introductory history course at Calvin Coolidge high school, his mother had him transferred to Hamilton Technical High School, where, although he received basic traditional educational courses, he could concentrate the majority of his time and talents on technical subjects. He graduated first in his class in the building maintenance curriculum--to his satisfaction and his widowed mother's pride.

For reasons unknown to himself, after arriving at Twilight Manor, Billy began collecting old time radio programs of the 1930s and '40s on cassettes--Jack Benny, Fred Allen and whoever else's comedy programs he could find. He had made his first purchase, "Fibber McGee Fixes a Porch Swing," when he had heard it being played in a small antique and gift shop in Braxton Falls. He never tired of listening to it. It made him laugh to hear how complicated McGee made such a simple task. And, he especially enjoyed hearing McGee's loving and ever patient wife, Molly, exclaim, "Oh, Heavenly days!" in response to one of Fibber's harebrained ideas, tall tales, skewed version of a historic event--or botched home repair project. After a busy day taking care of the four rectangular wings that comprised the Village's building, Billy enjoyed relaxing evenings in his basement apartment, with lights out and eyes closed, listening to his old time radio tapes. He had listened to his small collection so many times he could recite the dialog along with the performers. Their antics formed the basis for several of the jokes and stories he shared with Village residents.

Billy had made many friends among Twilight Manor's population, but none stranger than his one with Dominic Graystone. Billy had only received one call from the man's apartment. His toilet was periodically flushing without any help from a human hand. Billy quickly and easily adjusted the tank's float ball and replaced the rubber flapper--and the problem was fixed. He was aware that Mr. Graystone didn't associate with any of the other residents and kept to himself, except when, of necessity, he had to be among them in the dining room during meals. In fact, until Dominic had called and identified himself and his apartment number, Billy didn't even know the man's name--or his existence. Other residents generally referred to Graystone as Mr. X. Perhaps they didn't know his name, either. Although Dominic's favorite preoccupation was with being depressed, it was difficult, even for him, not to catch some of the contagious cheerfulness of this smiling, whistling young maintenance man. Although Dominic had difficulty relating to women, he was somewhat more at ease in the company of men. He found them less intimidating.

Upon entering Dominic's apartment, Billy noticed a three color movie poster on the wall advertising the crime genre movie, "Angels Don't Die." Billy, a fan of old movies, had recently watched this film on late night television, and mentioned it to Dominic, telling him how much he had enjoyed it. Perhaps Billy had an old spirit, and, in addition to old time radio programs, he enjoyed old movies, and sometimes stayed up much past his bedtime to watch one of the television filler films shown at one or two o'clock in the morning. At the mention of the movie, Dominic's eyes seemed to lose their hood and Billy experienced the strangest smile he had ever seen. He had to wonder whether the man was actually smiling or merely sneering. It was difficult to tell. But, Dominic's eyes lit up and the pair spent the next two hours talking about that movie, Dominic's role in it, and movies in general. In that short time, Billy learned more about the reclusive man than probably the rest of the Village's population as a whole knew. He was fascinated by the behind the scenes stories of moviemaking, and Dominic's talking about his stunt performer days. Their conversation came to an end when Billy's beeper went off.

"I'm sorry, Mr. Graystone. Duty calls," he said apologetically.

"Call me Dom. Everybody does," came the unexpected reply. That sounded odd to Billy. He had never heard anyone refer to the man by his real name.

"OK, Dom. Call me Billy. I've really enjoyed our talk. You sure know a lot about movie making. We'll have to talk more about it again some time."

"OK." But, Billy could see Dom was beginning to retreat back into himself--his eyes again hooding to safety from the world. But, Billy was determined to draw out this unhappy, and obviously lonely, man.

"Right! I'll talk to you later, then," Billy said as he left.

"OK. Later," Dom replied softly. The door had been opened a crack and Billy was determined to get it to swing open even wider. He had called Mrs. Milford from Dom's apartment, telling her he was on his way, and his mind refocused to her stopped up sink.

After Billy left, Dominic felt a loneliness sweep over him. He slumped in his easy chair, staring blankly at the poster on the wall. It was nice talking to someone about his life and profession. And Billy seemed like a nice kid--old for his years. Dominic remembered his life at that age--working as a stage hand and gofer, running errands for anybody and everybody on a movie set. That had not helped bolster his self esteem. It was, "Boy, get me some coffee." "Boy, run this manuscript over to soundstage seven." Day after day, it was boy, do this, and boy, do that. But it was a living and had kept his mind off his problems--real and imagined. One day, when delivering some script pages to a director, the man seemed to be staring at him. Looking Dominic up and down, he asked, "You ever do any stunt work, boy?"

"No sir. But, I'm sure I could," Dominic quickly added."

The director looked at him again. Dominic was solidly built, with good shoulders and a mass of unruly black hair.

"Would you like to?" came the next question.

"Uh, I guess so. Sure!"

"Do you know how to fall?"

"Uh, I've fallen down a lot, if that's what you mean." The director couldn't help but laugh at Dominic's reply.

"Do you think you could fall off that building over there--into that net?" the man asked, pointing at each of them in turn.

"I-I think so." There was some hesitation in Dominic's voice as he mouthed the words.

"Want to give it a go? It pays twenty dollars." That settled it. Dominic would do almost anything for that amount of money--so long as it was legal. His next reply was stronger, and more full of confidence--or perhaps bravado.

"Sure. I don't see why not."

"Good. Go over to wardrobe and tell Marie you want the jumper's cowboy clothes."

"OK." Dominic trotted off, wondering what he was getting himself into. But, whatever it was, twenty dollars was a lot of money just to fall down. He was dressed and back in the presence of the director in a matter of minutes.

"Well, you look like a real cowboy. What's your name, son?" the director asked. Then, he added, "just in case we have to have a tombstone made for you." He followed the remark with a hardy laugh, at what he considered a humorous comment.

"Dominic Xavier Graystone, sir!" Dominic replied, not quite sure how to take the director's comment.

"Whoa! Back up the wagon. How about I just call you Dom? OK?"

"OK." Dominic could not stop thinking about the easy twenty dollars he was about to make for just a few seconds work.

"Good boy! See that ladder next to that building there?" Again, the director pointed--directing Dominic's eyes to a twenty foot ladder leaning against the side of a two story western storefront facade. He thought, that's not too bad. And that's a big net to fall into. He reasoned that he couldn't possibly miss hitting it. He obeyed the director's instructions and hurried up the ladder to the roof of the building. Somehow, it looked a lot higher from the roof top than it had from the ground. But, there was twenty dollars at the bottom. This eased whatever qualms Dominic was beginning to have about his assignment.

"OK, now. See that rifle next to the ladder?"

"Yeah!"

"OK. Now pick it up and point it at the cowboy across the street. He's going to shoot you. When you hear the sound of his gun, drop your gun, grab your chest and fall into the net."

"OK." Dominic thought, I can do this. Twenty dollars. He pointed the weapon in the direction of the cowboy actor across the street. He heard a loud noise, dropped his rifle, grabbed his chest, and fell clumsily forward, landing awkwardly in the net below. He was surprised how easy it had been. Before climbing out of the net he stretched his arms and legs. Everything worked. He breathed a sigh of relief, accepted the offered hand of a crew member and crawled out of the net.

"Good job, son. I've got a few other jobs I can use you for now and again, if you're interested."

"Sure," Dominic replied without hesitation. Thus began his unplanned career as a stunt man, earning the beginner's customary twenty dollars a stunt. Overall, he recollected, he had fallen off buildings and horses, been shot in gunfights and beaten up in brawls in over a hundred movies. The one he most remembered was the bar room fight where another stunt man accidentally broke his nose. The other man later apologized and told Dominic that, if it was any consolation, his crooked nose gave him character. Of all the movies in which he performed, his name appeared in the credits of only seven of them. But, that was all right. He was still getting paid. That is, until a balky horse ran away, dragging Dominic along with him, his foot caught in the stirrup. This virtually ended his career. At the time, he was earning one hundred dollars a stunt, more money than he had ever made before.

The beginning of his new career as a character actor came by way of apology from the director in whose film he was injured. For twenty five years, Dominic enjoyed a small, but steady income in an acting career that included much of the same type action he had performed as a stunt man--only not quite as physical. He still got shot, hit over the head with bottles, crawled out of wrecked cars, and leered menacingly while stabbing or shooting heroes and other villains. But, no more falling off buildings or riding horses, or doing any of the other myriad of high impact and dangerous activities he had been involved in previously.

Dominic's head fell to his chest and he began snoring quietly--his reminiscing ended for the time being.

Chapter 11

POP BATES

ALTHOUGH JASPER BATES was younger than many of the residents of the Village, he was known affectionately by one and all as "Pop." He had inherited this name as a result of his responsibilities for keeping the aging steam boilers in the basement--which he referred to as his "babies"--working properly. He was a well known and well liked character around the Village and in nearby Braxton Falls. He had been responsible for building maintenance and power plant engineering at Twilight Manor for over twenty eight years. He had earned his engineer title more by experience than by education. He had barely finished the tenth grade in school. When he was sixteen years old, he enlisted in the Army--successfully lying about his age and education. There had been a war on at the time, and the recruiters accepted the word of prospective enlistees with a wink. He had tested high in mechanical aptitude, and after completing basic training, he was transferred to Camp Osborne, Alabama, to attend technical school in mechanics. After completing his enlistment, he volunteered for three more hitches. During those years, he advanced from private to technical sergeant, the second highest enlisted rank, and earned the revered classification of Master Mechanic. In addition to being a good mechanic, he had a natural talent for fixing practically anything else that could be taken apart and put back together. After being honorably discharged from service, he used the proceeds of his mustering out pay to open a small, one man fixit shop in Des Moines, Iowa. He worked on everything from toasters to electric motors and gasoline engines. His motto was "Anything you can break, I can fix," and he proudly spent several years proving his claim. Then, an upturn in the economy led him into bankruptcy, contrary to the conventional causes of such financial failures. In the repair business, when times were good, consumers were more inclined to buy new items instead of repairing their old ones. Pop had his own way of explaining it. "How many shoe repair shops do you see these days?" It came to a point where it had begun to cost Pop more in labor and parts to repair some items than a new one could be bought for. With business continuing to slow, to stay competitive, he frequently charged only for the retail price of parts, and waived his labor costs. At the end, in many instances, it was costing him more to repair an item than what he charged a customer. Although Pop was a skilled technician, he was not a very good business man.

Pop's story of how he came to the Village of Twilight Manor was vague at best and changed with each telling. When anyone inquired about his past life or work history, his explanation was seldom the same. The "facts" changed from time to time to fit his mood of the moment, or the gullibility of his audience. To say that he was not above exaggeration and embellishment would be an understatement. But, even if all of his stories were not true they were always interesting, colorful, filled with intrigue, and included, of course, claims of successful and failed amorous affairs with beautiful, mysterious women.

Pop was not an imposing figure of a man. Physically, he was small and wiry, the same of which could be said about his head of sparse gray hair. He walked with a slight limp. Depending on his mood and the amount of curious attention exhibited by a listener, he would attribute the cause of his irregular gait to anything from a wound received in combat, to falling off a bar stool in Madagascar--or, when he did not feel creative--a case of the "rheumatiz." Inquirers were free to believe whichever version they chose.

When young Billy Inch came to work at the Village as Pop's apprentice, Pop was in his seasoned years. He had recently celebrated his seventy second birthday and his twenty eighth anniversary at Twilight Manor. His eyes were still sharp and his hands were rock steady. Ladders, however, had become his downfall--so to speak. Once he came under the tutelage of Pop, Billy quickly became his legs, inheriting the high work-- tuck pointing, gutter cleaning, shingle mending, exterior and interior painting and the like. The more chores Billy took over, the more Pop retreated to his first love, babying the complex assortment of the Village's boilers and other power plant equipment. During his watch, there had never been a complaint from any of the residents that their apartments were not warm enough or cool enough. Pop saw to that and was proud of his record. He had described and explained to Billy--too many times to keep track of--every intimate detail of every boiler and steam pipe in the complex, which ones had threatened to fail--and the tricks of the trade he had used to prevent them from doing so. He also enjoyed regaling Billy with how he had done the same with every electrical wire and connection, and every air conditioning unit. Although, frequently, the secret of his success, especially with electrical and plumbing equipment, was to replace it with new, rather than repair the old. Billy learned more about power plants, electrical systems, air conditioning and general maintenance from Pop than he could have learned at a technical college. In spite of Pop's lack of formal education, he was a good teacher as well as a good yarn spinner, not only about the history of technical problems that had challenged and been defeated by his skilled hands, but also, telling anyone who would listen, stories about his adventuresome life as a young man during his wandering days--before age and common sense had settled him down somewhat. Whether true or a fabrication of Pop's creative mind, he told of having been married to an English lass he met while stationed at Blandford Camp, outside of Salisbury, England. According to him, she had died in childbirth shortly before her twenty fourth birthday. Only Pop knew if that was true. What he never talked about was what happened to the child of that marriage. No one was ever quite certain about--but never questioned-- the veracity of Pop's stories.

Billy had on several occasions visited Pop's single room, with bath, located in a dark corner of the sub basement near the boilers. Pop called it his "hideaway." He much preferred that arrangement to living above ground in one of the complex's more spacious and comfortable apartments. "Too fancy," he would say when the subject came up. Nowhere in his Spartan room was there a picture of any kind to be found, except for one small, curling and faded three by four inch black and white snapshot of a smiling young soldier in military uniform, with his arm around an attractive young woman. It was barely noticeable, being sandwiched haphazardly between the mirror and the edge of the wooden frame of his dresser. When Billy asked about it, Pop told him that it was taken when he was in the big war. When Billy suggested that Pop was not old enough to have served in World War Two, Pop, never short for an answer, replied, "Son, when you're in a combat situation and bullets are whizzin' 'round yer head, there ain't no such thing as a small war."

Pop, a simple man, preferred living the simple life. His main source of entertainment was driving to Braxton Falls every Saturday night and nursing two domestic beers--his self imposed limit--at Larry's Office Bar, an old fashioned tavern on Grand Avenue, just off Main Street. Usually, during such times, he was successful in corralling a game of Dominoes or Billiards, with one or more of the older, regular patrons. He rarely won at

Billiards. He seldom lost at Dominoes. But, he always told the best--and tallest--stories of the evening. Billy admired him and looked upon him not only as a mentor and friend, but also as a father--or perhaps a grandfather-- figure. Billy's father had died in a more recent war, and Billy missed the years they could have had together, but were unable to.

Pop did not take his influence on the young man or his responsibilities to him lightly or for granted.

Chapter 12

LOVE IN BLOOM?

THE AFTERNOON WAS warm and sunny. A light southwesterly breeze played gently across the rolling hills of the surrounding countryside. Billy was on his way to 18D--again--to change a light bulb for Mrs. Murtenson. It had become practically a ritual. The woman was nocturnal by nature. Whenever he passed by her window, no matter the time of day or night, all her lights were on. She was a nice lady, barely five feet tall, and on the light side of ninety pounds. She had been a third grade school teacher for forty two years, and delighted in recounting tales of her student's antics and accomplishments. She and her husband had had no children of their own, but she had felt a special bonding with each pupil in each of her classes--no matter how gifted or slow in their learning ability or potential. She had taken pride in being able to give each child the individual attention and help he or she needed. This had not always been easy, considering the size of her classes--but she tried--and most of the time she succeeded. Like Billy, she wore a seemingly perpetual smile. Whenever he arrived at her door, her first act was to offer him a cup of coffee and a home baked cookie. No matter how busy his schedule, Billy always found a few minutes to share her small kitchen table and listen to her tell him about her teaching days and her students--or gossip about the other residents. None of the gossip was malicious, of course, just humorous tidbits she had overheard or observed during her occasional meanderings around the hallways and strolls down to the lake to feed the geese that occasionally came to visit. And, of course, she was always pleased to share detailed descriptions of her latest twinge of fibromyalgia, or bursitis--although often she was not quite sure which one was bothering her at the moment. But, in spite of her discomforts, she remained cheerful and had a zest for and devotion to her reading. Her apartment was an overflowing library. She quickly devoured her daily morning newspapers and dispatched them to the Village's tree saver bin. Her favorite sections were the comic pages and the crossword puzzles—which she usually completed. Her other reading was eclectic--romance novels, biographies, history and travel books, and weekly news magazines. One could usually tell when she discovered a steamy novel that held her interest. On those occasions, she would not be seen in the dining area for two or three days, remaining curled up in her quarters, reading and snacking on potato chips and cheese dip, to which she had become addicted. During these periods of solitude, the room monitors regularly checked on her to ensure that she was not ill, but merely preoccupied. Amazingly, in spite of her almost constant eating, she never seemed to gain a pound in weight. When asked how she managed to stay so trim, she would attribute it to a fast metabolism--rightly or wrongly--but her answer seemed to satisfy the curious.

Billy had taken a short cut across the quadrangle from A wing to Mrs. Murtenson's apartment at the far end of D wing. He was by nature an outdoorsman and took every opportunity to enjoy the weather--fair and foul. Other than what was on his tool belt, he rarely carried anything else. He could take care of most maintenance and repair problems with what was around his waist. Nor did he have any light bulbs with him. He had pre-positioned in Mrs. Murtenson's kitchen cabinet a supply of every wattage bulb he might need, knowing it wouldn't be long before he would again be called back to her apartment to brighten it.

Halfway across the quadrangle, Billy saw two women slowly coming toward him. They seemed to be deeply engrossed in conversation. He immediately recognized Ms. Stratton, but not the woman with her. She looked like a shorter, younger version of her companion. And she walked with a bouncy step, as opposed to Ms. Stratton's slightly tentative gait. As the three intersected, Billy smiled and said, "Hi, Ms. Stratton. Beautiful day, isn't it?" To Billy, every day was beautiful. Then looking at Christine, he asked, "Is this your sister?" Emmy laughed, and replied, "Flatterer!" The younger woman smiled shyly. Billy noticed how white and straight her teeth were. Then his gaze rose to her eyes, their pale blueness seemed to innocently see right into him. Billy liked women, but in his job, he rarely had time or opportunity to see or talk to any his age. There were no women younger than fifty five at the Village, and with his work schedule, he didn't get to town very often. He figured that this newcomer was somewhat younger than he was, probably eighteen or nineteen. He noticed she had an unblemished complexion and soft features, in contrast to her strong cheekbones. In his opinion, which he felt would be shared by a majority of other young men, she was very attractive. Then Emmy said, "Billy, I'd like you to meet my favorite niece, Christine." This was the family's standard inside joke. Emmy had only one sister and one niece, so they either had to be her favorite or her least favorite. In both cases, they were always her favorite, even when they disagreed on an issue or observation, which was seldom.

With the smile still on his lips, Billy bowed slightly and held out his right hand. "I'm pleased to meet you, ma'am." He was surprised how small and soft her hand felt in his large, rough, working man's hand.

"It's nice to meet you, too, Billy. Call me Chris." Her voice was as soft as her hand and had a lilting cadence. Billy knew immediately that he would enjoy hearing more of it.

"Chris has come to visit her old maid aunt for a couple weeks to keep me out of trouble," Emmy volunteered--then added, self-deprecatingly, "As if I needed it."

"I don't know. Two lovely ladies like you, out on your own, should probably have a chaperone." As soon as he said it, Billy thought how patronizing the words must have sounded. But, Emmy and Chris appeared to accept his comment graciously. He felt relieved. Although he was friendly with all the residents of the Village and joked with most of them, for some reason, he felt that these were two special people and deserved special attention and treatment--especially Chris.

"So, where are you rushing off to, Billy," Emmy asked.

"Mrs. Murtenson's", he said, rolling his eyes upward.

"Oh, another light bulb job?" she asked, smiling.

"Good guess. But, then, I suppose it's common knowledge about her and light bulbs."

"It's the talk of the town," Emmy replied, again laughing, softer this time. Chris had a puzzled expression on her face, so Emmy explained about the woman's reading habits and her leaving lights on twenty four hours a day, even on sunny days.

"Chris, I know I said I'd show you around the Village, but my leg is telling me that it wants me to get off it for awhile. So, could we do it later? My age must be catching up with me." She grimaced slightly.

"Why, you're still a young woman," Billy said. "You've got lots of years before you need to start worrying about age."

"Why, thank you, Billy. That's sweet," Emmy replied, the light smile on her lips betraying her feeling of pain.

"If you want, Ms. Stratton, after I take care of Mrs. Murtenson, I'd be glad to show your niece around the place," Billy offered--hopefully.

"I'd like that," Chris answered quickly, before Emmy could reply.

"You would probably make a better guide than I would, anyway," Emmy told Billy. Then she turned to Chris and said, "Why don't you meet me in the dining room about five? Billy can show you where it is." Billy nodded affirmatively.

"OK. Settled. See you then, Aunt Em." With that said, Emmy turned back toward her apartment. Her limp felt more pronounced than usual.

Billy pointed to the wing at the front of the complex, and the pair started toward it.

"So, do you go to school?" Billy asked, as they approached the back door of the main entrance.

"Yes. I'll be a senior at Boston College in the fall."

"Really? You don't look old enough to be in college." Chris accepted the intended compliment with a silent smile. "What's your major?"

"Psychology."

"Uh, oh! I better watch what I say, then." Billy wrinkled his brow and recoiled in mock fear.

"I wonder why everyone thinks that if you're a psych major you're constantly analyzing their behavior?"

"I don't know. It just goes with the territory, I suppose. It can be kind of intimidating to us common folk." Another laugh was shared.

Before they realized it, they had reached the front of the building. Pointing, Billy said, "This is called Building A, although all four sides of the complex are connected. It's also called Wing A--depending on your preference. Offices, reception area, front desk, lounge, library and dining area. Wings B, C and D are residential apartments. Downstairs we have the swimming pool, fitness center, game room, power plant, and my humble abode."

"Really? You live in the basement?"

"Only temporarily--just until I become general manager."

"My. You do aim high, don't you?"

"Whenever possible." Again, they laughed.

Chris and Billy felt at ease with each other, much like old friends who had come together again after an absence. Although Chris and her former boyfriend Brad had dated for almost a year, there had remained an unspoken feeling of distance between them. Chris found herself becoming more relaxed and comfortable with this young man she had just met than she had, on many occasions, with Brad, who had no noticeable sense of humor. Chris often felt she had to filter whatever she said to him so as not to offend him, or have explained to her why what she said was wrong, inappropriate or stupid. If asked to sum him up in a few words, she would have to admit that he was overly stiff and serious, especially for such a young man. Their relationship had been a sputtering one, and not a particularly romantic one. It had not progressed beyond kissing and some clumsy fondling attempts by Brad. But, Chris had enjoyed his company and had stoically accepted his low key, non-emotional ways. Basically, he was a good person, but often their personalities clashed. When this occurred, Brad would brood over some imagined or unintentional slight by Chris--or correct her on some fine point during a conversation. With the optimism of youth, in spite of their differences, she had thought the two of them would eventually rise above their differences and be able to have a future together some day, and, that with time, Brad would become more outgoing and romantic. She rationalized that, with her sense of humor and easy going ways and his serious, no nonsense ones, it was just a matter of the "opposites attract" cliché. She had hoped that eventually they would come to terms with their different needs. But, now that Brad had ended their relationship, this was merely a rhetorical point.

"Hellooo? Are you there?" Billy asked, noticing the far away look in Chris's eyes. She had not been aware that her mind had wandered from the uncertain present into the unchangeable past.

"Oh! I'm sorry. My mind seemed to have just left my body for a moment."

Billy resisted the temptation to say, "And a nice body it is." Instead, he segued with "And now, for the underworld tour. After descending a stairway to the lower level, Billy pointed, and said, "Zero floor. Swimming pool, fitness center, game room, and my subterranean penthouse apartment."

Choosing to ignore the last part of Billy's remark, Chris said, "What a nice pool. And I brought my swim suit with me."

"What a coincidence. So did I." They both laughed at the absurdity of Billy's remark. "Maybe we can test the temperature of the water while you're here."

"I'd like that," Chris replied, so softly Billy barely heard her.

"It's a date then. You can bring your aunt to be our lifeguard and chaperone--if you want."

Chris didn't mention how self conscious her aunt was about the scars on her leg and that it was highly unlikely she would join them in the pool. But, she said, "I'll ask her, although I don't think a chaperone is necessary. I trust you."

"Ah, lass, that may lead to your undoing," Billy replied, twisting an imaginary moustache in the manner of Simon LeGree.

"Sir, you are a cad," Chris replied mischievously, batting her eyes innocently and folding her hands together in playful coyness. They were enjoying their silly banter, which they both felt comfortable engaging in. Chris could not believe how easy it was to talk and joke with someone she had just met. She was enjoying herself.

Changing the subject, Billy said, "And here's the game room. Billiards, ping pong, shuffleboard, darts, dominoes, checkers, chess--dancing 'til dawn. Just kidding about that last one."

"I like ping pong", Chris offered.

"And you're probably some kind of pro, who could destroy my fragile male ego with a single wicked backhand."

"Possibly," she said, demurely.

"Well, we'll just have to see about that then, won't we?"

"I think so."

"When?"

"Let me check with Aunt Em and see what her schedule for me is."

"OK. Next attraction, one flight up, is our nine hole golf course and luxurious putting green--behind Wing C."

Chris looked at her watch. The time had passed more quickly than she had realized--or wanted.

"Oh, no! I'm twenty five minutes late. Aunt Em will think you've kidnapped me. I guess our next stop needs to be the dining room."

"Already? We've barely scratched the surface of the grand tour. And I want you to get your money's worth. Shall we continue tomorrow?" Billy asked hopefully, adding, "There's a lot more to see and do, not to mention the ping pong."

As receptive as she was to the idea, Chris didn't want to neglect spending time with her aunt, so she replied tentatively, "Let's see what tomorrow brings."

Chapter 13

TODAY'S ANOTHER DAY

DAWN HAD YET to break over Twilight Manor. Most of its population slept peacefully in their beds. There were some exceptions. Mrs. Murtenson, as was her habit, lay motionless on her couch, engrossed in reading a new novel, "Love Tales of the South Sea Islands." Bits of broken potato chips were scattered in a crazy quilt pattern across the front of her time worn terrycloth bathrobe--a present from her late husband a few months before his death. She had been an avid reader ever since she could remember, and had promised herself that when she retired, she would catch up on her pleasure reading. She had spent seven years in college with little time to read anything beyond textbooks and professional publications. Now she read for herself--not for school, not for work, not for others. She and her husband had enjoyed their early retirement years traveling and doing whatever they chose to do rather than what others expected or demanded of them. They were free to travel the world, and did, until that fateful day when he was unexpectedly taken from her. She treasured the countless memories of their lives together.

Now she had only her books to comfort her. They were her daily companions. Granted, they were no substitute for her husband, but, nevertheless, she considered them good friends.

Dominic had lain awake most of the night, eyes staring blankly at the dark ceiling, worrying about a rattle he had heard the previous day in the passenger door of his car, and wondering what it felt like to have a serious disease--no particular one--just any of the countless number that existed. Surely, sooner or later, he would get one of them, he knew. It was just a matter of which one and when. His health and his car were his two main preoccupations. He worried about both. He felt that he had little or no control over either. But, at the moment, he was too tired to get up and too worried to sleep. So he laid there and continued to worry. It always made him feel better when he had something to worry about. It filled his mind and his time. He felt that he had no friends. He was not an unfriendly man. He simply felt that he didn't fit in anywhere socially. He considered himself clumsy, unlearned and with no talent for anything beyond falling off horses and playing dead--or preparing to play dead--in B movies. Not much of a life, he thought. But, it was all he had, and in a perverse way, he enjoyed it. Perhaps, with his penchant for worrying, enjoy is too strong a word. But misery fit him nicely. It was his hobby. And although he often was depressed, he really wasn't unhappy. He was a living contradiction without realizing it. On the positive side, he did seem to be able to talk to the Village's young maintenance man on occasion. What was his name? Dominic had always had a problem with names. As he got older, he worried more and more that he was becoming senile. After all, he was sixty years old. His parents had both died in their early sixties. He was sure that was to be his fate, too. There seemed to always be something to worry about and to negatively occupy his mind.

Emmy had spent a restless night. Her back had been paining her since the day before. Her orthopedist had explained to her that this was caused by the misalignment of her spine due to her shorter leg, which resulted in pinched nerves in her back.

Sometimes, even the orthopedic shoe she wore didn't help. Other times, around the apartment, she chose to wear soft slippers and walk on the ball of the foot of her bad leg. She and Chris had gone into town to shop the day before, and in the enthusiasm of having Chris visiting her, Emmy had walked more and had been on her feet longer than usual. She reminded herself to make an appointment with her doctor to see if her special shoe needed to be adjusted or replaced.

Chris was sleeping comfortably and quietly. She was not an early riser. This had caused an occasional problem with early morning classes at school, especially when she could not schedule a required course late morning or mid afternoon. Some classes were only available first hour so she would defer taking them, hoping they would be offered at a later time the following semester. She and Emmy had stayed up late the previous night catching up on each other's lives. Emmy had decided to stay in bed awhile longer and try to get comfortable--and hopefully, be able to go back to sleep. She wasn't successful in doing either, and arose in the dark and quietly limped into the kitchen, careful not to disturb her sleeping companion. Her stealth was unnecessary. Her sister had once told her that Chris slept so soundly even a train going through her bedroom wouldn't awaken her. Emmy put on the kettle, lifting the spout to prevent it from whistling. When the water was ready, she prepared a cup of instant green tea and took a chocolate chip cookie from the cookie jar. She allowed herself only one cookie, twice a day. Not that she had to worry about gaining weight. It was more habit than anything. Many mornings this was her breakfast. She sat at the kitchen table, alternately looking at her reflection in the still dark window and working the paper's crossword puzzle. She needed to plan what she and Chris would do today. Having lived a solitary life for so long she was out of practice at entertaining others. Chris was young and energetic. Emmy decided that she would tell her what there was to do and where there was to go and let Chris tell her what she preferred. After yesterday, Emmy wasn't sure but that it might have something to do involving Billy. Or was she just imagining that they had already made a connection? After all, what did she know of such things? Was she beginning to think like an old maid aunt? She hoped not. Soon the sun would begin its rise and signal the beginning of another day for the community's residents.

Billy had been jarred awake at 4:30 by the ringing of his telephone. The Schultz's were having a problem with their toilet. It had decided to overflow again. During Mr. Schultz' fourth visit of the night to what he referred to as "the throne room," he had accidentally knocked a plastic bag of cotton balls off the top of the toilet tank and into the bowl as he flushed it. The bag had refused to complete its unplanned journey and had become lodged in the curve of the bowl, causing the toilet to back up and overflow onto the bathroom floor. Although extremely nearsighted, Mr. Schultz never bothered to put on his glasses when he went into the bathroom. Nor did he bother to turn on the bathroom light. His wife regularly chastised him for both actions, or, more appropriately, omissions. Although, in his mind, he was not entirely to blame. His wife had the single vanity neatly and completely covered with her assortment of cosmetics, skin softeners, shampoos, and other bath and beauty aids. Running out of room on the vanity, she had expanded her storage area to the top of the toilet tank. Besides his clumsiness, Mrs. Schultz had other complaints about Mr. Schultz's bathroom habits. For one, his aim was unpredictable in the dark. At least once or twice a week she had to scrub the bathroom floor around the toilet bowl. For another, he never put the toilet lid back down. On one occasion, when she had an urgent need to use the toilet, she backed up and sat down on the exposed, cold porcelain rim with the resulting sensation of cold water on her bare bottom. Toilet etiquette, or lack thereof, comprised a large part of the couple's daily conversations. As might be expected, Mrs. Schultz's complaints and reminders fell on deaf ears--although, for his age, Mr. Schultz' hearing was adequate. His standard excuse for not complying with her wishes was that he forgot. And, he added, an eighty seven year old man shouldn't be required to concern himself with such trivial matters. After all, he countered, it was easier for her to remember such mundane things since she was only seventy eight--so why couldn't she remember to put the toilet lid back up after she finished. This conversation had volleyed back and forth between them for most of their fifty some years of marriage.

This wasn't the first time Billy had to unstop the Schultz's toilet. He too, had reminded Mr. Schultz on previous visits to put the lid down, if only to avoid knocking things off the tank and into the bowl. Usually, when Mr. Schultz had a mishap, he merely fished the errant object out of the bowl and returned it to its place on the tank top. However, some small objects had neatly flushed themselves away forever. Mrs. Schultz had lost several tubes of lipstick as a result of her husband's carelessness.

Billy retrieved the errant cotton balls and mopped the floor while the Schultz's had their latest conversation on the subject of bathroom protocol. By the time he returned to his room, Billy was wide awake from his labors. It wasn't yet five o'clock--too early to stay up, and too late to go back to sleep. So, he lay in bed on his back, hands clasped behind his head, and closed his eyes. His thoughts turned to Chris and how nice she seemed. She was so easy to talk to. And she smelled good. It was a shame she lived so far away. Billy wasn't exactly sure how far Boston was from Braxton Falls, but he knew it was too far. Even if it was geographically closer, they would still be a world apart socially. She was a soon to be college graduate, and he had only graduated from a technical high school. "Two different worlds," he heard himself say. "Two different worlds." But, on the plus side, she wasn't uppity like some girls would be in her position. And they did seem to share similar senses of humor. He knew that she was too good for him, but he couldn't erase from his mind the memory of her face and smile. Finally, he forced himself to turn his thoughts to more practical matters. He needed to check with Mrs. Barquette to see what color she wanted her living room repainted. And Mrs. Leighton had told him that her oven wasn't heating properly--that whatever she put in it came out undercooked. He had been tempted to suggest she just let food cook a little longer, but, he told her he would look at it and see what he could do. He turned toward the digital redness of his clock radio. It was only an hour before he would start his day. His thoughts faded--and he was asleep.

The other residents of the Village were attending to whatever it was they did at that time of morning. Most were still asleep. Others were flushing toilets, hopefully without anything that didn't belong in them. Some were early risers. Many enjoyed jogging or a brisk walk in the crisp morning air before breakfast. Still others preferred to sleep late and enjoy a light breakfast of cereal and fruit in their apartments and start their day slowly with a newspaper and a cup of coffee. Then, there were those, especially residents with kitchenettes and spouses, who preferred to have a leisurely traditional hot breakfast. And there were those who preferred to eat a more robust meal in the cafeteria.

Each resident was uniquely different and special in his or her own way. Yet, what they had initially lacked in common with each other--backgrounds, religions, talents, beliefs, prejudices and preferences--seemed to meld into a cohesiveness of community as they settled in and became an integral part of their new home. Villagers came from many parts of the country, and from a multitude of previous lifestyles. The majority were physically, mentally and financially independent. Only a few of the long term older residents required some assistance in managing their lives and activities. But, regardless of who and what they had been in their pre-Village days, they now shared a bond of togetherness--with the possible exception of Dominic Graystone, who just didn't seem to fit in anywhere.

For those residents now awake or awakening, the sun was beginning to slowly reveal itself to them from behind the distant mountains in the northeast. Today was another day, and each resident of the Village would deal with it in his or her own special way.

Chapter 14

DECISIONS

BILLY TRIED TO put Chris out of his mind. What was the point of thinking about her? Admittedly, she was attractive and had a nice personality. And he felt very much at ease around her. But, again, what was the point? She was here for a few days to spend time with her aunt, and then she would be gone. Forever! And, besides, why would she want anything to do with a common laborer like him? She could do so much better. There were probably a lot of boys at college who were better suited to her likes and tastes. After college, she would probably marry a lawyer, or maybe even a doctor, and live in a big house. Of course, Billy, in his reasoning, had no way of knowing that Chris's ex-boyfriend, Brad, had ended their relationship once he had been accepted for medical school.

Billy's mental wrestling failed to succeed in removing Chris from his mind. He realized that he was acting like a teenager with his first romantic crush. But, then, he rationalized, she was here. He enjoyed her company. And he believed she enjoyed his. Nothing lasts forever, he told himself. So, in the middle of painting Mrs. Barquette's walls for the second time in six months--he made his decision. He would spend as much time with her as she would let him, and, of course, that his workload would permit. His mind suddenly seemed clearer. Whistling, he directed his full attention to the half painted wall in front of him and looked forward to his next opportunity to be with Chris.

Chris finally struggled slowly from her bed. Emmy could hear the shower running. Although a tea drinker, she knew that Chris liked her coffee in the morning,+ and had bought a small jar of instant for that purpose.

"That smells good, Aunt Em," Chris said cheerily as she entered the kitchen, still drying her hair, her feet slapping lightly against the tile floor.

"It's instant. I hope that's OK."

"That's what I drink at home. Actually, I think I enjoy the smell more than the taste."

Other than on weekends, Chris rarely ate breakfast, especially when she had an early class. Sleep had always held more of an attraction for her than food. But, for some reason, she had an appetite this morning. Perhaps it was because it was closer to lunch time than breakfast time.

"How did you sleep last night?" Emmy's question was a rhetorical one. While she had lain awake trying to find a position that would give her some relief from pain, she could hear Chris's soft, even breathing. She hadn't moved all night.

"Wonderful, Aunt Em. It must be this country air. And it's so quiet here." Emmy laughed. "I know. They should have named this place Peaceful Valley. I can fix you some cereal--hot or cold--pancakes, bacon and eggs, toast and jelly." Emmy shrugged. "I'm sorry that's all I can offer you at the moment. Or, we can go down to the dining area and eat, if you like." She looked at the clock on the wall, and added, "It's less than an hour until they start serving lunch."

"The cafeteria sounds fine. I don't usually eat anything before noon, anyway--except when I'm home and mom fixes pancakes."

The two drank their beverages in silence, Emmy studying the world news section of the paper and Chris scanning the comic page, occasionally chuckling softly to herself. The pair's main focus, however, was on their thoughts. The only sounds in the room were the steady ticking of the clock and an occasional rustling of a newspaper page. Emmy didn't want to disappoint Chris, but with her recent lack of sleep and some still lingering pain, she really didn't feel like being too physically active. Chris's mind vacillated between thoughts of her ex-boyfriend and Billy. They were so different. She began wondering what she had ever seen in Brad. He was such a snob--and so self centered. He had grown up as a spoiled rich kid, whereas Billy . . . . She wasn't quite sure what to make of Billy. What she knew about him was superficial, at best. He was friendly, open and down to earth--and had an engaging sense of humor. She liked that. She felt as though she had come to know him better in a day than she had Brad during almost a year.

"What would you like to do today?" Emmy asked, interrupting the silence. "We can go into town and I'll show you around. Or, we can drive out to Stone Rings Park. It's very scenic this time of year." Emmy told Chris how, in the late 1920s, an eccentric and reclusive millionaire had begun to build a castle deep within the woods of the park. When the depression came in 1929, he went bankrupt and only the outside stone walls were ever completed. "It's been a point of curiosity and tourist interest ever since. Or, we could spend a lazy day here."

"I wouldn't mind a quiet day here," Chris replied. She sensed that Emmy wasn't feeling well and she didn't want to be a burden on her. She came mainly to spend time with her aunt, whom she rarely saw, and didn't feel a need to become a tourist, or to be entertained.

"You sure?" Emmy asked, questioningly.

"I'm sure," was Chris's reply in the positive.

"OK. That's fine with me. And, we still have a lot of catching up to do on what's been going on in each other's lives." Looking again at the clock, Emmy saw it was almost noon. "Feel hungry? How about having some lunch?"

"I'm ready." Chris was still in her bathrobe. "Give me a minute to put on some clothes and I'll be right with you."

There were only a scattering of people in the dining room when Emmy and Chris arrived. Many residents had already eaten and others preferred to eat later. Emmy pointed to a table near the window, overlooking the courtyard. Chris nodded. On the way to their destination, Emmy noticed Dominic seated alone, his back to the wall and his head down, srudying his food. He looked so forlorn and lonely, she felt a need to stop and say hello to him.

"Hello. Remember me? I'm the clumsy woman you rescued from an unfriendly sidewalk in town."

"Oh, yes! H-hello," Dominic replied nervously, half rising, practically upsetting his chair in the process.

"Have you met my niece?"

"Uh, no, I don't think so." Dominic stood to his full height to acknowledge her presence, an awkward one sided smile forcing itself onto his face.

"This is Christine or Chris, as I call her." Dominic bowed slightly, and said, "Pleased to meet ya." There was an awkward silence. Finally, Emmy said, "I'm so sorry; I don't remember your name." All she could think of was Mr. X, by which she was certain he would not appreciate being called.

"Uh, Dominic. Dominic Graystone." His swarthy complexion betrayed a slight additional coloration.

"I'm Mary Elizabeth Stratton--Emmy for short. We occasionally see each other in passing. I suppose we should at least know each other's names."

"Pleased to meet ya," Dominic repeated, once again bowing slightly.

"Chris is visiting me for a few days, and we're trying to figure out how to spend the time."

"There's a craft show at the high school in town, with home made quilts and lots of other stuff, if you like that sort of thing." Emmy's pale blue eyes held Dominic's gaze. He seldom looked into another's eyes. Usually, he looked at the ground or to the side when forced into a situation where he had to communicate directly with someone. But, this woman was different. He didn't feel as awkward talking to her, even though he couldn't really think of anything to say. This was probably the most he had said to a female since he could remember. Emmy was surprised at how dark and deep his eyes were, as though they hid the secrets of the universe, but weren't able to express them in words.

"What do you think, Chris?" Emmy asked, a positive inflection in her voice.

"Sounds interesting," Chris replied.

"Well, we better get something to eat before the food's all gone," Emmy commented, changing the subject. "It was nice talking to you," she said, her eyes still holding Dominic's gaze.

"It was nice meeting you, Mr. Graystone," Chris added.

"You, too." Dominic attempted a smile, once again bowing. Then, the two women continued toward their table.

"What an unusual man," Chris offered. "I didn't want to say anything, but he was the man who stopped and changed the flat tire on my way here. I guess he didn't recognize me."

"Maybe, with the way he always seems to be looking at the ground, he didn't see you. And, you said it was dark. He seems like such a lonely man," Emmy said, a sad tone to her voice. "I feel kind of sorry for him. He doesn't seem to have made any friends since he came here. It's too bad. He seems like a nice enough man, even though he's obviously painfully shy--and a little unusual looking--as I'm sure you noticed. But, he can't help how he looks, can he?"

"Why, Aunt Em! If I didn't know better, I'd think maybe you had a thing for that man."

"Oh, don't be silly." Emmy's pale skin was suddenly pink. "You know me. I've always had a weakness for stray animals. And, anyway, what would any man see in an old cripple like me? Chris shot her aunt an uncharacteristically stern look. "Aunt Em! You're far from old and even farther from being a cripple. Could it be you're experiencing a bit of self pity?" Emmy was taken aback by Chris's outspokenness. It wasn't like her. Maybe, Emmy thought, she really was being somewhat insecure about herself and her future. She made a mental note to try to be more cheery and make Chris's visit an enjoyable and memorable one.

Dominic finished his lunch and returned to his apartment. On the way there, he felt a little weak in the knees. Talking to a woman normally was very stressful for him, but he felt something unusual in the presence of Mary Elizabeth Stratton. He liked that name. It seemed to roll musically off his tongue. He suddenly felt an inner peace--if there was such a thing. He couldn't find anything negative or depressing about her. She seemed so full of life--so outgoing. And her eyes. Those eyes. She had beautiful eyes. Such a contrast to his own, dark hooded ones. Hers seemed to glow with life. She was the nicest person he had met since coming to the Village--except for Billy. But, of course he was a man. Men were always easier to be around and talk to. But, there was something special about this woman. What, he didn't know. He hoped he would have occasion to encounter her again. He looked forward to the possibility. He would behave more gentlemanly the next time, he vowed. Then, returning to his normal attitude about life, he felt that this would never happen. But if it did . . . . The thought gave him something else to worry about.

Chapter 15

THE MEETING

EMMY AND CHRIS leisurely strolled down Main Street, occasionally stopping to examine a store window. Emmy wasn't feeling well. Between her lack of sleep the previous night and the radiating pain in her leg and back, each step became more difficult. Although she rarely used her cane, today she felt she needed its support and reassurance. She was enjoying the pauses before the reflective glass of the shop fronts more than the walking, since the pain subsided somewhat when she stood still. Chris was only going to be visiting a short time and Emmy didn't feel she should complain about her discomfort. Her obligation was to ensure that Chris had a good visit with her only aunt.

"Oh, look Aunt Em!" The reason for Chris's outburst was a bright pink sweater she had noticed in the window of the Bon Venture Boutique. "Let's go in, shall we?" Emmy smiled through her pain and nodded. She could tell that light conversation was going to be difficult for her today. Chris was through the doorway before the forced smile had left Emmy's lips. She was pleased to see that there was a visitor's chair in a corner of the shop, near the fitting rooms. She limped heavily toward it, saying, "You go ahead and look, Chris. I think I'm going to sit for a minute." Chris looked at her, concerned, a furrowed brow replacing her smooth features.

"Are you OK, Aunt Em?" she asked.

"I'm just a little tired from getting up too early this morning. And I'm not as young as I used to be. Youth has its rewards, doesn't it?" She forced another wan smile. Chris had sensed at breakfast that her aunt wasn't feeling well. She was hesitant about going into town, but Emmy had insisted that she was all right. Chris accepted Emmy's explanation at face value. She didn't want to embarrass her by seeming over solicitous about her health. As long as her aunt was willing to make the effort, she would act as though she hadn't noticed the color drain from her face, which, by this time, had become chalky white. Also, the limp had become more pronounced. Chris decided she did not need the sweater and that this would be their only stop. She suggested to her aunt that they have an early return home.

The pair had gotten a late start on their day and Chris was getting hungry. Ever since arriving at the Village, she seemed to have a perpetual appetite. At home, between being preoccupied with school work and the demands of Brad before their recent breakup, she had been a light eater. She thought about her mother repeatedly telling her she was getting "skinny as a rail," whatever that meant. This was an exaggeration, of course, as she had gained five pounds since Brad had become her ex-boyfriend. As a psychology major, she had a tendency to over analyze whatever happened in her life. She reasoned that her loss of appetite and weight were attributable to the stress of maintaining a fine line between the school's and Brad's demands on her and her time. Once he had severed their relationship, her appetite increased considerably. Their situation had never been easy for her. At best, it was never what she could look back on as fulfilling. They seldom went anywhere or did anything together. Rarely had they gone out to eat or to a movie. Brad's priorities for the allowance he received from his parents were mostly on clothes, tennis lessons and maintaining his car. He had rarely bought Chris anything or taken her anyplace that involved having a dollar sign attached to it. His main interest in her had seemed to center around talking about himself and his accomplishments, and awkward and unsuccessful attempts at what he considered lovemaking, which Chris regarded only as self indulgent and crude slobbering kisses and pawing.

"Are you getting hungry?" Emmy asked, seeming to have read Chris's mind.

"As a matter of fact, I am. I don't know what's come over me lately. All I want to do is eat and sleep. By the time I go home, my parent's won't recognize me. I'll look like great aunt Tillie." Emmy mentally visualized her aunt. She was a large woman. Almost six feet tall, and big boned--which was the family's delicate way of expressing her extreme overweight. Chris on the other hand, was small boned, five foot four inches tall and weighed at most a hundred and fifteen pounds.

"I wouldn't worry about it, dear," Emmy said. She and Chris came from a line of women who were tall--and excluding aunt Tillie--slender. Chris was the shortest one in the family, after her father. And, it was doubtful she would ever have a weight problem, no matter how much she ate or how old she got.

"There's a sandwich shop down the next block," Emmy continued, pointing her finger in its general direction.

"Lead me to it," Chris said, her eyes opening wide, her expression a feigned look of hunger. She felt this had not been a good day for her aunt to go on a shopping trip. Probably getting her off her feet for awhile was a good idea.

The café was small and not busy. Chris and Emmy chose a table near the window, where they could watch the passing parade of cars and people, which were few at best. Other than some locals moving from one place to another in pursuit of their occupations, there was not much vehicle or pedestrian traffic. The work week was not a busy time for the tourist trade, which seemed to swell the town's population to double or more on weekends. Emmy ordered a tuna melt sandwich and a small green salad. Chris ordered a soup and sandwich combination. Both of them selected iced tea as their beverage. As they ate their food and relaxed, Chris could see some color returning to her aunt's cheeks. Still hungry, Chris ordered a piece of apple crumb pie with two scoops of vanilla ice cream--quickly finishing them off. After completing their meals, they lingered over their drinks and talked about nothing in particular. Emmy began to tell Chris what else there was to do in town, but Chris thought that further exploration should be saved for another time, when her aunt was feeling stronger. She was about to suggest this when the bell on the eatery's door tinkled. Looking up in unison, they saw Billy entering. He spied them immediately. A smile split his face and he headed toward their table.

"Hi, you two," he said. "Looks like you were hungry, too."

"Hi, Billy," Emmy replied to his greeting. This young'un has about worn me out. We're just resting until I get my second wind."

"Actually, we were just thinking about heading back to the Village. What are you doing in town?" Chris asked.

"I had to come in to get some supplies from the hardware store. It seems Mrs. Barquette has changed her mind again about what color she wants her living room walls painted. She seems to think that the color I was using clashed with her drapes, and as she explained it to me, paint is cheaper than drapes." Billy rolled his eyes. "And Mrs. Murphy needs a new outlet." His face reddened at his poor choice of words to describe Mrs. Murphy's problem.

"Actually, Mrs. Murphy doesn't need a new outlet. Her kitchen counter wall does--an electrical outlet. She continues to insist on trying to plug her appliances in with the big end and little end backward. She doesn't seem to understand that today's electrical plugs are polarized for safety and will only go in one way. She keeps telling me that in her day you could plug them in either way. And she won't accept that she can't still do it that way. Old habits are hard to break, I guess."

"Old dogs and new tricks," Emmy said. Billy and Chris stared blankly at each other as though they had not heard this expression before. "Sorry. I guess it's a generational thing," Emmy apologized. "Won't you join us Billy?"

"Thanks. If it's OK." He looked at Chris for approval.

"No! We'd rather you just continue to stand there," Chris said in mock sarcasm.

"OK. I can eat standing up," Billy replied, unabashed.

"Don't be so silly. Sit down." Chris felt at ease teasing Billy in this way. It was something she could never have done with Brad--without getting a puzzled look in return or a lengthy and detailed explanation of how and why her comment was not only inappropriate, but also was stupid.

Billy sat down and ordered a chocolate milkshake. Chris continued her teasing.

"Is that all you're going to eat? No wonder you're so skinny."

"OK. So, maybe I'll get a cookie or two to go with it. Will that make you happy?"

"I guess we'll just have to wait and see, won't we?" The two were smiling at each other, enjoying their word play. What made Chris happy was that she could share such lighthearted back-and-forth with Billy in good fun, without being accused of being mean spirited. The more she was around him, the more she wondered how she could have put up with Brad for so long. Maybe, she rationalized, he was just meant to be a class project.

Emmy was in obvious pain. No matter which way she adjusted her sitting position, there was no relief. "I hate to be a wet blanket, but I think maybe we should return to the apartment," she said. Pain was etched on her face.

"Oh, I'm so sorry, Aunt Em. I should have known you weren't feeling well." Turning to Billy, she said, "Well, it's been nice talking to you, Billy. But, I think we better be getting back." Chris noticed that Billy was visibly disappointed by her declaration. He had been so preoccupied with talking to her that he had momentarily forgotten that Emmy was there. Emmy was aware of this. Perhaps, she thought, there was a way all three of them could benefit from her discomfort.

"I've an idea. How soon do you need to be back at the Village, Billy?" she asked.

"Why do you ask, Ms. Stratton?"

"Well, if you aren't in a big hurry, I can drive home now, and perhaps Chris could ride back with you later--if that would be OK."

"Would it!" Billy instantly realized that his answer had probably sounded a little too enthusiastic. "I don't need to hurry back. Mrs. Barquette will probably change her mind about the color of her walls two or three more times before she finally settles on a color. And Mrs. Murphy eats dinner in the dining room and shouldn't need to plug anything in for awhile. I'd be happy to be Chris's tour guide for the afternoon." Looking hopefully at Chris, he said, "If that's OK with you, of course."

"I'd like that," Chris replied quietly, her eyes looking down at the table top.

Billy and Chris escorted Emmy back to her car. He opened her car door and helped her into the driver's seat. "Are you sure you feel well enough to drive back by yourself?"

"I'm fine, Billy. I just need to rest awhile. A nap and I'll be good as new," she said, hoping she sounded convincing.

Billy and Chris stood at the curb and waved as Emmy pulled away and drove off toward home.

"Well, since I'm going to be your baby sitter for awhile . . . ."

"My what?"

"As I was saying, since I'm going to be your guide and designated driver, I feel it's my responsibility to ensure that you receive your money's worth during your Braxton Falls totally tailored tour.

"I certainly hope so, young man, or else I'll be obliged to dispatch a letter of complaint to the management of the BFTTT," Chris responded. She and Billy continued to pursue this lighthearted line of conversation. She couldn't help but wonder if Brad had been as open as Billy, whether their relationship could have lasted. In her heart, however, she knew that with Brad, it would have never been possible. The most important things in his life, besides his car, were his continuing education and future success. It had become obvious there was no room in his long-range plans for her. This had initially hurt Chris. But, on another level, she was relieved by Brad's initiating what could only be the inevitable outcome of their relationship. She wasn't certain whether Brad had outgrown her, or more likely, she had outgrown him. Either way, she was now convinced that their going separate ways was for the best.

Her thoughts were interrupted by Billy's voice. "Well, what would you like to see first, madam? The zoo, the planetarium, the history museum, the thirteen hole golf course, city hall, the bowling alley, the roller skating rink, the pool hall, the flea market, the yacht club, the antique mall and its thirty two spin-off antique shops and crafts stores, or, uh . . . ." Billy paused, out of breath.

"Really? You have a yacht club? The only water I've seen so far is the lake at the Village--and it's hardly big enough for a yacht. And a thirteen hole golf course? Do they have such things? And where are the "falls" in Braxton Falls?"

"Well, maybe I did exaggerate a bit. I was just checking to see if you were paying attention. But, Braxton Falls does have a nice museum, a bowling alley and a roller skating rink--and more antique shops than I can count. And, of course," here Billy took a big risk, "if you look to the west, you can see Grant's Bluff. It was named after President Ulysses S. Grant way back in 1868, after he dedicated a tree near the Civil War monument there. If you squint, you can just see the top of the monument. Sadly, the tree died that same winter. Today, the bluff's main claim to fame is as a place for the town's young people to go to watch the submarine races while the sun sets. Or, so they tell me. Have you ever seen a submarine race?"

"Are you flirting with me, Mister . . . ?"

"Come to think of it, I don't know your last name."

"Stoopnagle. William Claypipe Stoopnagle."

"Really?" Chris's mouth dropped open.

"No, of course not. It's Everett Randolph William Stoopnagle." Then, he added, "the third." Chris slapped Billy playfully on the shoulder. "Seriously, what is your full name?"

"How soon do you need to know?" Billy asked, tauntingly.

"Right now. Or I'll punch you harder."

"All right. All right. Don't hit me again. I bruise easily. My full name is William Elsworth Inch." Chris gave him another playful punch on the shoulder.

"No. Seriously. That's my real name. William, after my grandfather, and Elsworth after Major Elmer Elsworth, the first Union soldier killed in the Civil War. My father was a history buff. Come to think of it, I don't know your full name either."

"Christine Anne Patric."

"That's a pretty name. Mind if I call you Cap, for short?" Billy asked.

"You do, and you'll receive some major pain. Seriously, though, did you say Braxton Falls has a roller rink?"

"One of the finest. Hodges Roller Arena. It's an open air rink. It has a wooden frame with canvas sides—and a roof, of course. During warm weather, the sides are rolled up--unless it rains. When the weather gets cold or it gets too windy, they are rolled down and fastened at the bottom. The rink's floor is one inch thick tongue-and-groove hard maple--110 feet wide by 220 feet long. It was originally the floor of the old Wonderland Roller Rink in St. Louis. The city council saw it advertised for sale in a trade magazine and bought it shortly before the Wonderland building was converted into a dairy."

"How do you know so much about it?"

"It's my job. Twice a year, I put a fresh coat of wax on the floor to keep it smooth."

"Can you skate?" Chris's question momentarily caught Billy off guard.

"Can I skate? Can birds swim? Can fish fly? Would you like a demonstration? Maybe tonight? The rink hours are from 8 to 10 PM." Billy cocked his head to one side in anticipation of Chris's answer. She opened her mouth as to speak, and then hesitated. She thought of her aunt at home, probably in bed with pain. As much as she would like to spend more time with Billy, her first obligation was to her aunt. So, she said, "Why don't you call me tonight . . . about seven?"

Chapter 16

TODAY'S THE DAY?

IT WAS THE beginning of a perfect day. The sky was dark. The clouds were gray and heavy with rain ready to fall on the unsuspecting sleeping residents of Twilight Manor. Dominic Graystone was happy. He was whistling. He had awakened early, showered, shaved and eaten one of the store of energy bars he kept in the top drawer of his bureau. "It won't be long now," he muttered. "It won't be long now." He enjoyed repeating these words over and over. He felt more alive than he could remember having felt in a long time. "It won't be long now," he said again, this time in a whisper. Hastily, he dressed, double checked that all his lights were turned off, appliances unplugged and drapes closed. He left his apartment, double checked that the door behind him was tightly closed and locked. He jiggled the knob. All was well. "It won't be long now," he again repeated, more audibly this time.

There was hardly any traffic on Junction TT to Braxton Falls. But, then, there seldom was more than a trickle. The county road was used mainly by the residents of the Village for journeying into town to do their shopping, or whatever else they found to occupy themselves with there. He really didn't care about traffic or anything else at the moment, because it wouldn't be long before his mission would be completed and he would finally be at peace.

His old gray Checker four door former taxicab rolled noisily into an empty space at the curb in front of a silver colored parking meter. He bounded athletically out of the car, slamming and locking its driver's side door, pulling twice on the handle to make sure it was locked. Satisfied his vehicle was secure, he rammed a hand into his pants pocket in search of a quarter for the meter. His removed hand held only several pennies, two nickels and a paperclip. This momentarily dampened his festive mood. But, then he thought, it won't be long now, so why worry. He stepped up onto the curb. Looking up Main Street, he saw the sign, which pointed at the street like a directional finger. It read "Three Balls Pawn Shop and Antiques." He hurried toward this neon beacon of light. Reaching the door, he pulled vigorously on its handle, only to be met with resistance. The door was locked. He looked at the sign on the glass. CLOSED. He read the smaller hours of business below the large, red letters. It was fifteen minutes before the store would be open. He really didn't want to wait, but had no choice. He impatiently walked back down the street. Looking through several storefront windows, he saw that a few merchants were already in their closed shops, preparing for another business day. Soon, the street would again become alive with people and activity.

After his pocket watch assured him that the pawn shop would now be open, he hurriedly returned to it. His efforts with the door handle proved more successful this time. Entering, his first sight was of a small, balding man behind the counter, attempting to load a paper roll into his adding machine. The man momentarily raised his eyes and silently acknowledged Dominic, then returned to his task. Dominic surveyed the contents in the array of glass topped cases. In the third one, he saw what he wanted. It was a silver 38 caliber, snubbed nosed police revolver. Six shots. Or, was it eight? He couldn't remember. He did remember, though, that usually they were black, not silver. He had used one much like it in one of his movies. He momentarily wondered why he usually had been cast as an evil doer and seldom as a good guy. Seeing his reflection looking back at him from the case's glass top, his question was answered. He had to admit that he looked more like a villain than a hero. Having finished his struggle with the paper roll, the clerk approached Dominic.

"Yes sir. Something I can show you?"

"Uh, could I see that 38 caliber revolver?"

"This one?" There were three similar weapons in the case. The one the man's finger pointed to was the one Dominic was interested in.

"Uh, yeah." Dominic's voice was so soft it was barely audible.

"It's a beauty, ain't it? A retired policeman brought it in a couple weeks ago. He took good care of it. Carried it with him for more than twenty years, he said. Kept him alive a couple times, he said." He handed the gun to Dominic, who hefted it in his large hand, turned it over, and opened and spun the cylinder. He nodded his head in approval.

"Uh, how much you want for it?"

"It's a steal at a hundred and twenty five dollars."

"Uh. Do you have anything cheaper?"

"Not of this model, in this condition. It's like new. Been tenderly taken care of. Never had a shot fired in anger, so I was told."

"Well, uh, I guess it's OK. I really don't like paying that much for a 38, though."

"Tell you what I'll do. I'll throw in a box of ammo free." That seemed to satisfy Dominic.

"OK." He reached into his back pocket for his wallet. "How much did you say?"

"One twenty five. And I won't charge you sales tax. Quite a bargain, in my opinion."

Dominic counted out the money--six twenty dollar bills and a five. The clerk rang up the sale and placed the small handgun and cartridges in a plain brown paper bag.

"Thank you, sir. Come again." The comment made Dominic laugh to himself. "If you only knew," he said under his breath.

"What was that, sir?"

"Nothing."

Leaving the shop with his package grasped securely in his hand, the weight and feel of it lifted Dominic's spirits. It was going to be a good day after all. Returning to his parked car, he noticed a yellow colored parking ticket on the windshield under the wiper blade. Again he laughed, at the incongruity of this sight. He removed the paper, briefly looked at it, frowned, crumpled it and stuffed it into his pants pocket.

Back in his apartment, Dominic took his purchase out of the bag and examined it more closely. He hefted it a few times to become familiar with its feel, pointed it at a mirror, closed one eye and took aim at his reflection. Pulling the trigger, the click on the empty chamber unexpectedly startled him. Was he beginning to have second thoughts, he wondered? No, he told himself. He removed the cellophane from the small cardboard box of bullets, and opened the lid. He gently removed a shiny brass bullet and placed it into an open chamber. For the first time in a long time, he felt happy. He would finally do something right in his life. He closed the cylinder, twirled it, pointed the gun at his temple, and pulled the trigger. His action was met by the hollow sound of the hammer falling on an empty chamber. Again, he spun the cylinder. Again, he pulled the trigger. Again, the hammer fell on an empty chamber. "That's two," he said. As he was preparing to spin the cylinder a third time, the doorbell rang. He jumped, startled, his concentration broken.

"Who is it?" he asked in a hoarse voice, while hurriedly placing the gun and box of shells in the drawer of an end table.

"It's Billy." Dominic started to ask what he wanted. But, the young man had been good to him, so instead, he got up from the couch, walked to the door and opened it.

"Hi Dom. I haven't seen you around for awhile. I was just wondering how you were doing, and thought I'd look in on you while things were slow."

"Come in, Billy," Dominic said reluctantly, closing the door after him.

"You sure keep your place looking nice. I wish all the residents were as neat as you." Then, spying the empty paper bag on the coffee table, he pointed at it and said, "Guess you haven't done your housecleaning yet today." His comment was intended as a joke, since Billy had never before seen anything out of place in the apartment.

"Uh, sorry. I bought some things in town this morning and forgot the bag was there."

"Just joking with you, Dom. So, how've you been?"

"Never better, Billy. Never better."

"Well, you're looking good. Whatever you've been doing has obviously been good for you."

"That's true," Dom replied, with a lopsided attempt at a grin.

"You'll never believe this. But, when I was in town the other day, I stopped in at the video store. A couple months ago, I gave the manager a list of some of the movies you told me about being in, and asked if she could special order any of them from her old time movie sources. And guess what? She was able to find a copy of "Restless in Life." Dominic's eyes widened and his mouth dropped open.

"I remember that. It was the only one of the two movies I was in where I played a good guy. I was a detective sergeant. I even remember my lines. 'It's Mrs. Philips, Captain.' And when he said, 'send her in,' I replied, 'Go right on in, Ma'am,' and held the door open for her. That was a long time ago. But, somehow it seems like only yesterday. Makes you wonder, sometimes, where all the years have gone, doesn't it?" He looked wistfully at Billy, who seemed pleased that he had done something to brighten Dominic's day, little knowing that the man had other ideas about how to brighten his day.

"Maybe we can watch it together, Dom. I'd like to see you in action."

"Maybe, Billy. Maybe. I'll let you know. Thanks for your thoughtfulness." In the back of his mind, Dominic still harbored other, more ominous plans for the near future. Although, he had to admit that it would be nice to see himself young again. At that moment, Billy's beeper sounded. He apologized and left to see what the Schwartz's needed this time, leaving Dominic alone with his thoughts.

Chapter 17

THE DATE

THE KEY TURNING in the lock woke Emmy. Having lived alone most of her life, it was a sound she was not accustomed to hearing. Two things came immediately to mind. She had no pain in her leg or back, and Chris was home. Instinctively, she asked, "Is that you Chris?"

"No. It's a cat burglar. Got any cats worth stealing? Of course it's me, Aunt Em. Or were you expecting your boyfriend?"

"Ha, ha. Very funny. How was your afternoon with Billy?"

"It was really nice, Aunt Em. I like him. We went to the Museum of Modern Art and saw a touring exhibit. Billy said he had done better work with a four inch brush. I'm basically a traditionalist and post-impressionist, but it was interesting. You can't argue taste. Afterward, we must have visited a dozen antique shops. I even bought you something.

"You shouldn't have!"

"When I show you what it is you'll change your mind."

Emmy sat up on the edge of the bed and put on her slippers. Chris had piqued her curiosity. "Well, come in here and tell me more about your day," she said. Chris entered, rattling a small ornate box.

"Oh, good. Just what I always wanted--a small, noisy box."

"Wait till I show you what's in it." Chris waved the box back and forth, teasingly, in front of Emmy's face. Then, with a flourishing bow, she handed it to her. Emmy opened the box and saw an ornate brooch. "Oh, you shouldn't have. You remembered how much I like cameos. This is beautiful." She held it up to the light. It was a small, oval black and white profile of a Greek woman's face, framed by a gold bezel.

"You can wear it as a brooch or a pendant. The antique store lady told me it was made in 1898, and was a fine example of some period I don't remember the name of. It's all hand carved and set in fourteen carat gold."

"It must have cost you a fortune."

"Not really. I only have to make monthly payments for the next five years, and give up my first born child. But, it was a bargain. It would have cost me twice as much back home."

Emmy was overwhelmed. She liked jewelry, but seldom bought any, her excuse being that she never went anywhere to wear it.

"Well, thank you Chris. That was so thoughtful. But, I still say you shouldn't have done it." She gave Chris a hug.

"I just wanted to get you some small token of appreciation for taking this poor orphan girl in for a couple weeks so her parents could gallivant around the world without guilt, and not have to worry about what trouble their daughter would be getting into. It's a small enough price to pay for your putting up with me."

A tear rolled down Emmy's cheek. Changing the subject, she asked, "What else did the two of you do this afternoon?"

"Do you mean besides making mad, passionate love in the backseat of Billy's truck?"

"Chris! Don't shock your old maid aunt--or make me jealous. Besides, Billy's truck doesn't have a back seat. Seriously, did you see anything besides the museum?"

"We mostly walked around downtown and Billy told me about the history of some of the old buildings. We even took a tour of a 1800s mansion. That's the way I want to live when I get married."

Emmy looked at the clock. It was just after five thirty. "Have you eaten anything?"

"Uh-huh. Billy took me to a quaint Italian restaurant. Do you know what penne is?"

"Of course. They're round, hollow pasta noodles."

"Well, I had some, in a creamy sauce, with strips of chicken. Brad never took me any place like that. But, more importantly, how are you feeling? You look better."

"I feel better. I don't hurt anywhere. Sometimes I get a little overtired and my body tells me to slow down. I'm fine now. So, what are your plans for this evening?"

"Why do you think I have any?"

"By that Cheshire cat look on your face."

"Is it that obvious? I don't really have anything firm planned. I first wanted to see how you felt and what you preferred to do this evening."

"Actually, I'm fine. And I'd be happy to stay in, relax and read a good book, if that wouldn't disappoint you."

With some hesitation, Chris asked, "So, you wouldn't mind me going out this evening and leaving you alone?"

"Not at all. What were you and Billy planning to do?"

"Well, since you asked, if you would rather be alone this evening, he's offered to take me to a movie and show me the view of town from Grant's Bluff afterward."

"And watch the submarine races?"

Chris's mouth dropped open and her face flushed. "Does Billy have a reputation for doing that?" Chris asked, surprised that her aunt knew about such things.

Emmy laughed. "No. But, I wasn't always an old maid aunt. Before my accident, I was known to socialize with the opposite sex on occasion. I don't want to shock you, but I watched a few submarine races during my misspent youth."

Chris was relieved. She didn't know why the thought of Billy being with other girls bothered her, but it did. Emmy said, "Go ahead. It'll do you good. You should spend some time with people your own age."

"I told him to call me about seven and I'd let him know if you and I had anything planned." She looked at the clock. It was almost six o'clock, past her aunt's normal dinner time.

"Well, then," since it's time for dinner, are you interested in going to the dining room with me, or are you even hungry?"

"I'm always hungry, Aunt Em. I've time to eat with you before Brad . . . oops . . . Billy calls."

Emmy and Chris returned from dinner ten minutes before seven. Chris immediately changed into a sweater blouse, keeping on the same pair of jeans. At precisely seven, the phone rang. Chris let it ring three times before answering. She didn't want to appear overanxious.

"Hello, Joe's Bar and Grill," she said.

"Oh, I'm sorry. I was calling a beautiful young lady. I must have misdialed.

"This isn't a beautiful young lady, but will I do instead?"

"Well, it depends. Her name is Cap. She's about five foot four, blonde pony tail, sky blue eyes, and a lilting voice. Can you compete with that?"

"Yes, except for the lilting voice. Mine is more like a fog horn. And my initials are C-A-P.

"Close enough. Are you available tonight?"

"That depends. What did you have in mind?"

Billy gave his best imitation of a wicked witch, and said, "You'll just have to wait and see, me pretty!"

"That sounds like an offer I can't refuse. I'm yours--in a manner of speaking."

"That's what I was hoping to hear. Do you like old movies?"

"Some. Did you have a particular one in mind?"

"The local theater is doing a retrospective series of nineteen thirty's and forty's films. Tonight's offering is Casablanca, with Humphrey Bogart and Ingrid Bergman. Have you heard of it?"

"Are you serious? That's one of my favorite films! I must have seen it three or four times. I cried every time. I'm surprised it's something you would want to see."

"Mr. Graystone in building C has a collection of old time movies on videotape. He lends me one now and then. And we talk about movies a lot. He was an actor in his younger days, bit parts mostly. But, he knows a lot about Hollywood and movie making. He's an interesting man to talk to, if you get him on the right subject. So, I guess you aren't interested in going to a movie you've already seen."

"On the contrary. My philosophy is that you can never read a good book or see a good movie too many times--especially this one."

"Good. The show starts at seven thirty. If I pick you up in five minutes, we can just make it. I'll even bring along an extra handkerchief."

"Sounds good. See you shortly."

"Oh, and bring a jacket. It gets kind of cool up on Grant's Bluff at night. Bye."

"What do you mean . . .?" Billy had hung up before she could finish her sentence. It was five after seven. She combed her hair and put on fresh lipstick, then turned to Emmy and asked her how she looked. She didn't quite know how to accept the answer. "You look like a high school girl about to go on her first date." Considering her tumultuous relationship with Brad, the statement had a ring of truth to it.

There was a knock on the door. Chris hesitated before opening it, counting to three before she did so. "I hope I'm not too early," Billy said, jokingly, since he had arrived in four minutes instead of five. "No, you're right on time, give or take a minute," Chris replied. "In spite of all your faults, I have to admit you're punctual."

"Faults. What faults?" Billy feigned a hurt look. Emmy walked into the room.

"Oh, hi, Ms. Stratton. I'll take good care of Chris. I'll have her back in a day or two."

"You two have a good time," Emmy said, laughing. She turned to Chris and added, "I'll probably be asleep when you get back. You've got a key, so just let yourself in."

"Oh," Chris exclaimed. She quickly disappeared into the bedroom and came back with a jacket over her arm.

Billy's pickup truck was several years old and rode like what it was, but Chris was enjoying this ride considerably more than the one's she had shared with Brad in his BMW. In the twilight, a full moon began casting filmy gray shadows over the countryside. It was only a fifteen minute drive to Braxton Falls, and they arrived exactly at seven thirty. Billy told Chris that Sam, the projectionist, who was in his eighties and getting a little absent minded, didn't always start the movie right on time. The couple chatted easily until the lights dimmed, five minutes late, and the screen lit up. Then they both sat silent, engrossed in the classic 1942 film. As Chris had warned Billy earlier, she began sobbing softly during the scene where the two lovers were to be parted. Without taking his eyes off the screen, Billy removed a fresh handkerchief from his pocket and offered it to her. Chris accepted it wordlessly and began drying her eyes.

As they left the theater, Billy asked Chris how she had enjoyed the movie. Her eyes were red and damp. She answered by nodding her head, afraid that if she spoke, her voice would crack. Billy asked if she was hungry. To her surprise, she wasn't. The popcorn and soft drink she had consumed during the movie were all she needed. They returned to the truck and Billy opened the door and helped her into the cab. Without a word, they drove out of town and turned off on a road that Chris didn't recognize. Soon, they were going up an incline, the truck's engine protesting under the effort. Billy made a semicircle turn at the top. They drove around a large, shadowy stone structure and Chris was suddenly exposed to an array of lights from cars, houses and street lamps shining below them. Billy was the first to speak.

"Well, what do you think?"

"Oh, it's beautiful. So peaceful." The sun had long since disappeared and they shared the darkness. Thousands of stars blinked on and off above them. Billy reached across the seat and gently took Chris's hand in his. They sat there, quiet, looking, in turn, at the small lights twinkling above and the display of larger moving and still lights below. They were content in each others company. Words were unnecessary. Billy helped Chris put her jacket on. He was right, it did get cold on Grant's Bluff at night. He slid his arm across the seat's back and around Chris's shoulders and slowly pulled her toward him. With his other hand, he lifted her chin and turned her face toward him. He softly kissed her lips. Warmness flowed through her. Chris couldn't help but compare Billy's touch and kisses to Brad's. The difference between them was that she enjoyed the one and had dreaded the other. The moon was proudly demonstrating its pale beauty. Two young people were feeling close in body and spirit under its pale light. The moment couldn't have been better for either of them. The future was unknown, but the now was everything one could wish for. They sat that way for several minutes, occasionally sharing longer kisses, their open mouths exploring each other's.

Chris felt safe and secure with Billy's arm around her. She found herself wanting more from him than kisses. But, her upbringing told her that it would be too much, too soon. She and Brad had never consummated their relationship, just engaged in some heavy petting. But, now, she was conflicted. Her mind and her body were sending different messages. She didn't want to lose his arm around her or the feel the warmth of his body pressed against hers, yet she knew it was probably best they start back to the Village, before she allowed her body to overrule her mind. She moved away from Billy and said, "I hate to say this, Billy, but I think we should be going." Billy sighed. He thought too much of this young woman to try to influence her or take advantage of her vulnerability and have her regret it later. He removed his arm from around her and started the engine. They drove back to the Village in silence, her hand covered by his. Arriving, Billy parked the truck in front of building B and they entered through the side door. It was eleven thirty three. Most of the residents, with the possible exception of Mrs. Murtenson, had probably retired for the night. Billy walked Chris to her aunt's door. Once there, he put his arms around her waist and pulled her to him. She was standing on her toes, her arms around his neck. They kissed long, deeply and passionately. His hands moved down from her waist to encircle her hips, pulling her tightly against him. Then one hand found its way under her sweater blouse and caressed her breast.

"Please, Billy," came her weak protest as she removed his hand. "I think I better go in, before I make a fool of myself," she said unconvincingly. "I'll see you tomorrow, OK?"

"I'll look forward to it," he replied. His heart was pounding and his breathing was labored.

"I really enjoyed this evening. Thanks for being so understanding," Chris said, almost apologetically.

"You're welcome," he replied. Realizing how weak a response that was, he added, "Good night. I'll talk to you tomorrow." Then, he turned, and quickly walked away.

Chris quietly unlocked the door and went inside. Her resistance to Billy had become borderline and she didn't trust herself as to what she would have done had they stayed together much longer.

"That you, Chris?" came a voice from the bedroom.

"Yes, Aunt Em." Chris was not in a mood for a witty response to the question.

"Did you have a good time?"

"Yes, Aunt Em."

"Who won the submarine race?" her aunt asked, hoping to elicit more than a three word answer.

"It was a tie," was Chris's subdued reply. With that, she went into the bathroom and prepared for bed.

Chapter 18

TROUBLE IN PARADISE?

IT WAS RAINING heavily and the sky was dark. There was a feeling of uneasiness in the air in the normally tranquil setting of the Village. Billy was reliving the events of the previous evening in his mind. He was feeling guilty and not certain why. Although he felt he had overstepped the boundaries of proper behavior in his aggressiveness toward Chris, he had no regrets. His main concern was how she would view him now, and whether she would want to see him again. He hoped so. He planned to apologize to her as soon as he had time. But, work had kept him from calling her. Demands on his time towards the needs of the Village ranged from feast to famine. Weeks would go by where he merely attended to routine maintenance and cleaning projects. Often, however, this would be followed by an onrush of priority and emergency jobs--repairing a major plumbing problem, rewiring an electrical circuit breaker, repairing one of the riding mowers that the contract lawn service personnel used to manicure the grounds, and frequent trips into town to buy repair parts and replacement items. Normally, this was fine with Billy. He enjoyed keeping busy. When things were too quiet and no one needed his services, he became restless and time seemed to stand still. Worse, his mind now was divided between his projects and wondering what Chris thought of him and his crude behavior. He hoped he hadn't offended her. He liked her and didn't want to do anything to cause a rift in their relationship. She hadn't acted offended, but with women, Billy rationalized, one could never be sure.

Mrs. Murtenson was in near frenzy. She had run out of reading material. She had finished her latest novel the previous night and had devoured the daily newspaper before breakfast. She had checked with the Village's librarian and was disappointed to learn that the novels she had ordered still had not arrived. "What was life without books?" she had asked the woman. She had even read the back of her cereal box twice while eating breakfast. Desperate, she began to re-read a novel she had only half finished because it had put her to sleep. It had the same effect on her second attempt. She was pacing and thinking. Maybe Gertie Raymond in 22C would have some reading material. Her phone call met with no answer. Gertie had been a physical education teacher, and still jogged down to the lake and back most mornings before breakfast, rain or shine. Mrs. Murtenson made a mental note to call her again in a few minutes. However, when the few minutes had passed, Mrs. Murtenson lay asleep on her couch, mouth open, snoring evenly.

Dominic was fighting an inner demon. He removed the revolver from its hiding place and closely examined it. He began to wonder if a 38 was too small a caliber gun to properly perform what he needed it to do. Maybe he needed t a 44 caliber--or perhaps a Magnum 357. He had used one of those once in a movie. He remembered it had quite a kick, even using blanks. Perhaps the 44 was the proper tool for the job. He decided he would give some more thought to the subject.

All was quiet in the Stratton household, although a sense of uneasiness could be sensed in the room. Emmy wondered what Chris was thinking about as she watched her sit motionless, staring out the window, seemingly entranced by the tiny rivulets of rain slowly cascading down the glass. She had been unusually pensive this morning--not her usual upbeat self.

Chris was upset with herself. Would Billy think she was a prude, or worse yet, a virgin, which technically she was. What Brad had considered sex was far different than her definition of the word. She worried that Billy wouldn't want to see her again because she had acted so childish. After all, she reasoned, she was a grown woman in every sense of the word. She continued to analyze her previous night's behavior. She had enjoyed Billy's holding her and kissing her--and touching her. She wanted to call him, but felt that would be too forward. Hopefully, he would call her. But, if she didn't hear from him by lunchtime, she decided that she would call--forward or not.

On the other side of the room, Emmy was deep in her own thoughts. The episode with her leg and back had her concerned. Normally, she went for weeks or months with little or no pain. She felt all right at the moment, but she wondered if the previous day was just the beginning of a new episode in her life. She had been feeling somewhat depressed lately. Chris's arrival had cheered her. Although they didn't see each other often, the times they did were pleasantly memorable. They enjoyed being together and their personalities and interests were similar. But, Chris was young and had her whole life ahead of her. Emmy wondered what her life would have been like, and be like now, had it not been for that unforgettable accident and long, painful period of recovery. She could visualize herself as a successful dancer with a long and rewarding career on the stage. She compared herself to a Roman candle--bright and fiery, but too soon burning out and becoming mere ashes. That was how she viewed herself--burnt out. During periods of depression, she wondered what the point of her life was. She felt that she wasn't contributing anything in her current role. She lived one day much the same as any other. She felt she was just taking up space in the world by not justifying her existence.

This line of thinking began to trouble her. She knew it wasn't a healthy attitude. But, sadly, she felt it was a realistic one. Perhaps, when she went back to her orthopedist, she would ask him for some tranquilizers to soften the sharp edges of her life.

Mr. Schultz was frustrated with what he considered the clutter of his wife's "bathroom junk." He had asked her many times if all those bottles, tubes and boxes were really necessary. After all, he wondered, who needs twenty tubes of lipstick? She only had one mouth. Surely, she could do with only one lipstick. That would be a big step toward reducing some of the problems in their marriage--as he saw them. Maybe the next time she was at the beauty parlor, he would throw half the items into the dumpster. She would probably never miss them. He doubted if she even knew what all she had. It was something to think about. He made himself a cup of strong, black coffee and planned his next move, while his wife Sadie napped innocently in the next room.

The half painted lilac wall was beginning to gnaw at Mrs. Barquette's nerves. She kept looking from the wall to her beige drapes, and back to the wall, doing a fair impression of a pedestrian attempting to cross a busy intersection. "It just won't do. It just won't do," she kept repeating. "I'll have to talk to that young man. This just won't do."

Mrs. Barquette had lived by herself some thirty years. That was how long it had been since her husband Clarence had passed away. While he was alive, they had frequent conversations. She talked and he listened. Now that he was gone, she continued to talk but there was no one to listen, although that didn't seem to make any difference to her. She continued to talk, anyway.

Colleen Murphy continued to stare at the shiny new wall plug like it was an alien from another planet. She cocked her head to the right and stared. And then she cocked her head to the left and stared. Either way, it looked the same to her. But, that didn't mean she had to like it. She couldn't help wondering why things had to keep changing. Once something worked, why couldn't they just leave it alone and quit tinkering? She couldn't abide change. Things were so much simpler when she and her late husband Fred had set up housekeeping. That was--she couldn't remember the year--but it was a long time ago, she knew that.

"The oven still didn't work right," according to Leia Leighton. She had told that nice looking young maintenance man time and time again, that it needed adjusting. And, she had become upset when Billy implied that perhaps she could adjust her cooking time to include a few minutes more, to see if that would correct the problem. That idea was unacceptable to her way of thinking. After all, she had been cooking for over fifty years. She certainly knew how to use an oven. She knew how it was supposed to work, and this one just didn't work right. "It's supposed to work right without having to tinker with it," she had told him firmly. She was still upset, and swore never to use that "devil contraption" again. Perhaps she should ask him to install a wood burning stove like her mother had when she was a girl--and cook on that.

Perhaps the edginess some members of the community were feeling had something to do with a change in the weather. Or, maybe it was just one of those cycles in people's lives which occasionally occur, when things just don't seem to go the way they want or think they should, no matter what they do. It's even possible that some residents felt that the excitement had gone out of their lives with the all too rapidly passing of time and loss of loved ones and friends. Normally, the population of Twilight Manor was a happy, outgoing, friendly and active group of individuals and couples who enjoyed sharing their lives and activities with others, while maintaining their independence and cherishing a degree of privacy. Most were happy with their situations in life. Others missed the challenges and responsibilities of the working world and family structure of yesteryear. To still others, the memories of the struggles and hard times of years past were forgotten, and the good memories came to be remembered as better than the realities.

Chapter 19

THE UNDERSTANDING

EMMY WAS CONCERNED about Chris. She was not her usual outgoing, energetic self. She seemed to be locked deep in thought. In Emmy's opinion, this was not a healthy sign in this vital young woman. When questioning her about what was bothering her, Chris gave the standard answer. "Nothing." But, her behavior belied her denial. Emmy did not want to overreact in expressing her concerns, but she felt that while Chris was in her charge, it was her responsibility to ensure that the young woman enjoyed her vacation, and that it was up to her to find out what the problem was, and how she could help resolve it.

At breakfast, Chris kept looking out the window. She seemed restless and upset.

"Do you want some coffee, Chris?" Emmy asked, hoping for an opening to a conversation.

"OK," came the terse reply.

"What would you like for breakfast?"

"Cold cereal is OK."

"I'm concerned about you. At the risk of sounding like a nosy body, do you mind telling me what's bothering you?"

Chris began to again say "nothing", but thought better of it. She knew that she owed her aunt an explanation. It wasn't fair to her to be so evasive. "Are you sure you want to know, Aunt Em?"

"Of course, I do. Your problems are my problems." Then, with an attempt at lightheartedness, she added, "at least until your mother comes home. And, after all, you are my favorite niece." This old family joke brought a slight smile to Chris's lips. She turned to Emmy and said, "It's Billy." Emmy wasn't too surprised that a boy was at the heart of Chris's problems.

"Oh, you mean that big ugly, good for nothing hired hand who pretends to work here?" Emmy said, teasingly trying to get Chris to open up to her.

"Don't talk about him like that, Aunt Em. He's one of the nicest people I've met. He's a lot nicer than Brad." As soon as these words left her lips, she realized she had made a mistake in comparing Billy to Brad. "I didn't really mean that. Brad was a good person--in his own way. It's just that his way and my way were different. So, now, when I find someone I really enjoy being with, shortly after meeting him, I make a mess of things.

"That's better. Recognizing a problem is half the solution, isn't it?"

"Are you sure you weren't in my Human Relations 101 class?" Chris asked, beginning to act more like herself again. "I realize that I've only known Billy a short time, but, somehow, it seems like I've known him all my life. I know that sounds like I'm a teenager having a crush on a boy. It's just that I feel so comfortable with him. But, then I have to go and act like a child around him." Chris went on to recount her and Billy's awkward good night kiss and parting--and how she had wanted more, but was too confused to trust herself. When Brad had acted like Billy, she resented and discouraged it. When Billy showed affection, she liked it, but now he probably thought she didn't want his attentions. She was not upset with Billy for what he had done. She was upset with herself for handling a delicate situation indelicately. Worse, she felt that Billy had felt rejected and probably thought that she was just a tease and would not want to see her again. Emmy did not know quite what to say. She had dated some before her accident, and experienced relationship situations similar to what Chris was talking about. That was a long time ago, and times change. She was not sure whether advice from someone her age would apply to a modern young woman of today. And with Chris being her niece, Emmy was wondering whether she could be objective in giving advice. As she was trying to think of the right words of encouragement or caution, the telephone rang. Standing near the phone, Emmy quickly answered it.

"Hello?" she said, half questioningly. She was thankful for the temporary interruption.

"Hi. Is this Ms. Stratton or Chris? Your voices sound so much alike."

"Oh, hi Billy. This is Chris's aunt. I suppose you want to speak to her." Chris's full attention was on her aunt's side of the conversation. She held her arm out toward Emmy in a silent request for the phone, which her aunt placed gently in her hand.

"Is that you, Billy?" she asked nervously.

"No, it's Christopher Columbus. My boat just got in and I thought I'd give you a call. You know how we sailors are, a girl in every port." As soon as he said it, he thought how insensitive it must have sounded. He too was nervous and not quite certain how to direct the subject of their conversation.

"Well, hi, sailor," Chris replied, cheerfully. "What's new?"

"I'm sorry I didn't call you sooner. Mrs. Barquette has been driving me up a wall-- literally. She changed her mind again, and I had to go back to town to exchange her paint. Nick at the hardware store is probably going to lock the door the next time he sees me coming. Guess what color she wants now?"

"White?" Chris guessed.

"How did you know? She decided the only color that would go with her drapes and furniture was a neutral one. And, in her words, 'white goes with everything.' I didn't want to tell her, but it's not that much different from the beige I started out with. But, if she's happy with white, I'm happy with white. And now, maybe I can have a little time for more important things--like you."

"You're just like all the other sailors I've known. Sweet talkers. Must be all that salty sea air." Emmy breathed a sigh of relief. Things were back to normal. She was relieved that her advice and counseling would not be needed--at least, not for now.

"Seriously though, I think I owe you an apology for my behavior when I took you home last night," Billy continued.

"Why?" was Chris's short reply. We're both grown up. At least, I am."

"Me, too. Almost! So, you're not mad? I was going to use the excuse that I had just washed my hands and couldn't do a thing with them. But, then I thought that's a pretty lame excuse for bad behavior."

"What bad behavior? I had a nice time, Billy. I enjoy being with you, if you can put up with my occasional adolescent behavior."

"No problem, there. I-I didn't mean you're an adolescent," he stuttered. "What I meant was . . . ." Chris interrupted him.

"Say no more. I think we can settle this case out of court with a plea bargain."

"Thank you, your Honor. Would completion of our Village tour be an appropriate place to begin?

"Accepted. And, I won't even put you under house arrest, or on probation." Hearing Billy breathe an audible sigh of relief, Chris laughed quietly, her hand over the mouthpiece of the telephone. Their conversation was becoming more relaxed.

"Would I sound overanxious if I suggested we do the rest of our tour this afternoon, and then go into town for dinner, and maybe go roller skating afterward?"

"Let me check my social calendar for today," she replied, looking questioningly toward her aunt for approval. Emmy smiled and nodded. Sensing that her presence was no longer needed, she quietly went into the bedroom so the couple could continue their phone play in private.

"I think I can fit you in. What did you say your name was again, sailor?"

"You can just call me sailor, although I answer to almost anything," Billy replied, feeling better about himself and his relationship with Chris.

"Just one caveat," Chris added. "What's your plan for holding up a skater with two left feet?"

"Just one what? You college girls sure use big words. Aren't caveats fish eggs?" Billy asked in mock seriousness.

"No, silly. But, I'll try to keep our conversation in single syllables for your benefit," Chris replied jokingly. Her voice had become relaxed and her conversation easy.

"I'd appreciate that. Actually, I've only roller skated once or twice, but it's probably like riding a bicycle. I'll hold you up as much as you need and hold you as close as you'll let me."

There was a slight pause in the conversation while Chris tried to think of a good reply. Finally, she said, "You sailor's sure know how to charm a girl. So, what you're really saying is that we can lean on each other to keep both of us from falling down and embarrassing ourselves."

"You see right through me, don't you?"

"Not yet. But, it's getting easier."

Chapter 20

DATING AND SKATING

IT WAS TWO thirty in the afternoon. Chris was deciding what to wear for her day with Billy. She reasoned that since they were probably going to go roller skating, jeans and her favorite blouse would be appropriate. But, for the afternoon, jeans and a T-shirt would do. She looked at the clock. He would arrive shortly. She nervously ran a brush through her ash blonde hair for the third time, then secured it into a ponytail with a green ribbon.

There was a knock at the door.

"I'll get it Aunt Em," Chris said. Opening the door, she laughed. Billy was standing there, a white sailor's cap cocked back on his head and a wide grin on his face. Instead of hello, he said, "Yo, ho, ho, lassie. It's eight bells and your sailor boy has docked." This was one of the things Chris liked about Billy. He could be serious, but he was not hesitant to be playful. Their conversations complemented one another's, with their offbeat senses of humor and quick witted responses to each others joking and teasing.

"Come on in, sailor. Are you ready to take me on my voyage around the Village?"

"My wish is your command, fair lady. Or is it the other way around? Either way, shall we be off?" he asked.

"I think we both already are," Chris replied, laughingly.

Emmy entered the living room, greeted Billy and smiled when she saw his cap and overheard the tone of their conversation. She turned to go into the kitchen to prepare her mid afternoon snack of tea and graham crackers. Her departing words were "Be back before nine," to which Chris responded with one of her "Oh, Aunty Em" looks.

As the couple walked down the flagstone path to the gazebo by the lake, Chris could not contain her curiosity, and asked, "How can you afford to take a whole day away from your work, Billy?"

"Pop's covering for me. He said he'll take care of anything that comes up, except for dealing with Mrs. Leighton. He doesn't have the patience or the tact to deal with her indecisiveness and imaginary problems. But, she can't come up with anything that won't wait until tomorrow."

Billy had brought some stale bread from the Village's kitchen and the two sat quietly and at peace on a bench at the edge of the water, throwing morsels to the transient geese which had settled onto the mirror smooth wetness. Several other geese, which had been sunning themselves at the edge of the lake, joined those in the water and charged around in a crazy quilt pattern, vying competitively for the small projectiles of food, flapping their wings and squawking noisily. A gentle breeze was blowing and at the moment, neither Chris nor Billy felt the need for any words. They were content simply being together.

After the bread was gone, the two walked back up the hill, hand in hand, toward the golf course. Once there, they each selected a "lucky" putter at the golf shack. Billy suggested that the first one who holed a twenty foot putt on the putting green would have their dinner paid for by the other one. Chris readily agreed.

She didn't mention to Billy that she had played golf in high school and was on the University's women's golf team. When she was the first to sink a putt, she passed it off as beginner's luck. Billy looked at her with disbelief, but quietly said, "I think you've played this game before." Chris said nothing, and, in false shyness, looked down at her feet.

The next stop on Billy's tour was the game room, where they played four games of table tennis, each winning two. Afterward, they visited the swimming pool and watched the aquacise class for a few minutes. All the exercisers, except for one man whose wife had insisted he join her, were women. Emmy had earlier mentioned to Chris how much the water aerobics classes had helped to ease her leg pain. At first, self conscious about her scarred leg, she had been reluctant to join the other women in the pool. When she finally did, no one seemed to notice. Some of the other women also had "battle scarred" legs, arms and shoulders. Others wore cotton T-shirts over their swim suits to hide their body's flaws--real or imagined.

Billy looked at his watch. It was five fifteen.

"Are you getting hungry, Chris?" he asked.

"A little," she replied.

"We've covered most of the tour, except for the fitness center, library, lounge, and, of course, my room." Chris's face reddened slightly at this last reference. Billy noticed, but chose not to say anything. Changing the subject, he asked if she would like to go swimming the next day. She nodded her head, and then qualified its movement with, "If Aunt Em doesn't have something else planned for me."

"OK. I'll take that as a maybe. For now, why don't we head into town and look the place over a bit before dinner?"

"First, let me run by the apartment to change. What does one wear on a combination fine dining and roller skating date?"

"You're fine just the way you are. Whatever you wear, I'll be the envy of every other man at both places."

"You sure know how to say the right things to a girl. But, seriously, let me go put on another top and pick up a sweater--in case it gets cold at the submarine races later. Billy did not know if Chris was teasing or serious, but he didn't want to press his luck by asking.

Chris made a quick stop at her aunt's apartment, and then she and Billy headed for Braxton Falls. The drive found them both in pensive moods. Chris commented on the picturesque old, faded red covered bridge, and how soothing it seemed going through it. She had a psychological explanation for this, but did not feel that this was the time or the place to expound on what Sigmund Freud had to say about such feelings. So, she kept her thoughts to herself.

Most of the antique shops had closed by the time they reached town. The large antique mall was still open, but would be closing shortly, so the couple browsed hurriedly through the cavernous building with its maze of treasure filled cubicle sized booths. Billy was attracted to a large, floppy Gay Nineties woman's hat and insisted on buying it for Chris. She wore it until they exited his truck at the Carriage House restaurant--which was doing a rush hour business. Billy and Chris had to wait several minutes to be seated. They filled the time easily with personal conversation. They were interested in each others lives, experiences, opinions, and feelings about life in general.

Once Chris and Billy were seated and had an opportunity to review the menu, a waiter who seemed to have appeared from nowhere, asked if they were ready to order.

"What do you recommend?" Chris asked Billy.

"Well, since I come here practically every night with a different young lady, I feel confident in recommending the caviar and pheasant under glass."

Chris shot him one of her "be serious" looks.

"OK. Seriously, the roasted chicken chardonnay is good."

Looking up at the waiter, Chris said, "I'll have the roasted chicken chardonnay, please."

"Good choice, ma'am. And what can I bring you to drink?"

"Just water, please."

"Yes ma'am. And you, sir?"

"I'll have the same--and a cup of coffee."

The waiter vanished as quickly as he had appeared and Chris and Billy continued their conversation until their food arrived. They ate quietly and thoughtfully, enjoying their meals. After dinner, they walked down Main Street and window shopped until time to go skating.

The rink, which sat on a hill just outside of town, was as Billy had earlier described it. The canvas sides were rolled up and a gentle breeze blew through the open space. It carried with it the faint sweet scent of a blossom Chris couldn't identify. They sat next to each other on the wooden bench that ran the length of one side of the rink, and laced up their rented shoe skates. Several skaters were already on the floor. The venerable Mr. Hodges, owner and floor manager, was leisurely skating backward, keeping an eye on his charges, occasionally warning a skater to slow down or to stop weaving in and out. This was accomplished with a shrill blast from the silver whistle that hung loosely around his neck on a white cord. Whenever the music from the overhead sound system changed from a waltz to a tango, skaters automatically quickened the pace of their progress around the floor. There was a full wall mirror at the far end of the rink, on the one solid wall of the building, making it appear twice its actual length. Most of the skaters were teenagers and young adults. Pre-teens usually filled the rink during the Saturday and Sunday afternoon matinees.

Their wooden wheeled shoe skates securely laced, Billy and Chris edged slowly along the railing and onto the outside lane of the polished hardwood floor. Billy took Chris's hand and bravely and carefully led her into the heavier traffic closer to the center of the skating surface. He put his right arm around her waist and held her left hand in the traditional partner's skating position. He was again reminded how small and firm her waist was. He enjoyed the feel of her close to him. This was the first time he had had skates on since he was a teenager and he was a little unsteady. Instead of him supporting Chris, she was helping hold him upright. When she was seven years old, she had learned to sidewalk skate, wearing strap-on skates with metal wheels. Years later, her mother had told her that every time she had seen Chris fall, she wanted to go pick her up and comfort her. But, Chris would always get right back up, brush imaginary dirt off her backside and continue back and forth on the walk in front of their house until she fell again, which, that first year, was often. When she was twelve, her father took her to a real roller rink, and she became a Saturday matinee regular. When she was fourteen, she took skate dancing lessons at the Crystal Roller Rink and became adept at two stepping, waltzing, fox trotting and tangoing with class partners. The rink had had live music. A gnome of a man sat in an elevated, glass windowed booth, his head barely visible over the top of an electric organ, and played skater's requests. So far as Chris knew, no one had ever requested a song that could be skated to, that the organist could not play. Chris had had a preference for waltzes, and frequently requested Beautiful Ohio and the Missouri Waltz. The music at this rink was provided by a sound system consisting of long play records on a turntable.

Billy continued to be impressed with Chris's abilities in so many activities. It seemed to him that whatever they did together, she was better at it than he was. But, this failed to dampen or damage his spirit. He was proud of her abilities. She had neglected to inform him of her skating background, but it took only a turn or two around the rink for him to realize what an experienced skater she was. The pair skated together in the "All Skate," "Couples Only" and "Ladies Choice" calls, sitting out only once, during the "Speed Skate" segment--an event which attracted mostly teenage boys. This gave Billy an excuse to rest his feet and legs. He and Chris shared a soft drink and enjoyed watching the skaters zoom recklessly around the length and width of the floor. Chris could not help but wonder what would happen if one of those skater's speed kept him from making a turn and he collided with the mirrored wall. Fortunately, this did not happen. The final call of the evening was for "Moonlight Skate." A large, rotating, faceted glass ball hung from a rafter at the center of the rink, casting snowflake-like moving dots of light on the darkened floor, providing the only illumination for the skaters. Chris felt warm and soft against Billy in the darkness. He leaned toward her and gently kissed her on the top of her head. She raised her face to him, offered her mouth, and he kissed her again. They held the kiss until they barely escaped running into a railing.

Chapter 21

THE LONG GOODNIGHT

IT WAS GETTING late. Billy and Chris had enjoyed their day, but now it was time to be getting back to the Village. As they walked to Billy's truck in the rink's parking lot they were tired but happy from their time together. During skating, Billy had taken several falls onto the unyielding wooden floor, once pulling Chris down with him--in spite of her best efforts to keep them both upright. This memory was quickly replaced by that of him holding her in his arms and kissing her in the darkness of the Moonlight Skate. A happy memory, indeed. Billy unlocked the passenger side door, holding it open for Chris to enter and helping her step up into the vehicle's high cab. Upon situating herself, Chris reached behind the seat for her new hat and put it on. She wondered how women of that era felt about wearing such apparel, especially during social occasions, when hats were customary--or required--attire.

Billy hurried around to the driver's side and was soon sitting beside Chris. He reached for her and she leaned in to him. His arms encircled her. They kissed long and passionately. She felt small in his arms, which were strong, yet gentle, holding her. The two held each other and kissed until Chris looked around and asked, "Where are all the other cars?" The parking lot was empty except for one other car at the far back end of the lot. "Probably the owner's," Billy said. They were amazed that a whole parking lot full of cars could leave without their noticing them. Billy sat back up in the driver's position, and said, "Well, I guess I better get you home before you turn into a pumpkin." Neither of them was ready to leave, but both knew they should.

Billy drove the entire way back to the Village with his right arm around Chris, her head nestled in the hollow of his shoulder. Neither spoke. This was another of those occasions when words were unnecessary. Although they were headed home, neither felt the night was over. As Billy's truck passed through the long tunnel of the old covered bridge, Chris felt a premonition. She did not know if Billy had the same feeling, but at the moment of exit, he looked at her, a caring smile on his lips. Before either of them was ready to, they arrived at the Village's parking lot. Billy parked in the employee's section at the far end. As soon as the engine was turned off, they again embraced, holding each other, tighter than the time before. Billy looked softly down at Chris and asked, "Would you like to see my humble abode?" Without a proper young lady's finishing school pause, Chris nodded and said "yes" in a voice that was barely above a whisper.

The time was eleven fourteen. Except for the main entrance, doors of the building were routinely locked to outside entry at eleven o'clock each night. They walked to the entrance to corridor C, and Billy let them in with his pass key. They quietly crept down the stairs to the lower level and then to the far end of the hall where Billy's apartment was located. He unlocked the door, holding it open for Chris. After a moment's hesitation, she entered. He followed her in, switching on a table lamp next to a settee. Chris was surprised to see how neat the room was.

"Oh, I like your apartment, Billy. I wish I had you around to help keep my dorm room this uncluttered."

"Who knows that the future holds?" he replied, in his best mysterious tone of voice. Looking around the room, he said, "There's not much to it, really. As you've probably figured out by now, this is the sitting room. To your right is the kitchenette where I prepare sumptuous gourmet meals, and straight ahead . . . " He paused, then added . . . "is my bedroom."

With false bravado, Chris replied, "Oh! Well, then. I better check to see if you made your bed, or if you keep only your living room this well tended for show." Billy led the way, reaching his arm through and around the inside of the doorway to turn on the light. With a bow and sweep of his arm, he ushered her into the bedroom, with, "After you, my lady." Chris entered timidly, Billy close behind her.

"You're not only a good fixer-upper, you're a spotless house keeper, too. Are you for hire?"

"Only for those with good references," he replied, smiling, his voice somewhat unsteady. Standing behind Chris, Billy lightly placed his hands on her shoulders and turned her slowly to face him. She looked up into his eyes and instantly felt his lips on hers. His arms folded her into him. Standing on her tiptoes, her arms instinctively went around his neck. They stood there several seconds, drinking in the warmth and softness of each others lips. Billy broke the silence. "I could hold you like this forever."

"Wouldn't it be difficult for you to work in this position," Chris asked, in an attempt to keep the conversation casual. The mental image of her question struck Billy funny. He stepped back for a moment, looked into her eyes, and said, "Good point!" He again pulled her to him and kissed her, this time with more urgency.

Releasing her lips from his, Chris said, "I realize this is probably terrible timing, but I really should be going."

"I know. But, I don't want you to. So, what do we do now?" Billy asked quietly. Both of them knew the question was rhetorical. He began unbuttoning her sweater blouse without encountering any resistance. She removed it and dropped it to the floor beside her. Then, she slowly began unbuttoning his shirt, which Billy removed and hung on the door knob behind him. With some fumbling, he managed to unhook Chris's bra and she slid it from her shoulders. Again, they kissed, the warm bareness of their upper bodies pressed firmly against each other. After another long kiss, Chris moved her face back from Billy's.

With firmer resolve this time, she said, "I hate to be a nag, but . . ."

"I know. Your aunt will be getting worried about you, and you need to get back before she sends out a posse looking for you," Billy said, reluctantly loosening his hold on her.

"I knew you'd understand," she said, apologetically.

"The sad fact is that I do understand. And I respect your wishes," Billy replied, in a less than convincing tone.

"Thank you, Billy. You just proved again that I wasn't mistaken about what kind of man you are." With that said, she picked up her bra and blouse from the floor where they had been discarded only moments before, and put them back on. Billy retrieved his shirt from the doorknob and also redressed. They walked to the front of Billy's apartment, arms around each other. Stopping at the door, they shared a tight embrace and a long, deep kiss.

"I'll walk you home," Billy said, when their lips parted.

"Again, I really do hope you understand, Billy," Chris said, having second thoughts about her reluctance to stay. She had never been with a man totally and this was new and terrifyingly strange territory for her. Worst of all, she could not yet bring herself to reveal to Billy that she was still a virgin.

"I do. But, we'd better leave before I start wondering if I really do," Billy admitted.

He walked Chris down the hall and up the stairs to her aunt's apartment. Arriving at Emmy's door, Billy looked at his watch and said, "Just past midnight, and you didn't turn into a pumpkin. That's encouraging." Both were still able to laugh at each others remarks, in spite of their emotions of the moment.

"Thank you for a wonderful day, Billy. I really had a nice time. I hope you know that." Her eyes gazed warmly into his.

"Me too," came his simple reply. "Maybe we can test the swimming pool water tomorrow--if you want."

"I'd like that. Give me a call in the morning and let me know what time's best for you." She unlocked the door, and by now, well practiced at standing on tiptoes, gave Billy a soft kiss.

"Goodnight, Chris. See you tomorrow. I mean, later today."

"It's a date! Goodnight. Sleep tight."

Billy slowly walked back to his apartment, head down, and his mind whirling with a mixture of emotions. He was not sure whether he would sleep at all, considering everything that had happened.

"Is that you, Chris?" said Emmy's voice from the bedroom. She had remained awake, reading, and waiting up for Chris's return. She wondered how many times her sister had done the same thing. Emmy thought it was probably a good thing she never had children, realizing what a worrier she had become.

"Yes, Aunt Em. It's me," Chris replied, too tired and emotionally confused to come up with one of her customary flippant replies.

"How was your date with Billy? You must have had a good time, or you would have been home earlier." Emmy could not help but notice when Chris entered the bedroom, that her blouse was buttoned unevenly.

"We had a great time, Aunt Em. Billy's good company. I really like him," she volunteered as she began undressing for bed. After a brief bathroom visit and settling into bed, she remained awake, staring at the numbers on the bedside clock, watching their digital redness continue to change shapes. Her mind was full of doubts and mixed messages. She lay there, questioning and second guessing her actions and words during her and Billy's time together. Fatigue from an active and emotion filled day slowly dimmed her thoughts and the need for sleep stilled them. Her last thought before falling asleep was that she had left her new hat in Billy's apartment. The red numbers of the clock continued to glow and change unobserved.

Chapter 22

THE MORNING AFTER

As much difficulty as Chris had falling asleep the previous night, she had even more trouble waking up. As she lay in bed, lazily stretching her arms and legs, she heard her aunt moving around in the kitchen. Something smelled good. Pancakes. They had been a favorite of hers since she was a girl. They had long been a family tradition on Sunday mornings. She arose slowly, the memory of what had happened the night before not quite clear in her head. Then, the events began replaying themselves in sequence in her mind. Once again, in an adult situation, she had acted immaturely. At college she felt like a grown woman, but in her personal life she still had some adolescent issues to face and overcome and some major womanly decisions to make. She had no regrets about Billy's actions, but continued to question her responses to them. She began wondering how B.F. Skinner would have analyzed her behavior. Although she knew the textbook answer of the famed psychologist, she chose, in her confused emotional state, not to acknowledge it. School was out. This was life. She was aware that sometimes reality and theory blend, while at other times they do not meet quietly, but crash noisily. She understood that she still had a lot to learn about psychology and even more to learn about life and the reality of transitioning from girlhood to womanhood. She was still only half awake and it was too early to deal with such weighty thoughts. She put on her slippers and stumbled listlessly into the bathroom to begin her morning routine. Above the sound of running water, she heard her aunt call out "Pancakes are ready. Come and get 'em while they're hot!"

Rounding the corner into the kitchen, her slippers flip-flopping on the wooden floor, Chris replied sleepily, "How can you be so cheery this early in the morning?"

"Pardon me, Missy. My clock may be wrong, but it says seven minutes after nine. The morning's already half gone. What did you do last night to leave you so tired and grumpy this beautiful morning?"

"You don't want to know," Chris replied, stifling a yawn.

"Oh? Anything you'd care to talk about with your old aunt?"

"No. Not really. You know what a stumble bum I am in the morning, even when you consider it half gone. I'm not much of a morning talker."

Chris was still in her pajamas, her robe hanging loosely around her, belt dangling. As she circled the kitchen table to sit down, she lazily brushed an errant strand of hair from her eyes with her hand.

"Well, don't you look like a Vogue cover? Although, I have to admit I've seen worse hair on some runway models. And they probably pay a lot of money to perfect the look you're sporting so casually."

"Ha, ha!" Chris replied in mock humor. "I suppose now you'll want me to share my beauty secrets with you. Short version--not enough sleep."

"Here. Sit down before you fall down," Emmy said, pushing a chair toward Chris. "My pancakes are guaranteed to put a smile on your face and a song in your heart."

As Chris slumped into a chair, she muttered, "It'll take more than pancakes."

"What was that, Chris?" Emmy asked as she flipped a browning disk into the skillet.

"Nothing. I'm just not awake yet. Forgive me, Aunt Em. As I said, I'm not a morning person. I bet you're glad you don't have to put up with me all the time."

"Nonsense. I really enjoy having you here. I feel younger and more alive just being around you--sort of a youth transfusion, you might say. You're good medicine for an old woman."

"Aunty Em. I wish you wouldn't keep talking like that. You are not old. You're a young and vibrant woman--at least you could be if you'd only loosen up a bit."

"Oh? Who's that from--Freud or Master's and Johnson?"

In spite of herself, Chris smiled. She enjoyed the give and take small talk between her aunt and herself. She felt that she could talk to her about things she would never even consider discussing with her mother. But, Billy was another matter. Chris would have liked to open up to her aunt about her confused emotions regarding him, but she could not--not yet, anyway.

"So, what are you and Billy planning to do today?" The sound of Emmy's voice brought Chris out of her reverie.

"That depends on you, Aunt Em. I haven't spent as much time with you as I should since I've been here. We can go sightseeing--or we can just stay here, eat ice cream and gossip about your neighbors."

"Actually, my leg has started to give me a bit of trouble again. If you want to spend time with Billy today, I'd be happy to just stay home and vegetate. Then, when you come back, you can tell me about all the wonderful things you two saw and did." This comment, made in jest, struck a sensitive nerve in Chris, with regard to where the direction her relationship with Billy was heading. She wondered if her aunt had some intuition about what was bothering her.

"We had talked about going swimming. But, I told him to call this morning and I'd let him know what you and I had planned."

"You two seem to have a good time together. If he has time to spend with you, take advantage of it. You're only young once. I'm an expert on that subject." Just then, the phone rang. Chris and Emmy both looked at the kitchen clock.

"That must be for you. I don't have any suitor's competing for my company these days," Emmy said in jest, but with a trace of sadness in her voice.

Chris lifted the receiver.

"Hello?"

"Hi, Chris. Billy. Are you still talking to me this morning?"

"Of course. Why wouldn't I be?"

"Just wondering. What are your plans with your aunt today? Pop Bates said he could do without me this afternoon. Things are pretty quiet. If you're available, we can go swimming. You do swim, don't you?"

"Like a fish--a flounder. Just a minute, let me check with Aunt Em."

Before Chris could say anything, Emmy gave her a nod and silently mouthed, "Go ahead."

"Aunt Em just gave me the OK sign. I won't have to fish you out of the pool, will I? It's one thing to pick you up from a hardwood floor and another to pull you out of soft water."

"I think I can manage to stay afloat. How does two o'clock sound?"

"Good. That'll give me time to lunch with Aunt Em and gossip about you and the other young women you entertain when I'm not around." Her teasing comment--for some reason--bothered Billy. But, he replied good humouredly, "I'm not sure four hours are enough time to tell you about all of them. Maybe she can just give you the condensed book version. I'll knock on your door at two."

"OK. See you then," Chris said, and hung up.

"Well, Aunt Em. You've got to put up with me for four more hours. Think you can handle it?"

"It'll be an effort, but I'll manage--somehow. Oh! I just remembered. Today's Tai Chi class. Eleven o'clock. Care to join me?"

"Sounds like fun. I don't know my Tai from my Chi, but I'll try anything once. I believe that's our family motto, isn't it?"

Arriving at the fitness center a few minutes early, Emmy introduced Chris to the instructor--a petite Chinese woman in her early sixties--and to the other arrivals. The warm up stretching; the slow, rhythmic movements of the form and the end of class meditation relaxed Chris's body, and more importantly, her mind. She felt refreshed. Her tensions and self doubts were forgotten for the time being.

"Ready for lunch, Chris?" Emmy asked as they left the fitness center.

"Ready. I'm feeling much better than when you first saw me this morning in my grrrrrr mood."

The pair went directly to the dining area, joined the cafeteria line and selected their food. They found a vacant table by a window looking out on the courtyard quadrangle. They could see several other diners scattered about outdoors, seated under colorful umbrella topped circular tables, enjoying the fresh air with their lunch.

"Don't look now, Aunt Em, but there's your boyfriend, Mr. X, at that table in the far corner. I don't like to sound like a broken record, but he does seem like a lonely man."

Dominic, in dark gray trousers and a navy colored shirt, blended so well into the shadows that he was barely noticeable to the casual observer. As was his usual custom, he sat hunched over, brow furrowed, eating and concentrating on reading a newspaper—his lips silently mouthing each word.

"I think he is," Emmy replied. "I never see him mingle with any of the other residents. He just keeps to himself. I sometimes wonder what he does with all his time. He just doesn't seem to fit in anywhere. He never attends any social activities." Emmy paused for a moment as in thought. "Although, I did notice him peeking in at us from the hallway one morning during Tai Chi class. Another time, I passed by the gym when there was no one else around and saw him exercising. I have to admit, he looks pretty good in shorts and T-shirt."

"Aunty Em! If I didn't know better, I'd think you had a crush on the man." Emmy's face reddened slightly at her niece's comment.

"Don't be silly. I just feel sorry for him. And he did help me up that time I stutter stumbled on the sidewalk in town. When his eyes are open they are dark, almost black. It's like they're looking into your soul. Most of the time, though, they're too hooded to be noticed." Chris looked at Emmy with surprise. "I can see I'm going to have to keep an eye on you. You're too young to have a mid life crisis."

"Don't be too sure, Missy," Emmy replied, her cheeks reddening even more.

"Well," Chris said, "I suppose I should get back to the apartment and find out if my swim suit still fits after all the food you've been making me eat since I've been in your charge."

As they were passing Dominic's table on their way out of the dining room, he looked up. His eyes were fully open, revealing a penetrating gaze in their direction. Instinctively, Emmy smiled at him and said hello. With a half smile, he returned the greeting--then his head again quickly sought refuge in his plate and paper.

"Why, Aunty Em. I do believe you were flirting with that man," Chris teased.

"You keep talking like that, young lady, and I'm going to have to ship you home early." Emmy laughed, but Chris noticed that her face remained flushed.

Chapter 23

WHAT NEXT?

AFTER LUNCH, EMMY and Chris continued to chat about family and long unheard from friends. They even had a brief conversation about Dominic Graystone. When Emmy had first learned his name, she felt it did not quite suit him. She had thought perhaps it would have been something darker or more ominous, like Boris Strangefellow, or something equally as sinister. She felt a sense of guilt thinking this way about a man she did not know--other than by sight and the occasional hello. She knew she should not judge him by his looks alone. Underneath his rough exterior, he probably was a nice man, possibly a widower with grown children and grandchildren somewhere, although, to her knowledge, he had not had a visitor since coming to the Village. Perhaps they lived far away, in another state or country. She could not help but conjure up all sorts of scenarios about his past life and livelihood. Chris remarked that Billy had told her that he occasionally visited him, and that they watched old time movies together. Chris had thought what an odd pair they made. Billy was so outgoing and friendly, and Mr. Graystone seemed so introverted and antisocial. Emmy was surprised when Chris told her that Billy said Dominic had been a stuntman and actor. She had pictured him as perhaps a kind hearted hit man or someone in the witness protection program.--but, an actor? She was certain she had never heard his name or seen a film she recognized him in. During their brief encounter in town, he had been polite--though painfully shy. His personality did not fit the profile of a rough, tough stunt performer. But, then she remembered seeing him in the gym, working out, and recalled that he did have an athletic body--when he stood up straight. Usually, when she encountered him, he appeared preoccupied with studying the nap of the hallway or dining room carpet.

"What are you thinking about, Aunt Em?" Chris asked, interrupting Emmy's thoughts.

"What? Oh, nothing profound. I was just thinking about Mr. Graystone and what you told me about him."

"Do I sense that my favorite aunt has a latent interest in the man?" Chris could not resist the temptation to tease her aunt.

"Oh, don't be silly. It's just that I've always had a soft spot for needy creatures that don't seem to fit in anywhere."

"Do you want to know what John Dewey said about that?" Chris queried.

"No thank you. I don't need a seven minute psychoanalysis."

"What makes you think Dewey was a psychologist?"

"If you brought up his name in a conversation, it doesn't take a Sherlock Holmes to make that deduction. It's just that Mr. Graystone seems so lonely and has such baleful eyes. I suppose I'm just nosy enough to want to know his story. Actually, I've been wondering how to help him become a part of the mainstream of our community."

"I suppose you feed stray animals, too."

"As a matter of fact, I do. If you would get up a little earlier, Missy, you could watch me feed Stray every morning."

"I assume Stray is either a dog or a cat."

"Cat. But, let's change the subject."

Emmy was beginning to get a little annoyed with where she felt Chris's conversation was heading. However, she was becoming even more annoyed with herself. Here, obviously, was a man who needed help, and she felt helpless to help him. She believed there must be some way to get him to open up and let others see the real him--whatever that was. Perhaps after Chris left, she would make him her pet charity project.

"You're drifting again, Aunt Em. I'm sorry for teasing you about a man you barely know. Let's talk about more pleasant things. What do you think of Billy? Really?"

"He seems like a nice young man. He's hardworking, outgoing, pleasant to be around, and not too bad looking."

This provided an opening in the conversation for Chris to tell her aunt about her experience with Billy the previous night. But, she still was uncomfortable broaching the subject. Maybe later, she thought. This still was not the time.

"So," Emmy asked, "what time is Billy coming by for you?"

"Two o'clock."

"It's almost that now," Emmy said. Without another word, Chris jumped up from her chair and ran into the bedroom. She still had some getting ready to do. Hurriedly, she put on her two piece swimsuit and looked in the mirror. She wondered if it was a little too daring. Then, she rationalized, Billy wouldn't see anything he hadn't seen before. She took her beach robe from the closet and put it on over the bikini. "That's better," she said, examining her slender reflection in the mirror. Sliding her feet into her floppies, she completed the effect. She was ready to go swimming. The bedside clock radio reminded her that it was two o'clock. Grabbing a towel from the linen closet, she entered the living room. Billy was already there. He and Emmy were standing just inside the door, chatting. Chris thought how nice he looked, dressed in colorful boxer trunks and white T-shirt, with a colorful striped towel draped over one shoulder.

"When you said two o'clock, you meant it, didn't you?" Chris said, smiling.

"Yes ma'am. As I always say, if nothing else, I'm punctual."

"Well, I'll give you a brownie point for that. I'm ready to go." Billy gave her a long, admiring look, but said nothing. Chris assured her aunt that she would be back in time for dinner.

She and Billy walked down the long corridor to the stairway leading to the floor below. When they arrived at the pool, the afternoon aquasize class was just finishing. The couple sat on a poolside riser and watched the exercisers perform their final stretching movements. After the class ended, two of the women remained in the pool for a short swim before leaving. Billy and Chris joined them, and soon had the pool to themselves. Billy was a strong swimmer. He and Chris swam several synchronized laps together, occasionally turning to push the other one's head under water. They were young, active and happy to be in each other's company. When they tired, they returned to the deck. "It's a shame there's no diving board," Chris lamented.

"Do you dive?" Billy asked, surprised.

"Like a lead weight," Chris answered.

"I'm shocked. You mean there's something you don't excel at?"

"More things than you know," Chris replied, too softly for Billy to hear her.

They patted themselves dry and sat by the side of the pool, watching some newcomers noisily splash around in the water.

"That was fun, Billy. We'll have to do it again before I leave."

"On that subject, when are you leaving?" Billy asked, apprehension in his voice.

"Day after tomorrow," came the unwanted reply.

"Just when I'm getting to know you, you're going to run away back to the big city."

"I know, Billy. I don't want to go, but as they say in the movies, duty calls. And besides, I need to get out of Aunt Em's hair soon, so that she can get back to her normal life. I've noticed she's gotten some more gray hairs since I've been here. I've probably been the cause of a few of them."

They sat quietly at the edge of the pool, their feet dangling lazily in the warm water, creating a small ripple effect. With entwined hands, they each began to think how different life would be when they could no longer be together like this. To break the somber mood, Chris jumped up and said, "How about a game of ping pong?"

"Dressed like this? And, we're still wet."

"So what? Just pretend we're on the beach in Hawaii, enjoying the sun, surf and sea breezes."

"Well, since you put it that way, you're on!"

They dried their feet and padded off to the nearby game room, which was empty except for them. As before, the outcome of their contest was two games to two. Neither of them wanted to outdo the other, so they decided not to play a tie breaker.

"There's still an hour before you have to meet your aunt for dinner. Would you like to stop by my room and look at my etchings?," Billy asked, hopefully, while doing a bad imitation of Groucho Marx, raising his eye brows and shaking imaginary ashes from an imaginary cigar. Chris cocked her head to one side and gave him an "I'd like to, but . . . " look.

"Can I take a rain check?" she asked, making it sound more like an apology than a negative answer.

"Anytime. My door's always open," Billy replied with false cheeriness. "How's this for an alternate plan? After dinner, how would you like to take a stroll down by the lake and feed the ducks, geese, and whatever other feathered creatures show up?"

"I'd like that. But, what will you do?" She asked coyly.

"Well, I had kind of hoped maybe you would invite me go along with you."

"Oh! That's an even better idea. What time will you ride up on your white charger?"

"How about promptly at seven?" he offered.

Chris nodded. "You know where to find me," she said, doing an imitation of a Mae West eyelash flutter.

Since there was no one in sight, Billy put his arms around Chris, gently pulled her to him and gave her a lingering kiss. They held an "I don't want to leave" embrace for a few more seconds, parted, and then Billy escorted Chris back to her aunt's apartment.

"See you at seven," he said as he left her at her door and reluctantly headed back to his own apartment.

Chapter 24

CONSUMMATION

DINNER WAS QUIET. Chris spoke hardly a word. Emmy sensed that something was bothering her, since being quiet for any length of time was foreign to Chris's personality. But, she restrained herself from asking about her niece's obvious subdued mood. She felt certain it had something to do with Billy. Emmy watched Chris pick at her food--which also was unusual--as she had always enjoyed a hardy appetite, and in spite of it remained trim. Chris noticed her aunt looking at her with the same furrowed brow her mother assumed whenever she was concerned about her daughter's health or behavior. Tension was rising at the table. It was inevitable that one of them would need to speak soon. Then, they both chose the same moment to break the silence.

"Chris, I . . ." "Aunt Em, what . . ." Their words overlapped. Then, Chris said, "You first, Aunt Em." Emmy paused, as though to organize her thoughts. She knew this was not going to be a comfortable conversation for either of them. But, she also was aware that communication was essential. She took a deep breath, and began speaking, slowly and deliberately.

"Chris, I'm worried about you. You haven't been yourself the last couple days. Is anything wrong?"

Chris, too, hesitated before speaking. Her impulse was to say no, but she knew that would be a wasted word. She felt compelled to give her aunt an answer--while telling her as little as possible of the details. Her words came slowly and with difficulty.

"I'm sure you know that it has something to do with Billy." Emmy nodded, but did not interrupt. She needed to know more about what was on Chris's mind before she ventured further into the conversation. "Well, as you know, Billy and I have been spending quite a bit of time together." Emmy nodded again, the lines across her brow now more prominent. Chris continued. "You probably also know that I haven't had much experience with boys--young men." She paused again. Her aunt's expression did not change. "The closest I've come to a relationship with a man was Brad, and that had limits to how far it went." Emmy's eyes involuntarily widened. "Billy is just the opposite of Brad. Brad was all about Brad. His needs and expectations were important to him, and he expected them to be just as important to me. We had several disagreements about what the structure of our relationship should be. Whenever he didn't get his way, he would sulk, and I wouldn't hear from him for days afterward. That bothered me. Yet, in another sense, it was a relief not to have him around pressuring me to be something or someone I wasn't--just to conform to what his expectations of me were. I don't know if it was my lack of cooperation that increased the distance between us or his looking forward to leaving for medical school--or a combination of both. I won't even attempt to analyze the narcissistic side of his character. That's the trouble with being a psych major. After awhile you begin to analyze everything you do or say, especially in regard to relationships with others. It's been said that you have to be a little abnormal yourself to be attracted to the field." Emmy continued to listen attentively, her body language and facial expression remaining unchanged. She could not help but think that this was the longest Chris had talked to her since meeting Billy. Chris continued.

"Unlike Brad, Billy is attentive, easy going, funny, and very open and easy to talk to and be with. It's almost impossible for me not to be attracted to him and want to please him." Then, as an afterthought, she said, "And, he's a lot more intelligent than he lets on."

At this point, Emmy felt it necessary to interrupt. "So, what are you trying to say, Chris? I still don't see why this would affect your mood, if you enjoy being with him so much. I would think you would be happy instead of being so mopey." Chris realized she had not begun to touch on the real issue, but had merely skirted around it. She was still not able to confide to her aunt the crux of her problem--which was that she was strongly attracted to Billy physically, but was afraid that because of her inexperience she would not be able to satisfy his needs or overcome her guilt or fear in attempting to do so.

Emmy realized that Chris had gone as far as she wanted to with this line of conversation, so she decided to change the subject.

"So, what would you like to do this evening?" she asked rhetorically.

"Billy asked me if I would like to take a moonlight walk down by the lake," she ventured bravely.

"Oh?" One of Emmy's eyebrows rose involuntarily. "And what did you tell him?"

"I told him to come by for me at seven--if that's OK. You're welcome to come with us."

"Did you ever hear the expression that three's a crowd?" Emmy countered, not expecting an answer. For some reason, she had a sudden flashback to her own youth, when she was a sophomore in college. She had had a relationship with a junior, which culminated with the two of them having sex in the back seat of his car in the parking lot of the football stadium one night after a game. It had been a first--and traumatic--experience for her, but apparently was satisfactory for him, although neither of them mentioned it afterward. Since he never seemed to have enough money for a motel, and the dormitories were segregated, every week or so--usually on a Saturday night-- he would find a dark, out of the way place to park, and they would have sex in his car. Occasionally, when weather permitted, he would spread a blanket next to the car, opposite the road side, or they would venture into a wooded area with the blanket. With her fear of their being caught, Emmy never became relaxed enough to enjoy the awkward and uncomfortable coupling. She was more interested in how quickly he could finish than in any potential pleasure. He seemed not to notice or be bothered by such details. On rare occasions, before taking her back to her dormitory, they would stop at a fast food restaurant for a snack. Nothing was ever mentioned by either of them about the prior events of the evening. He was usually relaxed and talkative afterward--about everything except them. Her only reaction to the rough and unwelcome sexual activity was usually an upset stomach. Try as she would, Emmy could not remember his name. As is the case with many strictly physical relationships, theirs lasted only a few months. After their break up, Emmy occasionally saw him around campus, smilingly escorting another girl who somewhat resembled her.

Chris repeated the offer, "You're certainly welcome to come with us, Aunt Em."

"You two young people go ahead. My leg is still troubling me somewhat. I don't think it would let me walk that far without complaining." Emmy realized that Chris's offer was more polite than sincere.

"If you're sure. I won't be out late. We might play some ping pong afterward. You're sure you don't mind being alone tonight?"

"No. I'll be fine," Emmy replied. She admitted to herself that since she had been alone most of her life, one more night would not make a difference one way or another.

Chris and Emmy lingered over their dinner until the dining room was almost empty and the staff was beginning to cover the tables with fresh linen. Shortly after they returned to Emmy's apartment, there was a knock at the door.

Billy was prompt, as usual. Chris invited him in and the three of them chatted for a few minutes about nothing in particular. Chris's mood had improved noticeably since dinner time. She and Billy laughed easily and teased each other good naturedly. Emmy was happy to see that, although she still had a foreboding concerning Chris's emotional state. But, she rationalized, her niece would turn twenty one the following month, and she had not done well enough managing her own life to feel qualified to pry into other peoples lives--or make judgments as to their behavior.

The evening was cool and a soft westerly breeze blew gently across the meadow. The sun was slowly disappearing behind the distant mountains. On their way to the lake, Billy and Chris passed several returning walkers and joggers. Some of them stopped and chatted briefly with them about the weather, or contributed a tidbit of local news or gossip they had recently heard. Twilight Manor was a friendly place and its residents, for the most part, were outgoing in spite of their various individual quirks or life styles.

By the time the pair reached the lake, the sun had almost hidden itself from view, and only a hint of light remained. They walked out onto the boat dock and sat at the edge of it. They removed their shoes and socks and dangled their feet in the sun warmed water, which in an hour or so would be too cold to comfortably do so.

"So, Chris, how was your day?" Billy asked, with obvious interest.

"My day was fine. Aunt Em and I spent most of it reliving the good old days, and me showing her some photos I brought from home. I can't help but worry about her, though. She seems so lonely. She gets these far away looks, and I wonder what she's thinking about--the past, what could have been, what is, or what's in her future? Other than my parents and me, she doesn't have any family."

"I wouldn't worry too much about her. She's got lots of friends here. Everybody likes her. She's active in most of the activities--except for the dances. I don't remember seeing her ever attend one. But, from what I hear, she's quite a Bridge player."

"Would you do me a favor, Billy?" Chris didn't wait for his answer. "After I leave, would you keep a close eye on her and let me know how she's doing--and if she needs anything?"

"You mean we're going to keep in touch after you go back home and have all those handsome college boys chasing you around campus?"

"I hope so," Chris replied wistfully. She somehow resented Billy's insinuation about her and other men.

"If I have my way, we will," Billy said, taking her hand in his and gently squeezing it. How different his hands were from Brad's, Chris thought. Brad had small, soft, almost effeminate hands, which probably would never know what a callus felt like. Billy's hands were broad and his fingers long. His palms were rough--working man's hands. But, Chris liked the touch of them on her face and body. Perhaps, she liked them too much, she reasoned.

They sat silently, drawing circles in the water with their toes. The sun had been replaced by a soft, silvery moon. All of the other people were gone from around the lake. One couple was still in the gazebo, seemingly deep in conversation. With his free hand, Billy turned Chris's face toward his and gently kissed her on the nose. His mouth moved to each cheek, and then lightly touched her lips. The kiss graduated from tender to needy. Chris felt her face reddening. Billy continued to kiss her sincerely and well. He said, "Why don't we go sit in the gazebo?" The solitary couple had just left and there was no one else around to share the encroaching darkness. She nodded. They arose, picked up their shoes and socks and walked, hand in hand, up the slight rise to the gazebo, its whiteness eerily reflected in the light and shadow patterns created by the moon. Once there, Billy put his arms around her and again kissed her. They both began to feel their passions rising. Their kisses became more intense and Billy's hands began caressing her, moving from her back to her breasts, which were small, but firm and well rounded. His hand cupped one of them. Chris had changed from her jeans into a sundress before their walk to the lake. Billy's other hand moved under her skirt and up her outer thigh. Chris could feel her panties being lowered. The next thing she remembered was stepping out of them. Billy's hand tenderly caressed her bare flesh. Chris's legs began to tremble and she thought for a moment she might fall. She leaned back against a post of the gazebo for support. She could tell that Billy wanted her--and she wanted him.

"Billy! Please-- not here." She was having difficulty with her breathing.

"Can we go to my room," he asked, also breathing heavily. She nodded assent.

The pair quickly arrived back at Billy's apartment. He nervously fumbled with the door's lock, seemingly unable to find the key hole. Soon, they were inside, with the world locked out on the other side of the door. They again began kissing passionately and exploring each other's body and mouth. Soon, Chris's sundress lay on the floor by her feet and Billy clumsily, but successfully, unsnapped her bra. He quickly removed his T-shirt, Khaki pants and briefs. Their bare bodies were pressed tightly against each other. They continued to kiss. Then, Billy easily lifted Chris and carried her into the bedroom, depositing her gently onto the bedspread. He lay down beside her and they rolled toward each other, locking themselves in each other's arms. They continued to kiss and caress each other. This was no time to tell him she was a virgin, Chris's mind told her. What happens happens. She was putting her trust in Billy. He had turned her onto her back and slowly lowered himself onto her. Then, a look of surprise came across his face. He stopped and looked down at her.

"Are you a virgin?" he asked, surprised at his surprise.

Unable to find her voice, she nodded.

"Do you want me to stop?"

She shook her head no. Billy continued, gently and patiently. She felt her body shudder as she put her arms around his neck, drawing him tightly to her. The sensation she was feeling was not what she had expected. In spite of some initial discomfort, she felt somehow fulfilled.

Afterward, they lay facing each other, bodies touching and arms encircling. Both of them were breathing too heavily to talk. They continued to kiss and enjoy the warmth of their bodies against each other.

After a few minutes, Chris said, apologetically, "I'm sorry about your bedspread."

"That's OK. I needed a new one anyway," Billy said. "I can't think of a better way to become motivated to get one." They both laughed, albeit, a bit nervously. Chris wondered if they had really been together, or if it was all just a dream.

Chris got out of bed, gathered up her clothing from the floor and went into the bathroom. Billy lay on the far side of the bed, savoring the memory of their togetherness. His pleasurable thoughts of what had just taken place were suddenly interrupted by Chris's voice from the other room

"Oh, no! I think I left my panties in the gazebo."

At this point, nothing could dampen either of their moods, and Billy said, "That's OK. "It'll give the early morning walkers something to wonder about then, won't it?"

Chapter 25

MEMORIES

WAITING UP FOR Chris to return from her date with Billy, Emmy began to wonder if this was what it was like to be a mother--listening for the sound of footsteps, a key in a lock, and the turning of a door handle. She had often thought about motherhood and wondered whether she would have been a good mother. She also thought about the responsibilities which accompanied that role. On occasion, she felt unfulfilled at not having married and having a family to care for. Other times, she felt she was not the motherly type. She enjoyed her independence and not having others in her life to worry about or be dependent on her. Was this, she pondered, why she had never let a man get close to her-- other than that time in college? She certainly did not consider that a happy memory of her youthful days. It had been merely a matter of taking the course of least resistance, giving in so as not to upset him or hurt his feelings. Perhaps, in her then young mind, she had considered the experience as satisfying a curiosity, a wick in the candle of her learning, which had long since blown out--or had never been lit.

She wondered about many things related to her growing up and blossoming into womanhood. After her accident, had she resisted relationships with men because she was ashamed of her marred body, thinking that no one would want her? Or, did she just use her scars as an excuse for avoiding close encounters with men? She had never been sure which, if either, of these reasons were valid. Normally, she did not burden herself with weighty issues and self doubts about her past behavior. But, having the responsibility for a girl-woman for two weeks had reawakened such memories and questions in her mind.

Soon, Chris would be gone and Emmy would return to her normal routine, mundane as it seemed to her. Nobody under foot to worry about. But, she knew she would miss her young companion, who had, for a short time, brightened her life with her youthful energy, outgoing personality and love of life. Emmy had enjoyed their talks, although she felt that there was still a submerged one that needed to be surfaced--an unspoken element of Chris's life that neither she nor Chris were anxious to address. In their last conversation, Emmy felt that they were near a breakthrough toward a core that, for some reason, just could not seem to be penetrated. She was somewhat surprised that Chris had been, up to a point, so open about her relationship with Brad. She had, however, been much less open about her relationship, short as it was, with Billy. Emmy felt that there was something bothering Chris she needed to talk about, that she was not yet willing or able to put into words. Whatever it was, if they were going to discuss it, they only had one more day to do so. Emmy would take Chris to the train station the following day for her trip back to Boston. And, who knew when they would again have another opportunity to be this close for this long.

Although Emmy was not one to intrude into others' affairs, she felt a frank discussion between Chris and her was merited. Unfinished business. Chris had returned about eleven thirty the previous night--seemingly preoccupied. When Emmy asked if she and Billy had had a good time, and how they had spent the evening, Chris had been evasive. Emmy had not pursued her questioning, since bedtime was not the time to begin a heavy conversation. Today would be the day. Emmy had decided. Not usually comfortable with confrontation or probing debates with others, once she made up her mind about doing something, she usually followed through. Her sister used to tease her, when they were growing up, about the stubborn Scots-Irish streak she had apparently inherited from their mother, a product of the Stewart clan.

The bathroom toilet flushed. Emmy looked at the kitchen clock. Ten thirty five. It would not be long until lunch time.

"You up, Chris?" she asked, loud enough to be heard through the bathroom door.

"Almost. What's for breakfast?"

"Pancakes, what else?" Emmy said. They had only missed having them for breakfast twice. Both times, they had decided to go to the dining area for brunch.

Chris stared at herself in the bathroom mirror. She still looked the same as before. She half expected that after last night, her reflection would be that of a changed woman, one with a more sophisticated and worldly presence. She was somewhat disappointed. She replayed the events of last evening in her mind, wondering if she and Billy would feel any differently toward each other today--or whether he would even want to see her again. She could not help but wonder if she had somehow cheapened herself by giving in so easily to him. She had no regrets about the act. It had to happen sometime. Growing up, however, she had fantasized about it happening on her wedding night, after her husband had carried her romantically across the threshold of their honeymoon suite. Imagination and reality frequently bear little or no resemblance to each other. Other times they clash without warning. One thing Chris had no doubts about was that she was happy it happened with Billy instead of with Brad. During their relationship, she could never picture herself being intimate with him. She remembered a saying, "live so that your memories will be an album of happiness, not a scrapbook of regret." She harbored no regrets about last night. She only hoped Billy felt the same. She was both anticipating and dreading their meeting today.

"Your pancakes are waiting. Better hurry before they get cold," her aunt called, interrupting her reminiscing.

"Be right there, Aunt Em." Chris quickly pulled on a pair of cotton shorts and a T-shirt and bounced into the kitchen.

"Well. You certainly look more chipper than you did yesterday. How did you sleep?"

"Good. If those pancakes hadn't smelled so tantalizing, I think I could have stayed in bed till noon."

"I'm glad you didn't. We need to organize the day and get you ready for leaving tomorrow. And," she added, "we need to have a heart to heart talk before you leave."

Color came into Chris's face. "I know, Aunt Em. But, could we put it off until after I talk to Billy?" Emmy nodded, her eyes looking understandingly into Chris's. They finished breakfast, talking about nothing in particular. Emmy mentioned that the Village was having a square dance this coming Saturday night, and that it was a shame Chris would be leaving before then.

"You're going, aren't you, Aunt Em?" Chris asked.

"I don't dance."

"You used to. Mom said you were the best dancer she ever saw. And the Rockette's thought you were good enough to dance with them."

"That was then. This is now. Times and people change."

"Well, I still think you should go. You'd probably have a good time." Chris was tempted to say maybe her aunt could invite Mr. Graystone, but decided against it. The conversation changed to the weather, what time the train left the following afternoon, and what needed to be done prior to Emmy's driving Chris to the train station. The telephone rang. Emmy looked at Chris and then toward the phone, her body language saying, "You answer it. It's for you, anyway." The side of the conversation that Emmy overheard consisted of, "Hello?" . . . Oh, hi Billy . . . Fine. And you? . . . Good . . . I'd like that, but let me talk to Aunt Em first, and see what's going on here today. Call me back in a few minutes, OK? Talk to you then. Bye." Chris hung up and turned to her aunt.

"Billy says there's a county fair over at Connor's Corners, and asked if I'd like to go. Would you mind?" she asked sheepishly.

Emmy had mixed feelings. They still needed to have their talk. But, this was the last day Chris would be able to spend with Billy before she left for Boston, and they would still have time to talk tomorrow morning, or later, during the drive to the station and waiting for the train's arrival.

"OK," she said, hesitantly.

"Thanks, Aunt Em, for being so understanding. With that, she gave her aunt a hug and disappeared into the bedroom. Emmy could hear her opening and closing drawers, followed by the sound of running water against the walls of the shower stall. Chris was still in the shower when Billy called again. Emmy told him that Chris would be able to go to the fair with him. She took Billy's message that he would come by for her at noon, and that they would eat there--if Emmy did not mind. She assured him that she did not, although she had some reservations. She could not keep from wondering if she was handling the situation properly, or if she was being too passive. But, there would be plenty of time to deal with her self doubts after Chris was gone.

As usual, Billy was right on time. Chris did not know what to expect from him. Would he be the same Billy, or a stranger she had spent part of a night with? She was relieved that, when she opened the door to him, he was his usual smiling and talkative self.

He invited Emmy to come with them, but as usual, she demurred. Her leg always gave her a ready excuse for not doing anything she preferred not to--even when it was not bothering her.

The couple walked to Billy's truck, holding hands and looking into each other's eyes, again engaging in their usual teasing-type conversation. As he opened the passenger door for her, he looked around, and seeing no one in sight, gave her a light kiss on the lips.

Connor's Corners was just under twelve miles the other side of Braxton Falls. They arrived there in less than half an hour. A large number of people had already congregated at the fairgrounds site. The day was warm and sunny, and the air was filled with band music and the sweet smell of funnel cakes. Billy warned Chris to watch her step, since the parking lot was normally where farmer Jenkins' cattle grazed. They managed to get to the fair grounds proper without misstep or mishap. Having been born and raised in a large city, Chris had never been to a county fair. Everything was a new experience for her. They watched the hog judging, the hog calling competition and presentation of blue and other colored ribbons in a variety of events. Food booths seemed everywhere. They enjoyed some local delicacies for lunch, washing them down with homemade lemonade. Billy demonstrated, unsuccessfully, the art of knocking over milk bottles with baseballs. After Billy's lesson, Chris took a turn, winning a small, stuffed teddy bear, which she hugged to her as they visited the various and seemingly unending other exhibits and merchandise booths. She particularly enjoyed the jewelry booths. At one of them, Billy bought her an ornate sterling silver ring centered with an unidentifiable stone, took her left hand in his and placed the ring on her ring finger. "Just so you won't forget me," he said quietly. Her eyes watered involuntarily. She squeezed his hand and they continued down the promenade, arms around each others waist.

At a T-shirt stall, Chris bought Billy a shirt with "Memories are from what dreams are made" across its front. As she handed it to him, she repeated his oath, "Just so you won't forget me."

He replied, "That's the last thing I'm likely to do."

Before leaving the fairgrounds, Billy insisted they ride the Ferris wheel, which was something Chris had never done. Initially, she had some apprehension about the height, but once they were up in the air, she enjoyed the view of farmland across the flat landscape and the feel of Billy's arm securely around her shoulder. They ate again before leaving the fair, and began the drive back--happy and at peace.

Arriving at the Village's parking lot, they wandered down to the lake and sat for several minutes enjoying the orange glow of the sun's slow descent behind its mountain home. No words were exchanged or needed. Billy finally broke the silence with, "Is it proper etiquette for me to invite you back to my rooms?"

"Everything considered, I don't see why not."

Once in Billy's apartment, they kissed and enjoyed the feeling of each other's closeness, and the fresh smell of the outdoors that still clung to them. This time, pressure free, their love making was unhurried and equally satisfying and fulfilling to both of them.

Afterward, they lay together, wrapped in each other's arms, secure and content in the knowledge that they had overcome the physical and emotional barriers between them. The one exception was Chris's leaving the next day, which they talked about, and how they both were dreading it. They discussed how meeting each other had changed their lives. They made promises to each other to be faithful to the memories of their togetherness and to not share with anyone else what they had had together. They were mature enough to realize that, over time, these might not be promises that could be kept, but young enough to be optimistic that they would.

Chapter 26

GOODBYE

DAWN ARRIVED BEFORE Chris was ready to accept it. She cast a sleepy eye at the clock radio. Seven thirty three. She decided there was no reason to get out of bed that early. Slowly propping herself up on one elbow, she looked over at her aunt, who lay unmoving in her bed. Chris could hear her slow, rhythmic breathing. This was the first time since her arrival that she had not been awakened by Emmy's puttering noises in the kitchen.

Chris quickly changed her mind about getting up. Her movement had caused her to feel the need to make a bathroom call, so she threw off her covers and shuffled unsteadily toward her destination. After completing the purpose for her visit, she flushed the toilet, splashed water on her face, and decided, since she was up, she might as well stay up. Perhaps she would surprise her aunt by preparing breakfast for her--for a change. This was to be Chris's last day at Twilight Manor. She would return home to Boston and start thinking about fall enrollment and other administrative details that needed attending to in preparation for beginning her senior year in college. And, then, of course, there were graduate school requirements to consider. She needed to bring her grade point average up to ensure being accepted. But, for the moment, her priority was to concentrate on making pancakes--which her aunt prepared from scratch. At home, they were made from a box mix, which seemed to her to be the more sensible and effective way to go about it. As Chris mixed the batter, she began thinking about Billy, and when, or if, she would see him again. In the past two weeks, her outlook on life had changed considerably. What had seemed important to her in the past she now viewed from a different perspective, one which she felt was more mature. She was both happy and sad at the same time--happy to have had an opportunity to visit with her aunt and to meet Billy--and sad to leave them both. Chris recognized that happiness was not only dependent on circumstances, but also on one's attitude about those circumstances. Sadness she had more difficulty rationalizing. This was the first time in her young life she had to face leaving two people she felt really close to and cared about. She thought about Abraham Maslow's hierarchy of needs. His theory was that a person's basic needs were physical-- food, water and shelter. She did not remember if sex also was included in that category. Once physical needs had been achieved, she recalled that he saw the next level of needs being safety--security, stability and order. Chris was uncertain how she ranked in this second level of needs. She had security, but was less than certain about having achieved stability and order in her life. In a sense, she felt that she had approached the third level--the needs of belonging and love. Her home life and school provided her belonging needs. She was not as yet clear in her mind about the love issue. Did she love Billy or was he merely a summer romance? She knew she cared for him and felt more alive and centered when she was with him than at other times. And, in spite of the differences in their upbringing and education, she felt that she had more in common with him than with anyone else she had known, outside of her immediate family. She believed that people never forget their first love or their first intimate experience. Billy was both. Was she now admitting to herself that she did love Billy? The more she attempted to analyze her feelings, the more confused she became. All her rationalizations did not help still the tightness in her stomach. Her conjecturing was interrupted by the unexpected sound of her aunt's voice behind her, "My, aren't you mother's little helper. What's gotten into you? When I looked over and saw your bed made and you gone, I thought maybe you had decided to run away from home. When I tell your mother you were up before me, fixing breakfast, she won't believe it. You may never live it down."

Chris smiled at her aunt's remarks. "Maybe I'm just a new leaf that's decided to turn over," she replied, continuing her stirring.

"Well, now that I've got you house trained, I hate to see you leave. Who's going to fix my breakfast tomorrow?"

Unable to resist the temptation, Chris said, "Maybe Mr. X will volunteer for the job."

Nonplused, Emmy replied, "Mr. Graystone to you, young lady. Somehow, he doesn't seem like the domestic type. Besides, I don't have an apron that would fit him."

Unable to hold her emotions in, a cascade of tears suddenly covered Chris's face. She threw her arms around her aunt, hugging her so hard Emmy had difficulty breathing. "I don't want to leave. I want to stay with you," Chris confessed. And Billy, Emmy thought, but said, "Now, now. What's happened to my grown up niece?" Emmy did not know much about modern young women. They seemed to mature earlier than in her day. But, she did know that although Chris would soon turn twenty one, she still had some more emotional growing to do. Not able to think of any words of comfort at the moment, she said, "Let's have breakfast and then we'll have a good old woman to woman talk about things. OK?"

"OK," Chris sobbed, dabbing her eyes with her pajama sleeve.

Breakfast was eaten quickly and silently. After the kitchen was cleaned up, Emmy took Chris's hand and led her to the living room couch.

"Now, first things first," Emmy said. "I know you've had some things bothering you the last few days, and we both know they include your relationship with Billy. So, here's where we step into the deep water."

Chris nodded her head in acknowledgement.

Taking the blunt approach, Emmy asked in a calm, even tone, "Have you slept with Billy? To Emmy's surprise, Chris, without any hesitation, again nodded and held up two fingers.

"Is that what's got you upset?" With the ice broken, Chris felt freer to speak openly.

"I don't know. That's part of it. I don't understand myself and the feelings I'm having--about Billy, school, my life. I feel that I haven't been fair to you, spending so much of my time with Billy since I've been here and not enough time with you--which is why I came."

"Well, put that part of your worrying aside. I've enjoyed having you here. In a way, I'm relieved you found someone to spend time with besides your old maid aunt. It took the pressure off me trying to come up with things for us to do. And, we've had lots of time for talking and enjoying being together."

"Are you sure, Aunt Em?"

"I'm sure," Emmy replied, with her reassuring smile confirming it. "Now, as to the other matter, that needs some talking about. What kind of understanding do you and Billy have between you, besides the obvious?"

"I really like him. It's too soon to say if I love him, but I really enjoy being with him--in every way. And I don't want our relationship to end. On the surface, he and I are total opposites, but underneath we're like one person. He makes me happy. I've never known anyone like him before. I don't want to lose him, but I know it's not practical to think that we can have a continuing relationship with me in Boston and him here.

"Why not? Although some people may think so, Boston isn't on the other side of the world, you know. And I know he gets three weeks vacation--and you have vacation breaks between semesters--and the summers. Why is it so hard to believe you can't continue to stay in touch? You both have telephones and know how to write. So, what's the problem?"

"You don't understand, Aunt Em. I'm afraid that after I'm gone for awhile, he'll lose interest in me and we'll drift apart. After all, absence makes the heart grow fonder--for someone else, as the saying goes. Dr. Foster says . . . ."

"Forget Dr. Foster, whoever he is," Emmy said, interrupting Chris in mid sentence. Does he know more than you and Billy about how the two of you feel about each other? I doubt it. So, think with your heart as well as your head, and don't blindly accept what some dried up old professor says--someone whose knowledge of life probably comes more from books than from living."

Chris had to laugh, in spite of herself. "You must know Professor Foster. He's never been married, and far as I know, he's never even had a girlfriend."

"There. What did I tell you? You can learn a world of useful things from books, but you can't live life merely by reading about it. That brings up the 'P' question." Emmy arched an eyebrow as she said it.

Chris hesitated before answering this unexpected question. "No, I'm OK there," she said, finally, although she had no concrete evidence to support her claim.

"Good. And how do you feel about these occurrences--emotionally?"

"Do you mean do I have any guilt or other negative feelings about what Billy and I did?"

"Yes."

"No. I don't have any regrets, other than it kind of complicates my leaving--after being so close, so to speak, in my relationship with Billy."

"And how does he feel? Have the two of you discussed the subject?" Emmy was beginning to feel that she was getting beyond her depth in the subject of the conversation. Her only experience dealing with an intimate relationship did not include any feelings of closeness or emotion, at least not on her part. With Del--she finally remembered his name--Delmar Brinkman--it had been strictly a superficial physical relationship--for his benefit only.

Chris continued. "We never discussed it. It just seemed that actions spoke louder than words, and we didn't feel the need to analyze it. It just felt natural to both of us. No regrets for either of us--so far as I know."

"Thanks for being so frank, Chris. I know this is not something that's easy to talk about, especially with a family member. Sometimes it's easier to talk to strangers about personal things than to those close to us."

"I don't know why, but I feel better now that we've talked," Chris admitted. "I guess I just needed to talk to someone--and I'm glad it was you. I hope you don't think I'm cheap or immoral because of what we did."

"Who am I to judge? Just between you and me--don't tell your mother--I had a similar experience when I was in college. Let me correct that. It wasn't similar. He may have gotten some animal level pleasure from what we did, but there were never any feelings on my part, other than becoming physically ill, to the point of sometimes throwing up afterward. But, I got over it by deciding that it was better to look ahead and prepare for the future, than to look back with regrets. And I learned a valuable lesson. Don't try to please others, if what you do isn't right for you."

"Thanks, Aunt Em."

"Oh, my, look at the time," Emmy said, feeling this was a good time to change the subject. "It seems that too often time runs our lives, doesn't it? But, we better start thinking about getting you packed, having lunch and getting out of here on time.

We don't want your folks waiting for you at the station and you not being on the train."

The telephone rang. Emmy and Chris, as had become their habit, looked at each other.

"Go ahead. Answer it. It's your last chance," Emmy told Chris.

"Hello?" Chris said tentatively.

"Hi Chris. I'm calling to volunteer to chauffer you to the train station."

"Oh! Hi Billy. Let me do a litmus test on that proposal." Turning to her aunt, Chris said, "Billy's offered to take us to the station--or would you rather drive?"

"I don't mind. He can drive you and I'll stay home."

"No. I want you both to see me off," Chris insisted. It'll make me feel important to have two people I care for waving to me as we pull out of the station." Chris turned back to the phone.

"OK, Billy. My train leaves at four forty. Aunt Em is going to go with us."

"I'll be there at three o'clock. That'll give us a bit of time to visit before you leave. But, I need to warn you, with three of us in the truck, you'll have to sit real close to me."

"You don't scare me, mister. I think I can handle it. See you then." Laughing, she hung up.

"So! What time is Billy coming by?"

"He said he'd pick us up at three. I assume 'promptly at' applies--as usual."

"Well, then, let's get you packed and go get some lunch so we'll be ready when he gets here."

By the time Billy's knock came, Chris's suitcase and garment bag were packed and sitting next to the door.

"Ready to go?" Billy asked, as Chris let him in. She was surprised to see that he was wearing a suit and tie. He handed her a bouquet of mixed flowers and a small box, with instructions that she was not to open it until she got on the train.

"Are you going to a party after you drop me off?" Chris asked, jokingly. "I've never seen you dressed up before. You clean up nice."

"Thank you ma'am. I try," Billy replied. I even washed my truck. Nothing but the best for my girl."

"Am I?" Chris asked, hoping he meant it.

"If I have any say in the matter," he replied.

"You do. And that goes for me, too," Chris said, a lone tear escaping from her eye.

"You mean I'm your girl?"

"You know what I mean, silly," Chris said, giving him a playful tap on his arm.

"You're my witness Ms. Stratton. You heard her make a commitment."

"I think you both just did," Emmy replied, softly.

The ride to the train station was uneventful and relatively quiet, until Chris spoke. "Besides you two, I'm going to miss this old covered bridge. Driving through it always gives me a feeling of peace and well being. It's an example of how, in the face of all the changes in our lives, some things remain the same. It gives one a sense of permanency."

Neither Billy nor Emmy felt any need to comment on Chris's words. They both knew what she meant.

The train slowly chugged into the station twenty three minutes late. This provided ample time for Chris to convince Billy he should let her open the box before boarding the train. When she did, she found a gold chain with a diamond-cut heart pendant attached. She pulled Billy close and buried her face in his shoulder, her arms tightly around him.

There were only two other people in the waiting room. They had no luggage visible, so it was assumed they were there to meet arriving passengers, who, shortly after the train came to a grinding halt, detrained to greetings and hugs.

Billy and Emmy escorted Chris from the station building to the platform. Emmy gave Chris a hug and a kiss on the cheek, and they exchanged words about how good it had been to see each other. Then Billy hugged Chris and kissed her, his lips lingering on her mouth for several seconds.

"All aboard!" the conductor's bass voice bellowed. Billy gave Chris another hug, as though to prevent her from leaving, and again kissed her, this time longer and more passionately.

"You've got my address and phone number, Billy. I expect to hear from you--often."

"Is every day often enough?" he asked.

"I guess so, if you can't do any better," Chris replied.

After several more quick hugs and kisses, Chris boarded the Pullman coach and seated herself by a window where she could see Billy and her aunt on the platform. Tears welled up in her eyes as she waved goodbye. As the train slowly pulled away, Chris was unable to see her aunt crying or Billy wiping his eyes.

All the goodbyes had been said.

Chapter 27

REFLECTIONS

THE MORNING WAS unusually dark. It had rained all night and Emmy had not slept well. She awoke and looked over to see if Chris was awake before remembering that she had left the day before. It had been a busy day. Chris had called her parents to tell them what time her train would arrive. With Emmy's help, she had packed her suitcase, which had resisted closing, being overburdened from the addition of souvenirs and gifts she had bought for her parents and her college roommate.

The trip to the train station had been an unhappy and unwelcome one. Emmy, Chris and Billy had all been in a somber mood, each for their own reasons. Saying goodbye had been done with tearful reluctance.

Emmy had become accustomed to sharing her apartment, and now, once again, she was alone. An emptiness enveloped her. Her stomach was unsettled and she felt as though she might throw up. Fortunately, she did not. Although the cause of her current upset was diametrically opposite from ones she had experienced during her youthful misadventures with Del, her physical and emotional sensations were similar. Dates with him had usually left her with stomach cramps and an empty feeling--and an inclination to vomit, which on occasion she did--once in the back seat of his new car. That was the beginning of the end of their relationship. His car was very important to him.

Emmy had read about parents experiencing empty nest syndrome when their children grew up and moved out of the house. If she had this much of a reaction after only two weeks with Chris, she marveled at how parents could adjust to their losses after eighteen or more years.

Following a habit of many years, Emmy arose, showered, dressed and in robot fashion, pointed herself toward the kitchen. Her only happy thought of the moment was that her leg was not paining her. There would be no pancakes or bright chatter this morning. Breakfast to her was more of a shared event than a solitary one. But, now it was back to tea and toast. They were her excuse not to have a regular breakfast without feeling guilty. She slowly and absentmindedly sipped her cooling tea and idly played with her burnt toast--remembering the happy glow and warmth that Chris had brought into her small apartment. Now, the glow and warmth were gone, having departed with Chris. Once again, here she was, a middle aged woman, alone and with no sense of purpose other than methodically and automatically moving from one day to the next, each of which seemed to blend into a flat line continuum that had become her sterile life. One day at a time had become her byword.

Emmy knew from experience that it was selfish feeling sorry for herself--and that selfishness led to loneliness. She resolved to remember the happy times she and Chris had shared during her all too brief stay, and her dark mood began to improve--although the weather did not. Rain continued to fall quietly and steadily and the sun was yet to make an appearance. The rain would end. The sun would shine. She would again see Chris. To combat her self-pity, she began thinking about taking a trip to Boston. She was long overdue in visiting her sister. It had been two years since she had been there, and there was no excuse now for her not to go. Except for an occasional twinge in her leg, she was feeling well, she could afford it, and she had no current commitments to anybody or anything--except the orphan cat, Stray. And she felt certain she could get one of her neighbors to feed him in her absence. These thoughts lifted her spirits. She would call her sister in a few days and find out when a visit would be most convenient. Perhaps she could even visit Chris at college. A feeling of peace and optimism washed over her, and the sun tried, with limited success, to overcome the dark clouds.

Chris's trip to Boston had been delayed half an hour while her train was switched to a siding to allow a westbound freight to pass on the one way track. Like her aunt, this was the first time she had been totally alone for two weeks. She unconsciously fondled the pendant on the chain around her neck as random thoughts ran uncontrollably through her mind. She remembered her time at the Village fondly. She felt that she had been changed by her life experiences during that time--emotionally as well as physically. She harbored questions and doubts about her future, and Billy's role in it. Their togetherness had altered her perceptions about life and how she wanted to live it. Before Billy, her goals had been simple and straightforward--to complete her college degree in psychology, continue on to a master's, and perhaps a doctorate--a requirement if she wanted to successfully pursue a career in psychology. She was still uncertain as to whether she would prefer teaching, becoming a therapist, or conducting clinical research. Her life had been changed and she had changed with it--at least insofar as questioning her plans and priorities for the future.

Chris missed her aunt and Billy. For two eventful weeks, they had been the center of her existence. They had filled a void she had not even known existed beforehand. New knowledge--but how should she react to it and use it? This was a question she was not yet able to answer objectively, or even subjectively. Perhaps, she needed to be more patient and not attempt to force answers about her future, in her present emotional state. She knew that patience was the forerunner of maturity and the proof of maturity was control. However, at the moment, she felt she lacked all of these qualities. Surely, with practiced patience, she hoped, maturity would follow. Control, however, at this stage, seemed an elusive concept to her. Soon, the intensity of her reflections faded, much as a dream faded upon awakening. And, in spite of babies crying, people coughing and heavy footed pedestrian traffic past her seat, she fell asleep.

Billy felt as though part of him had been surgically cut away. He never thought he could miss someone that he had known for such a short time—so much. He replayed their time together in his mind, alternately smiling and frowning. He thought of things he wished he had said to Chris, but had not, and wished he had used better words in expressing those things he had said. Light conversation came easily to him. Serious communication was not one of his better skills. He found himself being overcome with hindsight. He had used up most of his vacation days to be with Chris, but he vowed to take a trip to Boston soon as he had again accumulated enough leave time, and when Pop could spare him. That is, if she still wanted to see him. He could not escape the concern that once she got back home and around her family and friends, he would be just another brief entry in her diary--if that. But, he promised himself that he would do his best to not let that happen. His preoccupation was interrupted by Pop Bates.

"How many times you gonna paint that piece of wall, son? You're gonna wear a hole plum through it." Billy suddenly realized that his brush was continuing to go back and forth over the same small area.

"Sorry, Pop," Billy answered, sheepishly. "I guess my mind isn't totally on what I'm doing."

"It don't surprise me none. I know you enjoyed your time off, but work's pilin' up. I put off all the ladder work best I could 'til you got back on the job."

"Thanks Pop. I appreciate you giving me so much time off on such short notice. I'll work double shifts to catch up."

"No need for that. I've got most everything else up to snuff. You just keep your mind on what you're doin', and I'll keep everything else under control. That little filly kinda got under your skin, didn't she?" he said with a knowing grin, remembering his youthful adventures.

Billy did not realize that Pop had paid that much attention to his comings and goings with Chris, but in a community as open as Twilight Manor, it was probably obvious to him, and to the rest of the Villagers, that he and Chris had spent a lot of time together. Billy, on the other hand, had barely noticed anybody else while Chris was there.

"Sorry, Pop. I'm back on the job. I'll get things caught up quick as I can."

"OK, lad. Stay with it." Pop patted Billy on the shoulder and walked away.

Pop genuinely liked Billy. He was like the son he wished he had had. He was happy to have him back full time--at least in body. He understood that Billy's mind would probably wander for awhile, now and then, back to those two weeks he had been able to spend squiring Ms. Stratton's niece around. Nice girl, he thought. Billy had made himself available to take care of any jobs Pop needed him for, and still found time to spend with that pretty young filly, as Pop referred to her. Billy's energy and enthusiasm for his work had impressed Pop from the first day he came to work for him. Pop could still handle any problem or project that came up in keeping the Village's facilities operating efficiently and the maintenance needs taken care of, but, sometimes his knees balked at ladders. He did not climb too well these days. With Billy's help, however, he had been able to reduce considerably the mileage on his aging joints, for which he was grateful. Pop had worried about Billy not having anyone near his age to spend time with. So, he was more than happy to give him as much time off as possible. His legs began to feel stronger as soon as Billy came back to work full time. He no longer needed to soak his feet or apply hot pads to his knees at night. When Pop mentioned his leg problems, which were obvious from the way he walked, he would usually finish his story with, "The legs are the first thing to go. I can't remember what the second thing is," he would say, laughing at this old saying he truly believed was original with him. No one was going to tell him otherwise and risk hurting his feelings. Everybody at the Village had probably heard his saying this at least once, and, more likely, several times.

Pop's main concern about Billy was that one day he would head for greener pastures. He was young, energetic, ambitious--and a worker. It did not take Pop long to learn that. Although Billy did not have much more formal education than he, himself, did, he was a bright and capable young man, and a quick learner. Pop hoped that Billy would stay on until he retired, and maybe even afterward, and take the head man's job at the Village. Pop felt that Billy could do everything he could, with the possible exception of keeping those stubborn old boilers running. But, the young man was learning. Given two or three more years, Pop felt he could retire and leave the care and upkeep of the community in Billy's capable hands. However, retirement wasn't in Pop's blood, and he used the word reluctantly. He lived for his work and he was never lonely. He enjoyed telling his tall tales to anyone who would listen, which was just about everybody who worked or lived in the Village, or frequented Larry's Office Bar in town. He even liked that Mr. Graystone fella, even though he was kind of an odd duck, to his way of thinking. But, a good fella, best he could tell. Just on the quiet side. Anyhow, he was sure glad Billy was back on the job.

Dominic had not been feeling well lately. He was weaker than usual. He had no energy and felt an occasional sharp pain in his chest. He recollected he had not seen Ms. Stratton's niece with her lately. He had seen Ms. Stratton at dinner just hours before, and she was alone. She looked sad. He knew the look well. It was there frequently when he looked in the mirror. At dinner, she had sat and stared out the window, as though in a trance, picking idly at her food. That was unlike her, Dominic thought.

She always seemed to have a good appetite. He wondered how she and her niece could put away so much food and still stay so thin. He had to work out in the gym two or three times a week to keep from having to let his belt out a notch or two. He had always been athletic and firm bodied, and did not like his present profile. He had been proud of his firm, flat stomach and was upset when he noticed it beginning to curve outward, as reflected in the bedroom mirror. "I've got to work harder and eat less," he would tell himself. Then, as an afterthought, he would question why he should even worry about it, remembering the small, shiny pistol now waiting patiently in a drawer of his bedside table for its intended purpose. He removed it and cradled it in his hand, feeling the weight of its cold hardness. Every time he decided life no longer had any purpose and there was no point in living, he would somehow be interrupted from his proposed solution to correct the situation. He liked that Billy kid, but he got to be a pest sometimes, always popping in on him at the wrong time. How could he plan anything if people wouldn't leave him alone? The question, of course, was rhetorical. How long did it take to do away with one's self? If he really wanted to, surely he could find a couple spare minutes to do what needed to be done. It wasn't as though he had any higher priorities in life. He was being pulled back and forth in this thinking. At the moment, however, he did not feel well enough to end it all, so he decided to wait until he was stronger and in the mood to perform the task.

Dominic's mind turned back to Emmy. That Ms. Stratton was a nice lady, he thought. He wished he had the courage to talk to her. But, what was the point? He was a nothing and a nobody, or, at best, a has been, and she was an attractive, classy lady. When he looked into the mirror on his closet door he would say to his image, "Beauty and the Beast," picturing in his mind the two of them together. "Why would she want to talk to me, and what do I know to talk to her about that she would even be interested in hearing?" he would ask himself. Nevertheless, he enjoyed watching her at dinner. She was so poised and delicate in her table manners. "A real princess," he would think out loud. He purposely took a corner table in the darkest part of the dining room so she would not notice him staring at her. If he were a handsome man, and could talk like the movie's leading men, he would approach her. As it was, all he could hope for was just to continue to be satisfied with an occasional glimpse of her beauty and grace.

Chapter 28

TURN OF EVENTS

IT MUST HAVE been something he ate, Dominic thought. The pain in his chest had worsened. Or, maybe it was a strain from working out in the gym the other day. But, he had never before experienced a pain quite like this one--not from all the horses he had fallen off, the windows he had been thrown through or the roofs he had jumped from. This was a new and peculiar sensation. He began to perspire. His arm tingled. Circulation, he thought. Was he catching the flu? He did not normally perspire except during physical exertion.

There was a knock at the door. Who could that be, he wondered? It was a rare occurrence. He limped to the door, bent over, holding his arm across his chest, as if to keep his heart from jumping through his rib cage. Upon opening the door, he saw Billy, smiling at him. That was the last thing he remembered. Then, a noise woke him. He recognized the sound of a siren. The first thing he saw was the white roof of a vehicle. He had the feeling of being in motion. A large man in a white coat hovered over him, peering into his eyes and doing other things he could not identify. He felt a slight jarring and saw sunlight. He closed his eyes to block out the brightness. There were unrecognizable voices and faces and once again the sensation of motion, occasionally accompanied by a slight jarring. He heard the whoosh of an automatic door, followed by a smooth gliding feeling. Where ever he was rolling to, it was being done hurriedly, of that much he was certain. More voices. More people. Strange faces looking down at him. It was like a dream. He had no idea where he was or why or how he had gotten there. He had a vague recollection of having been put in a small room with a myriad of machines, hoses and tubes, some of which seemed to be coming out of him. His chest? His arms? He could not quite be certain. He felt cold. Then events ceased.

"How is he, Doctor?" Billy's voice asked, with obvious concern.

"Too soon to tell, until we run some tests," was the emotionless reply. "Nurse, would you please take Mr . . . ."

"Inch. William Inch."

"Would you show Mr. Inch where the waiting room is, please?"

"Yes, Doctor," the nurse replied smartly, as she took Billy's arm and guided him through a corridor to a room full of chairs. "We'll let you know how Mr. Graystone is as soon as the doctor finishes examining him" With that said, she gave him a tired smile, turned, and left the room, returning the way they had come.

When Billy had seen Dominic slump to the floor after opening the door to him, he did not know what to do. As soon as he realized the man was not moving, he used Dominic's telephone to dial 911. An ambulance arrived within minutes. To Billy, it felt like an eternity. He let in the two paramedics. They nodded to him, asked him to step aside, and immediately began checking Dominic's vital signs, quickly and expertly hooking him up to portable heart monitor and blood pressure machines. He heard one of the men say to the other one, "He's in cardiac arrest." They quickly had him in the back of the waiting ambulance, telling Billy to follow them to the hospital in his car. Billy insisted on riding in back of the ambulance with Dominic. He told the examining medic Dominic's name and approximate age. The medic continued his administering. Billy felt helpless. All he could do was sit tensely by and watch. His stomach churned and he felt light headed. He took several deep breaths, which helped, somewhat. The siren's blare stilled as the ambulance backed up to the Emergency Department's door. Billy breathed a sigh of relief. At least, Dom was now where he could get proper help.

As he sat in the waiting room, nervously waiting for someone to come in and tell him something, Billy thought how fortunate it was that he had stopped by Dom's apartment at just that particular moment. There had been no particular reason for his visit, other than that he had not seen or spoken to him since Chris arrived. Up until the time she had left, he had been occupied fully with spending time with her and taking care of work assignments for Pop. He could not help but wonder what would have happened if he had not, on a whim, decided to stop by and say hi to Dom and to apologize for not coming by sooner.

A man dressed in green hospital scrubs approached Billy and introduced himself as Dr. Greenberg. He informed him that Dominic had suffered a mild heart attack. It was not fatal, but he would need to be admitted to the hospital for observation and treatment for a few days. Billy had never thought of himself as a religious person, but when he heard the doctor's words, he looked toward the ceiling and said, "Thank you!"

"Mr. Graystone's conscious now," the doctor informed Billy. "If you would like to see him for a minute--no longer than that--you can. We sedated him, so he'll be asleep shortly. We'll keep him in the emergency room for observation for awhile before we move him into a room."

"Thank you, Doctor," Billy replied, and started quickly back toward the Emergency Department area and Dom's curtained off cubicle. On entering, Billy saw that his normally hooded eyes were open even less than usual. When Dominic saw him, he gave Billy a forced, lopsided grin, and asked, "What happened?" His memory of how he came to be on his back in a strange room was a blur. Billy briefly explained the series of events that had brought Dominic to his current location. With some effort, Dominic said, "Thanks," his eyes closed and he was asleep, his heart monitor displaying a normal rhythm signal. A nurse pulled back the curtain, smiled, and said, "You need to go now. He'll sleep for awhile. On your way out, would you stop by the nurses' station? They have some papers that need to be filled out." Billy thought of another saying that Pop took credit for, "A job's not finished until the paper work's done." In spite of the current situation, Billy could not help but laugh to himself about Pop and his sayings. He seemed to have one for every occasion and considered most of them original with him--however, probably few, if any, were.

After filling out the medical history form with as much information as he could about Dominic, and handing it to a nurse, Billy realized that he had no transportation back to the Village, having ridden to the hospital in the ambulance. Now, he was stranded without transportation. He searched the hallway until he found a wall telephone.

"Hello, Ms. Stratton," he said. "This is Billy. I hate to impose on you, but could you possibly come to County General Hospital to get me?" Then, as a second thought, he said, "Or, I can call the office and see if somebody there can come for me."

"What happened, Billy?" she asked, concern obvious in her voice. "Are you all right?"

"Oh, it's not me. I'm fine. But, Mr. Graystone's had a heart attack and I came to the hospital with him in the ambulance."

"Is he OK?" Emmy asked, as she caught her breath.

"I think he'll be OK. They said it was a mild heart attack, if there is such a thing. They're monitoring his heart activity, which seemed to be normal when I left him, but they want to keep him a few days for observation."

"I'll be there soon as I can, Billy. Where should I meet you?"

"I'll be at the Emergency Department entrance," Billy said.

Emmy hung up the phone, quickly grabbed her purse and car keys, and headed for the parking lot. Her self-pity and personal problems were put behind her for the moment. As she pulled up in front of the Emergency Department entrance, she saw Billy standing by the doorway, leaning against the wall. He opened the door and got into her car. His face was ashen gray, and his hands were trembling.

"Thank you, Ms. Stratton. I hated to bother you, but you were the first person I thought to call."

"I'm glad you did, Billy. What are friends for?" she asked, smiling, in an attempt to help calm him from his obvious nervous state. "Just one thing. Do you think we should check at the nurses' station before we leave, just to make sure everything's OK?"

"Sure," Billy said, angry with himself for not having thought of it. Emmy pulled her car into an Emergency Department's parking space, and the two of them hurried into the building and over to the island that was the nurses' station.

"Pardon me, Miss," Emmy said. "Could you tell me how Mr. Dominic Graystone is doing? He was brought to the Emergency Department awhile ago."

After shuffling through some papers on a clipboard the nurse replied, "As of ten minutes ago, he was resting quietly. If there's no change, he'll probably be moved to an intermediate care unit in a day or so." She smiled, hoping to have allayed some of the couple's concerns. She gave Emmy a card with the nurse's station telephone number and her name on it. "You can call tomorrow to check on his status and location."

"Thank you very much." The two left, still concerned, but somewhat relieved that Dominic's condition was stable, and confident he was in good hands.

The drive back to the Village seemed a long one. During it, Billy explained how he had come to take Dominic to the hospital, and that it was coincidental that he had decided to stop by and see him at that particular time. In all the excitement, Billy had temporarily forgotten about Chris. "Have you heard from Chris lately?" he asked.

"I heard from her this morning, in fact," Emmy replied. She's getting ready to enroll for the fall semester at college. She told me to say hi to you when I saw you and tell you she loves the necklace and pendant you gave her. She told me she doesn't plan to take it off and asked when you and I are coming to Boston for a visit." This information made Billy feel better, knowing she had mentioned him and liked the jewelry he had given her. It helped to ease his insecurity about her forgetting him when she got back to her normal life.

Chapter 29

A BLOSSOMING

THE DAYS THAT followed saw Billy and Emmy regularly visiting Dominic at the hospital. When Billy's work schedule permitted, the two of them went together. On days when Billy was unable to go, Emmy went by herself. Two days after his arrival, Dominic had been moved to an intermediate care room. Fortunately, tests revealed that there had been no damage to his heart, and his doctor assured him that, after his release in a few days, he could again return to a normal life. Dominic met this news with mixed feelings. He was not sure what a normal life was. Had his life been saved just for him to bring it to an end later? Now he had unlimited time to think about such questions and his thoughts ran the gamut about his future, or lack thereof. He enjoyed and looked forward to visits by Billy and Ms. Stratton--especially her. Just looking at her made him feel better. And her soothing voice comforted him. She always seemed to have a smile on her face, which he considered beautiful. He had never before seen anyone with such a symmetrical face and such smooth skin, even among the actresses in his B movies, who generally needed considerable makeup to cover their facial flaws. From his mid thirties, his skin had been coarse and his face etched. He had never liked to look at his image in a mirror and, except for shaving, seldom did, even when combing his coarse, thick salt and pepper colored hair. He had even considered growing a beard to conceal more of his features.

It was about time for his visitors to arrive. They usually came around two in the afternoon, shortly after lunch. Dominic had even, after a few days, felt comfortable enough to begin to have real conversations with Ms. Stratton. She had told him to call her Emmy, but he felt that was too informal for the short time he had known her. He lay on his back, staring at the ceiling, thinking about her, his life, and life in general, forming no conclusions about any of them. He wondered, after what had happened to him, what life would be like after he left the hospital. He heard a light knock on the door as it slowly squeaked open.

"Anybody home?" Emmy asked, her head preceding her body through the doorway. She entered quietly--smiling brightly. She held a milk white vase with a bouquet of colorful flowers in it. Dominic turned his head toward her and noticed them. As she sat them on a utility shelf, she said, "I thought these might brighten up your room a little. I hope you like flowers." Dominic had never thought much about flowers. He was indifferent to them. But, to him, these flowers were special, because of the person who had brought them.

"They're very pretty," he said, adding, to himself, "and so are you." Instead of mouthing this last thought out loud, he merely replied, "Thank you."

"I hoped you'd like them. Flowers always seem to cheer me up when I need it. I hear they're going to parole you tomorrow for good behavior." She gave a little laugh for being so casual in her conversation with someone she barely knew. She noticed that his eyes were completely open and she once again was able to see how gentle, yet deeply dark and penetrating they were. Even his smile seemed more normal and sincere, not the lopsided, forced one she had previously been exposed to. It was as though his medical mishap had changed his appearance. The lines in his face were less noticeable. He was almost handsome, in a mature, rugged sort of way. And his black, wavy hair, with it's speckling of steel grayness added favorably to the effect.

"That's what they tell me," he replied, simply. "I'll be glad to get out of here. The food's not near as good as at the Village. And neither is the scenery," he added, with an oblique reference to Emmy.

Emmy smiled, and wondered if this man could possibly be flirting with her? Whether or not he was, it gave her a warm inner feeling that she had not experienced for many years.

"That's true," she responded. "Maybe if they had a lake and a gazebo and a nine hole golf course, they could compete with the Village." They both smiled, realizing they were communicating with each other on two levels--spoken and implied. Changing the subject, she said, "Billy told me to apologize for his not being here today. Pop's got him busy doing some high ladder work that he can't do himself."

"That's OK. He's a good boy. I probably owe my life to him. Who knows what would have happened if he hadn't gotten me to the hospital when he did."

"He thinks highly of you, too. He told me how much he enjoyed visiting with you, talking about movies and watching old ones on video. He mentioned that you had been a stuntman and an actor. How did you ever get into that line of work?" Emmy asked, partially out of interest and partially out of curiosity.

"It's kind of a long story. I just sort of fell into it, you might say. I never did anything important in either job, but it was a living, so I can't complain. Nobody's ever asked me for an autograph, or told me how much they liked watching me fall off a horse or get knocked through a plate glass window. But, I enjoyed my work. I guess my favorite movie role was getting beat up by Robert Mitchum. And my most memorable dialog was "Oh, you got me!" He laughed at these references. Emmy noticed what a nice smile he had, and how white and even his teeth were. She wondered if they were his. They were. One of the fringe benefits Dominic had received from his movie work was that the studio paid to have his crooked teeth straightened and capped.

"Well, I better be getting back to the Village before they miss me," Emmy said humorously, knowing there was no one there who would, although she was friendly with and well liked by all who knew her. "I'll give you a call in the morning to see what time they're going to release you." As an afterthought, she said, "Would you like me to drive you home tomorrow?" She was surprised at herself for offering. Was she being too forward? It had been a long time since she had been this close to a man, even in conversation.

"I'd like that, Ms. Stratton," Dominic answered.

"Emmy. Please call me Emmy. That's short for my initials, M and E--for Mary Elizabeth." She wondered why she had even bothered to tell him that.

"OK, Emmy. Call me Dom. Short for Dominic."

"OK, Dom. I'll talk to you tomorrow morning and be here when you let me know what time."

"Thanks, Ms. . . . Uh, Emmy. I'll look forward to it," he said, flashing his impression of a matinee idol smile.

As Emmy drove back to the Village, her mind was a mixture of unrelated thoughts. She sometimes thought that she thought too much. Then she thought how redundant that thought had been. She had seen a different side of Mr. Graystone--Dom--than she had ever seen at the Village. But, this was the first opportunity they had had to have a real conversation. Although, he seemed to be more of a listener than a talker. The time he had helped her up after falling in Braxton Falls, their words had been sparse and the meeting somewhat awkward and embarrassing--especially to her. Maybe the town should change its name to Emmy Falls, she thought. As she approached the entrance to Twilight Manor, her focus turned to finding a parking space and wondering what was on the dinner menu. As she alit from her car, she realized that her leg had not pained her for several days.

Now alone in his hospital room, Dominic studied the flowers, thinking how thoughtful it had been for Emmy to bring them. She was right, they did brighten the room, but to his mind, she had brightened it even more. In a way, he was in no hurry to leave the hospital. He was enjoying all the attention he was receiving from the doctors and nurses, and the daily visits from Emmy and Billy. After all, how often did he get a beautiful lady knocking on his door everyday? And the food, although not as good as at the Village, was brought to him--he didn't have to go to a dining room to get it. Nor did he have to make decisions about what to eat. He ate whatever they brought him. He did not want to admit it, but he was feeling happy, at least by his definition of the word.

Dominic was uncertain as to what to expect after he returned to his solitary apartment. Probably the only change from his pre-hospital life would be whatever prescription medicine he would be required to take, possibly the rest of his life, however long that might be. And he was still undecided about that. But making a decision with regard to his future somehow didn't seem nearly as important as thinking about Emmy's arrival tomorrow to take him home.

Chapter 30

GOING HOME

THERE WAS A crispness to the morning air. Nature was providing one of its periodic reminders that winter was not far off. Dominic's doctor had signed his release papers the previous evening, and he would be going home today. He arose early, exchanged his hospital gown for the wrinkled trousers, shirt and black shoes and socks he had been wearing when admitted. He had not shaved during his confinement. Looking at himself in the bathroom mirror, he combed his thick, black hair, noticing how much more gray seemed to have crept into it since he had been admitted to the hospital. Probably just the harsh lighting in the bathroom, he thought. With razor in hand, he paused, then decided to leave on his short growth of beard, which had considerably more gray than the hair on his head. He carefully replaced the shaving instrument in the plastic toiletry kit the hospital had provided. In his opinion, his stubble-start toward a beard gave him a certain sophisticated air, and even better, it softened the lower half of his craggy facial features by covering them.

Dominic was not anxious to leave the hospital, but he was looking forward to Emmy coming to drive him home. He wondered whether anyone other than she or Billy even knew he had been gone. Probably not. Why would they? He had not exactly gone out of his way to try to make friends with any of the other residents. He had been too self absorbed with his personal problems and worries to open himself up to others. During most of his life, he had lived in an insular shell and had resisted becoming a part of the greater world. The only people he had mixed with to any extent had been his fellow stuntmen, and that one B actress, a memory he chose not to dwell on, and tried, semi-successfully, to forget. Theirs had been a brief relationship that ended badly and abruptly. He had taken the blame--for what, he could not remember. In retrospect, she had probably just found someone who could better satisfy her needs. But, that was history--and one cannot change history. He had learned that lesson well. Soon, he would move from the world of the hospital back to the world of the Village.

When Emmy called Dominic, shortly after he had finished breakfast, he told her he was ready to leave. She said she would be there within the hour. While waiting for her arrival, he sat slouched on the side of the bed, staring blankly out the window at the parking lot below, deep in thought. Thinking had long been a dangerous activity for Dominic. Seldom were his thoughts positive or productive ones. They continued to center on his troubles, and recently, before his heart attack, on the shiny gun in a drawer in his apartment. His only present, non-negative thought was about Emmy's coming to take him home. Even that had a negative edge to it. What would he have to talk to her about on the drive back? He had no social graces or gift for small talk. Was it in a Mitchum movie he had heard the line that careful listening is the best remedy for loneliness? He wasn't sure. And, to his mind, it didn't matter. He continued to look at his watch every few seconds. Time seemed to be moving in slow motion. The minutes dragged slowly by.

Emmy was nervous. She had not had a man friend since college. And that was an experience better left unrecalled. Of course, she could not consider Dominic a friend. He was a casual acquaintance of circumstances, at best. She put him in same category as Stray--a creature who needed her help. Stray cats and stray men. Was this to be her lot in life? That was not her preference in how to spend her middle years. But, when a being, human or animal, needed her help, she felt she had a responsibility to provide it. What was life about, she reasoned, if not to help others smooth out the bumps in their rough roads of life? She had always been a caring person, which, on occasion, had led to sacrificing herself to the needs and pleasures of others. But, she realized that remembering regrets merely wasted energy, and in the long run, accomplished nothing. But, what else did she have in her life to occupy herself with? Too much thinking, she thought. She remembered something William Arthur Ward had written, "Will someone else's life be brighter tomorrow because of what you have done today?" She took some solace in hoping so. Would her being there for Dominic help make his life better? Would her talks with Chris make her better able to cope with life's unexpected twists and turns? Emmy was not sure whether she had contributed anything positive to either of them. She still felt troubled about Chris and wondered whether she had been too passive in her attempt to help her. Perhaps she had just abetted her, especially in regard to her relationship with Billy. It was so difficult to run one's own life, she thought, without attempting to influence or change the lives of others. Perhaps she needed to examine her own priorities. She felt that she had not made much of a success of her own existence and was, therefore, not qualified to help or advise others in the direction of their lives. But, it was not her nature to ignore the needs of others, if she could be of help. She harbored hopes that at least a few of her attempts to help others would somehow benefit them, as she believed one of the greatest gifts a person can give another person is the gift of encouragement. She wondered how she could encourage Dominic. She still had difficulty thinking of him as Dom. Again, too much thinking. She had once been told that she had a subconscious need to be needed. She had not yet settled in her mind whether she agreed with that statement.

She finished her tea and toast, continuing, against her will, to think about that sad, lonely looking man in the hospital, that confused young woman entering her graduation year in college, and that directionless young man so full of potential and not realizing it--and the lack of focus in her own life.

On the drive to the hospital, random thoughts continued to flood Emmy's mind, occasionally overlapping one another. Thoughts that lead to actions or solutions are beneficial, but how many thoughts lead nowhere, other than to despair and indecision, she wondered? She chose not to dwell on that new area of thought, and attempted to dismiss it before it gained control over her.

As usual, traffic on Junction TT was light. Emmy particularly enjoyed this stretch of road, and looked forward to the old covered bridge, which gave her a sensation of returning to the womb. Did other residents of the Village have as many unanswered questions about life as she did, she wondered? They all seemed as though they had control of their lives and had not a worry in the world. Or, were they just good actors? She was thinking again. She made a resolution to stop doing that unless she had an answer to her questions about life and other people's lives. She turned on the car radio. Maybe that would help drown out her thoughts.

She reached the hospital almost before realizing it. It had seemed like a short drive to her. The front of the parking lot was full, as usual. Emmy had to make several trips up and down aisles looking for an empty space. She finally found one at the far end of the lot and eased her car in to it. Half way to the building, she found herself walking easily and briskly, and realized that her leg was not paining her. Ironically, it had not caused her any discomfort since Dominic had gone to the hospital. Coincidence? Or was it because her mind was on someone other than herself, for a change? Regardless, she liked the freedom the feeling gave her.

As was her habit, she knocked on Dominic's door before entering.

"Come in," Dominic said, in a cheerful tone--rare for him.

"Well, you look a lot better than that first day. You've got some color back in your face." She paused, and then said, "You look different."

Dominic gave her a full smile, and said, "Probably the beard."

"Oh, I didn't notice," she replied with some embarrassment. "It looks fine."

"Do you think so?" Dominic asked, pleased with her positive reaction to his facial hair.

"Yes. It makes you look outdoorsy," she said, lacking a better choice of words.

"Is that a good thing?"

"I think so. This is an outdoorsy part of the country. You fit right in."

"Good. Maybe I'll keep it." Dominic was surprised at how comfortable he was talking to Emmy. That was unusual for him. Normally, he would become tongue tied around people he did not know well--especially women, who, generally, tended to intimidate him and make him nervous. But, he was pleased with himself that he was able to communicate with this attractive woman.

"What did they feed you this morning?" Emmy asked.

"Pancakes, orange juice, decaffeinated coffee, and green Jell-O."

"Do you like pancakes?" Emmy asked, in an attempt to make further small talk.

"When I can get them. I haven't had any for a long time."

"Well, you're looking at probably the second best pancake maker in the country."

"Oh? Who's number one?" Dominic asked, with seeming interest.

"My younger sister in Boston. That's because she's had more practice. She makes them for her family's breakfast often, especially on weekends. It's become something of a family tradition, passed down from our mother and grandmother. So, if you'd settle for second best, I could whip up a stack if you ever feel a craving for some." She surprised herself. She was being more forward to this almost stranger than she thought prudent under the circumstances.

"I might just take you up on that," Dominic answered, feeling more relaxed than he had in a long time--the creases on his forehead and around his eyes barely noticeable.

Changing the subject, Emmy asked, "You ready to leave?"

"Everything I need to take, I'm wearing. Oh, and my hospital toiletry kit. I think I'll take it with me as a souvenir of my vacation." Dominic laughed. It had been awhile since he had smiled, let alone had anything he felt laughing about. He could not believe how easy it was for him to talk to Emmy. She seemed to inspire conversation even without saying anything. And her hair. There was something about the way she wore it--pulled back into a flowing blond pony tail. It reminded him of sunlight. It suited her, he thought. He imagined her with a sweater tied loosely around her shoulders, and a tennis racket in her hand. He mentally pictured the two of them on a tennis court--which was a stretch-- since he had never played the game. What an odd couple they would make. She was gracefully tall, slender and blonde. He was short, dark, graying, and clumsy. But, he enjoyed the image. Some things, however, just were not possible, he admitted to himself. His thoughts about her were interrupted by her voice.

"Ready to go, then?" she asked.

"I'm ready," Dominic replied, their conversation having stilled his nervousness.

At that moment, the door opened and a nurse entered, pushing a wheel chair ahead of her.

"Thanks, nurse. But, I don't need that," Dominic said when he saw it.

"Hospital policy, Mr. Graystone. All discharged bed patients need to be taken to the front entrance in a wheel chair."

Before Dominic could argue the point, Emmy said, "I'll go get the car and meet you at the pickup area at the front door."

All Dominic could think of to say was "OK!"

The nurse directed the chair toward him, helped him be seated, and gently placed his feet on the footrests.

"Drive on," Dominic said, in a happier mood than was typical of him.

Down the hallway they went, to the elevator--a short wait--and then down to and through the lobby. By the time he was escorted outside, Emmy was parked at the entrance. She started to get out of the car to help him in, but before she could, he was out of the wheelchair and in the passenger seat.

"I can see you're anxious to get home," Emmy said. Dominic smiled, but said nothing.

The drive back to the Village was a quiet one. The mountain range in the distance belied its name, with the high, late morning sun glinting brightly against its normally somber gray face. After his stay in the hospital, Dominic was ready to return to his apartment--and the comfort of his own bed. They had just entered Braxton Falls when Dominic broke the silence. "It's almost noon. Feel like stopping for something to eat?" he asked.

"That sounds good. I had an early breakfast."

Emmy navigated easily through town to the Dutch Maid Café. The normal weekday lunch crowd had already filled its tables and booths. There was a several minute wait before they were ushered to a rear booth. Maybelle, the solitary waitress, was futilely attempting to catch up on her order taking, limiting her opportunity to exchange her friendly, light banter with her customers. This gave Emmy and Dominic a chance to continue their conversation. Instead of talking further about themselves, they talked about Chris, Billy, Pop Bates, the Village and its residents. They also discussed what little was known about the history of Twilight Manor before it became a senior's community.

Dominic mentioned that his apartment was located above a wine cellar. On warm days, he told Emmy he could sometimes smell a light aroma of the wine that had once been stored there. Billy had told him that when the management renovated the facility from a convent to a senior's residence, they decided to leave the cellar and its outside entrance intact. Emmy mentioned the rumor that there had once been an unmarked cemetery on the grounds, and some of the other stories the residents passed among themselves. No one knew for certain how many of the tales told were factual--or merely conjecture. But, rumors continued to persist and grow, to the delight and speculation of the Village's residents. The most popular one was about the fortune supposedly buried somewhere on the premises during the Great Depression. Regardless of the facts, it made for interesting conversation and speculation. And Dominic, never having heard the stories, showed an obvious interest in Emmy's telling--or, perhaps, even more, in the teller.

After the pair returned to Twilight Manor, Dominic walked Emmy to her door. He thanked her for being so thoughtful and such good company. They shook hands and Dominic returned to his world as he knew it before its unexpected interruption by a hospital stay. But, recent events had changed his attitude about life, somewhat. In a strange way, he felt as though he had been reborn. As he walked away from Emmy's apartment, he looked straight ahead-- not down at his feet. He even said hello to two passersby when he met them in the hallway. This prompted one of them to turn to the other and ask, "Who was that? I don't remember seeing him around here before." Her companion merely shrugged.

Emmy was glad to be back home. She had a feeling of relief that her responsibilities toward Dominic were over and that he had recovered from his heart attack without any complications. She wearily kicked off her shoes, turned on her television, laid on the couch and reminisced about the events of the week. She missed Chris. Her apartment seemed empty without her. Fatigue from recent activities took over her body, and free from pain, she was soon asleep.

Chapter 31

UNCERTAINTIES

On the surface, life appeared to be peaceful and active for most of the Village's population. For some others, however, there were still issues to be confronted. Dominic was grateful for the quiet of his apartment, although he missed the attention he had received at the hospital. It had made him feel important. He had become accustomed to the steady stream of men and women in white coats or colorful nurses smocks--and a myriad of technicians examining him, drawing blood, supervising him on a treadmill, taking pictures of his chest, and showing an unflagging interest in his general well being. He also had become accustomed to answering the frequent, "And how are you feeling today, Mr. Graystone?" inquiries from a variety of concerned and smiling faces. He had not received anywhere near that much attention during his last hospital experience--years ago--as the result of just barely catching the corner of an awaiting airbag after being thrown off a roof. The director had wanted another take, but Dominic was in no condition physically to oblige him. But, that time it was only a two night stay--for observation and taping his rib cage. Three days after his release, he repeated the stunt, and landed squarely in the center of the bag, much to everyone's relief, most of all, his.

Now, with unlimited time at his disposal and nothing in particular to fill it, he could again concentrate on becoming depressed about his problems, although, at the moment, he was troubled that he could not come up with any specific ones. Then, he thought about that Ms. Stratton woman--Emmy. It was worth the temporary inconvenience of a heart attack to receive that much attention from such an attractive and charming person. Idly pacing the perimeter of his apartment, he found himself in the bedroom. On approaching his bedside nightstand, he thought of the revolver nestled within its confines. He sat on the edge of the bed and slowly and quietly opened the drawer. The silver weapon glistened from the reflected glow of the lamp above it. He removed the gun and spun the cylinder. He liked the sound. It soothed him. He opened the cylinder to expose the five brass rounds hidden there. Old thoughts of using the weapon to end his unhappiness with life played against a mental image of Emmy. He could not get her out of his mind. He silently wished he had the looks and words--and confidence--to invite her to have dinner with him sometime. But, this idea seemed a foolish one. Why would a woman like her, with everything, want to spend time with someone like him, who had nothing to offer? After all, he wasn't gifted with interesting conversation or witty sayings, and there was nothing in his life history to talk about that a refined woman would be interested in hearing. He again closely examined the gun. He felt a sense of relief in the knowledge that there was no need to make any decisions about what to do. The choice had been made for him. He was holding in his hand the cold, emotionless instrument needed to carry out his plan.

Emmy sat thinking. There would be no Tai Chi class this week. The instructor was continuing to recover from a sprained ankle, which had swollen into a purplish black mass, requiring her get from here to there on crutches. This left an even bigger emptiness in Emmy's schedule. What were her alternatives? Chris was gone. She had no reason to drive into town since Dom was home from the hospital--and now, no Tai Chi. But, there was still Stray to feed, brush and talk to. That took care of twenty minutes or so of her day. Now, all she had to do was find something to occupy the remainder of her waking hours. She supposed she could drive into Braxton Falls—if only to window shop or have lunch, but such solitary activities did not appeal to her at the moment. One is a lonely number, she decided, and so she chose to do nothing beyond preparing a cup of tea and enjoying the view from her kitchen window. The mountains were only a distant gray shadow, but the trees in the nearby meadow were proudly displaying their multicolored autumn foliage. What a contrast the two wonders of nature made.

Billy had been busy catching up on the various jobs he had postponed to spend time with Chris. Pop's arthritis, or "reumatiz," as he called it, was acting up, so Billy had not only his own backlog of work to deal with, but he had to take over some of Pop's projects, too. To Pop's credit, no matter how much pain he was in, he never neglected attending to his beloved old boilers. He claimed they were better than a woman. They responded favorably to his coaxing touches, kept him warm on cold winter nights, and were always there for him. And they didn't get headaches.

Billy had telephoned Chris regularly since she left. He enjoyed hearing her voice, but it was a poor substitute for being with her and able to look into her warm, pale blue eyes during their conversations. It was as though they saw into his very soul. She had begun her first week of college classes a week after returning to Boston. Billy was worried that with her school work, and the longer they were separated, she would lose interest in him. She had invited him to visit her during the holidays, but that was still a long time away. A lot could happen during that time to change their relationship and cause them to move in opposite directions. Before he met Chris, Billy had been in the habit of living from paycheck to paycheck, and did not have enough money for a train ticket to Boston. After he met her, and she had suggested he come there to see her, he had begun saving part of each week's pay. He resolved to have enough money saved to be able to go by Thanksgiving, or at the very latest, by Christmas. That was, of course, unless she changed her mind before then about wanting his company. To earn more money, he had even considered taking the part time job he had been offered at the hardware store in town while there recently to buy supplies. Any trip east would also depend on Pop's health and whether he could spare him for a week or so. Pop was not getting any younger and was making occasional noises about retiring. Billy felt that his own life was getting complicated and the future was becoming more and more uncertain. He liked his job, but he also wanted to spend time with Chris--as much, and as soon as possible. He did not want to lose her from his life, but he did not know if he would be able to keep her in it now that they were again living in two different worlds. As far as he was concerned, the decision was entirely up to her. He felt certain that his feelings would not change.

The semester was not starting well for Chris. One of the required upper level courses she needed to graduate was not available for the fall semester, so she had to take an elective survey course instead. Another class she needed was only being taught by Professor Kraus, who informed her students on the first day of class--with obvious pride--that she never gave an A grade. The students were expected to maintain A level work just to receive a C. This could affect Chris's grade point average, and even cause her eligibility and acceptance to graduate school to come into question.

Chris was lonely for Billy. And her period was late. This could result in a major impact on her being able to complete her degree requirements--not to mention how her parents would react to news that their daughter was pregnant. She had not yet mentioned this concern to Billy. She felt that he had enough on his mind with work, and did not need any distractions, especially a major one like this. She did not want to further add to his burden the possibility of becoming a father. There was no one she could confide in about her concerns--not even her aunt. She knew that Emmy would be understanding about the situation, but would probably feel in someway responsible for letting it happen. And, if she mentioned the subject to her room mate, it would soon be all over campus. Gloria was a nice enough girl, but she had no concept of keeping a confidence. Chris was looking forward to Billy's call that evening. She always felt better after hearing his voice. However, she felt she was going to have to force herself to sound cheerful during their conversation, in spite of the weight of uncertainties about her future that were troubling her.

The more Pop Bates' arthritis bothered him, the more serious thought he gave to retiring. He had worked, part time or full time, for almost sixty of his seventy four years. He did not feel his age particularly, except when he suffered inflammation and swelling in his knees. But, if he retired, he wondered what he would do with all his new found spare time. You can only play so many games of pool or dominoes, he reasoned--and he had never been interested much in golf. Another saying he took credit for was, "Never retire from something. Always retire to something." He had forgotten where he had first heard that, but since he could not remember, he felt it was legitimate to claim it for himself. But, there was currently nothing he could think of to which he really wanted to retire. Although, there was Maybelle, that waitress he chatted with during occasional dinners at the Dutch Maid restaurant in town. They were both outgoing, never-met-a-stranger types, and it had not taken long for them to form a bonding--of sorts. She must like him, Pop reasoned. Why else would she tolerate an old codger like him hanging around? It couldn't be for the tips, because he seldom did so. It was not in his nature. Whenever he went into the diner, she would sneak a piece of apple pie ala mode onto his tray at no charge. She was a widow, with six grown and scattered children. But, he wondered if she was too young for him. She was probably no more than sixty five, he figured. But, they seemed to have a lot in common, if their freewheeling conversations were any indication. They both liked the outdoors--and fishing. And how could you not like a woman who liked fishing--especially nowadays? Pop had no answer to that question. But, it was definitely a point in her favor, far as he was concerned. In addition, she was a fine looking woman, except for her bottle blonde hair. He didn't much care for that, but, he should not hold that against her, he supposed. And, she had a nice little, paid for, white frame house just at the edge of town. He occasionally did some fixing up and repairs to it, and, in return, was rewarded for his efforts with home cooked meals. She was a good cook. That was another point in her favor. And, it was time he began thinking about settling down. It was definitely something to think on. And, one of these days he needed to remember to ask what her last name was. He felt that he still had a lot of good years ahead of him. His maternal grandmother had lived to ninety four and his mother worked in the fields until she was eighty two, and was ninety eight when she passed on from a lack of will to live. So, he could probably expect to be around for another twenty or so years. Anyhow, that was the way he had it figured. But, on the other hand, the men in his family tended to die early. His father and grandfather had both died young--not from any particular health problems, but from foolish living. He knew better than to make that mistake. Pop made a mental note to seriously think--sometime soon--about his future and Maybelle's place in it.

Chapter 32

A NEW BEGINNING

FRIDAY'S DINNER CHOICES were meatloaf and salmon. Emmy did not eat much red meat, but the chef at the Village had a special meatloaf sauce she liked. She had toyed with the idea of going into town to a movie, but the more she thought about it, the less appealing the idea became. And, it looked like rain. She had not felt comfortable driving in rain since her accident. It brought back bad memories--and during wet weather, her leg seemed to bother her more. It took only the flimsiest of excuses for her to decide not to do something or go somewhere. Sometimes, she felt she was becoming agoraphobic. So, she decided she would stay home, have a leisurely dinner in the dining room and afterward catch up on her reading. The magazines she had received during and after Chris's visit lay unopened in a neat stack on the coffee table. She had become tired of walking past them and they were beginning to create negative energy for her.

Emmy napped in the afternoon and slept longer than planned. When she awoke, it was almost an hour past her normal dinnertime. She hurriedly splashed cold water on her face, combed her disheveled hair and adjusted and re-banded her ponytail. She began wondering whether she was too old for a pony tail. Perhaps she would make an appointment at the Village beauty salon. She was probably overdue for a change of hair style, anyway. She had had the same one since college. It had looked good on her then, when she had a brisk walk and her hair swung like a pendulum across the back of her neck. She did not like to remember how many years ago that had been. Where had the time gone? she wondered.

When arriving at the dining room, she did not see any empty tables. Her eyes instinctively darted toward the dark inside corner of the room, an area the sun never touched. There sat Dominic, alone as usual, head down, concentrating on his food--as usual. She approached his table.

"Hi, Dom. Would you mind if I joined you? It seems all the other tables are taken."

Startled by the sound of a voice above him, Dominic looked up from his plate and seeing Emmy before him, immediately stood bolt upright, looked at her and said, "Please," motioning his hand toward an empty chair. He stood in this military position until Emmy had seated herself.

"It seems more crowded tonight than usual, doesn't it?" she said, in an attempt to open a conversation. She noticed he still had not shaved and his beard had progressed to that awkward stage of looking scraggly instead of stylish.

"Seems like it," he replied, softly.

"So, how have you been feeling since you came home from the hospital?"

"Good. Good," he repeated.

"You look like you've lost some weight."

"A little," Dominic replied. He was not an easy one to engage in conversation, unless the other person was willing to do most of the talking. Billy had told Emmy that Dominic liked old movies. She knew very little about them, but had watched an old film noir the previous evening on the classic movie channel, as there had been nothing else that captured her interest.

"Billy tells me you're an old time movie buff. Is that right?"

"You could say so," he replied, matter of factly.

"I was watching one last night," Emmy said. "I think it was called 'Times of Panic,' or some such." She saw Dominic's eyes open wide and look piercingly into hers.

"It couldn't have been 'Crimes of Panic,' could it?" he asked, eagerly anticipating her answer.

"As a matter of fact, I believe that's what it was. Do you know it?"

"Know it? I was in it," he replied proudly, sitting straighter in his chair, his face coming alive. Emmy had captured his attention.

"Really? It's a small world, isn't it? What part did you play?"

"Actually, I had two parts--one as a stuntman and one as an actor. Do you remember the scene where the man gets knocked off the roof?" he asked, hopefully.

"Was that you? It looked like a terrible fall."

"It was. I spent some time in the hospital as a result." He told her about missing most the main part of the airbag that was supposed to break his fall.

"Oh, how awful!" Emmy exclaimed.

"Oh, it wasn't that bad," he said, with a touch of bravado. A few days later, I did it again--the right way. We always considered any stunt you could walk away from 'the right way.'"

"That sounds like a dangerous occupation."

"Only if you think about it. More stunt people get hurt thinking about getting hurt than from actually doing the stunt. As long as you prepare properly beforehand and keep your focus, it's no more dangerous than being a bus driver."

Emmy had a little difficulty with the analogy, but said, "I had no idea!"

"That's the truth," he said, as though it was important for her to believe him.

"So, what was your acting role in the film?"

"I'm almost ashamed to say. In my scene, I'm leaning against the bar in a tavern, when another actor bumps into me and spills my drink. I say 'Watch, it Bud,' push the other actor and we get into a fight. He ends up knocking me through the doorway, out onto the street. Actually, he had better dialog.

"I remember that," Emmy said, proud of her memory. "He looked at you from the doorway and said, 'you'll think twice before messing with Cavanaugh again, Bud,' or something like that."

Dominic laughed. "That's it exactly!" He marveled that Emmy had remembered the line. Now, she had his full attention. "And do you remember the mob scene on the street corner?" Emmy was not certain she did. Perhaps she had dozed off at that point, but she said, "Were you in that?"

"I was. Remember the man with the derby hat pulled down over his eyes and a cigarette dangling from the side of his mouth?"

Rather than admit that she did not remember seeing it, she said, "Was that you?"

"It was. No dialog and I didn't even get beat up. I was what you call a face in the crowd."

"How interesting. What other movies were you in?" After asking this question, all Emmy needed to do for the next forty minutes was nod her head, show surprise, and raise her eyebrows at appropriate times. Dominic did all the talking. She learned much about the inner workings of a film studio, and, to her surprise, she was not the least bit bored. Dominic was in his element and thrilled to have someone to talk to about movies.

"Whew," Dominic said finally, catching his breath. "That's more than I've talked to anyone, except Billy, in the last twenty years."

"I enjoyed it," Emmy said, without exaggerating. "Maybe we can talk again sometime."

"I'd like that," Dominic said. For some unknown reason, Emmy felt she would, too.

Having gained some confidence, Dominic said, "Uh, speaking of movies, there's an old time film festival at the Varsity Art Theatre tomorrow evening and Sunday afternoon. Tomorrow, it's a Louise Brooks silent movie double feature. Back then, movies only ran for an hour or so. Oh! And on Sunday, there's a Marx Brothers double feature, talkies. Would . . . would you consider going with me?" he asked apprehensively, the confidence in his voice trailing off slightly in mid sentence.

"That sounds interesting." Emmy took a pen from her purse, wrote her telephone number on a napkin and handed it to Dominic. "Why don't you call me tomorrow morning and we can talk more about it." She knew how much courage it must have taken for Dominic to ask her out, and she did not want to crush his ego by immediately turning him down. Between now and tomorrow morning, she was certain she could think of a polite excuse for not going with him.

"OK," Dominic replied. "What time?"

"Any time after nine." Emmy rose from the table and excused herself with, "I'll talk to you tomorrow."

"I'll look forward to it," Dominic replied, standing at the same time and smiling at her with his movie star teeth.

As Emmy walked away from the table, she asked herself what she was getting into. She did not want to hurt Dominic's feelings, but she was not anxious to spend the day with him either. And, she did not care much for his beard. She had always preferred her men clean shaven, few though there had been.

At three minutes past nine the next morning, Emmy's phone rang insistently. She was in the bathroom with a tooth brush in her mouth. She put the brush down, quickly rinsed and headed to the phone.

"Hello?" she said, wiping her mouth with the end of the towel she had wrapped around her wet hair.

"Hi, uh, this is Dom!"

"Oh, hello. What time is it?" she asked.

"Just after nine. I didn't call too early, did I?"

"No, I'm up. Just getting ready to fix some breakfast." This was somewhat of an exaggeration. Some mornings she did not even bother to eat breakfast, and some mornings she woke up slowly. On those days, even a shower did not fully awaken her. This was one of those mornings--for both events.

"Good. I mean, good I didn't wake you." Dominic felt clumsy in his attempt at social conversation. "So, what do you think about going into town to the movie festival?"

Emmy had not as yet come up with a plan for telling him no gently. She could not think of any reason that would not sound like an excuse.

"Uh, well, I don't know. What time would we have to leave?" Maybe there was still a believable reason that would come to her if they talked long enough.

"Oh, I don't know. The movies don't start 'til about six. If we got to town about four thirty or five, we'd have time to get something to eat before we go."

Emmy's mind was still slightly foggy, and alibis were not her strong suit at best. With nothing better to offer, she took the course of least resistance, saying, "Well, OK. What time should I meet you?"

"Why don't I come by there about four? It doesn't take long to get to town."

"Uh, well, OK." Her mind was beginning to clear, but not fast enough.

"Good. I'll see you then. Oh, by the way, what's your apartment number?"

She had to stop and think. "It's 27, corridor B."

"OK. Good. I'll see you then," Dominic said, hanging up quickly so as not to give her a chance to change her mind.

"What have I gotten myself into," she asked herself. Visiting Dominic at the hospital and bringing him home from there was one thing, but a date! "Good Lord," she said out loud, "what was I thinking?" But, she had committed herself, and it was too late to back out. So, she would make the best of the situation. "A Date? I haven't had a date in almost thirty years. I don't even know how to act on a date." Actually, she did have one date while living in the apartment, before moving to Twilight Manor. Another tenant in her building had invited her out to dinner. The meal had been nice, and the conversation flowed easily. But he had expected dessert afterward, and the evening ended up becoming a wrestling match in his car. She was eventually able to convince him that no meant no. He never spoke to her again. When they passed in the hallway or met at the mailboxes, he either looked away or straight through her. Fortunately, until now, she had erased that incident from her mind.

Three fifty five. The doorbell rang. Emmy opened the door to be greeted by Dominic, smiling--not his crooked smile, but a genuine one. Again, she noticed his perfect, white teeth. And he had made a partially successful attempt at trimming his beard. She could see two places where he had nicked himself with a razor. He was neatly attired in light gray dress slacks, a navy blazer and a white open collared shirt. Emmy had to admit he looked much nicer than she had ever seen him. He had even put something on his hair to hold it in place, controlling its usually tousled look.

"Am I too early?" he asked, anxiously.

"No. You're right on time. Come in a minute while I get a jacket. The evenings are beginning to get cooler."

"OK. I like your place. It's so, uh, neat."

"Thank you," Emmy said from the bedroom, where she had hidden the magazines that had previously been aging on her coffee table.

The drive to Braxton Falls was a quiet one. Dominic's car rode smoothly, if not quietly.

"What kind of car is this, Dom?" Emmy asked.

"Actually, it's a classic--a Checker cab. I bought it at an auction of a taxi company that was going out of business. I like them because they're built sturdy, and run forever. I had the interior reupholstered. That seems to be where taxis get the most wear, on the upholstery."

"It looks like you take very good care of it."

"Thank you. It's got over two hundred thousand miles on it, and runs as good as the day it came off the assembly line. Of course, I get a squeak or a rattle now and then. But, I like it. It suits me and gets me where I need to go, and back again."

Dominic and Emmy decided to have dinner at the Dutch Maid restaurant. Although there were better and more expensive restaurants in town, the menu at "The Dutch," as it was commonly called, was extensive and the food usually was well prepared. Afterward they walked down Main Street, stopping in two or three shops that caught their interest. Without warning, Emmy laughed.

"Did I say something funny?" Dominic asked--puzzled.

"No. It's just that this is where you picked clumsy me up when I fell that time."

"Oh! So it is. Watch your step." Pointing, he said, "I think that raised piece of sidewalk there was what tripped you." He gave it a kick with his toe. "We don't want déjà vu all over again, do we?" Emmy laughed and shook her head in agreement. She was warming up to Dominic. He was a kind man, gentle, although rather odd in a quiet way, but she felt comfortable with him. When she talked he listened attentively, often nodding his head in response to something she said, smiled when she said something amusing, and laughed when she said something funny--and he did not seem to notice her awkward gait. He was so unlike the men she had known in her younger days. All they seemed to want to do--other than try to seduce her--was talk about themselves and how important they were, and how lucky she was to be out with them. They reminded her of a joke she had once heard about an egocentric movie star, who on a date, talked only about himself. Then, finally, he said to his companion, "But enough about me.

Let's talk about you. How did YOU like my last movie?" Dominic was not like that. He seemed genuinely happy and appreciative to be in her company, and she was enjoying being in his.

Emmy was less impressed with the silent black and white movies than she was with her attentive escort. But, he seemed to enjoy them. On the way home, he told her about Louise Brooks, a silent era film anti-star. She was a beautiful brunette who was too intelligent and independent for her era. She had begun her show business career as a dancer in the Ziegfeld Follies. This led to a movie contract at nineteen, and she had small parts in several movies of the 1920s. American directors did not like working with her, as they felt she was too headstrong and opinionated. Her career did not flourish until she went to Europe to work for the German director G. W. Pabst in movies with such names as "Pandora's Box" and "Diary of a Lost Girl." Dominic admired Brooks for the way she stood up for herself and refused to be intimidated or controlled by the Hollywood power brokers. She was his favorite silent film era actress. Emmy was impressed by his encyclopedic knowledge of movie history and film lore. During these times, he spoke easily and articulately. She was beginning to see him as a much different person than when she had thought of him simply as the strange Mr. X. She felt that he was just shy and hid it by living within himself.

Dominic escorted Emmy to her door. He did not attempt to kiss her, but merely held out his hand to her, said good night and walked away. To her surprise, she had had an enjoyable day with this strange, yet not so strange, man. Lying in bed, she wondered if he would call again. She hoped he would.

Immediately upon returning to his apartment, Dominic went into the bedroom, opened the drawer containing his revolver, took it in his hand, opened the cylinder, removed the bullets and put them back in their box. He then took the box and the gun and put them at the back of the top shelf of his closet. For the first time since he could remember, he was not depressed. He enjoyed the feeling.

Chapter 33

AFTERTHOUGHTS

Some actions and occurrences do not stand the tests of time well. Emmy's encounters with the opposite sex had proven to be less than successful. In the past, her limited experience with men, combined with self consciousness about her body, had proven to be obstacles to forming any successful relationships. She had accepted that she was probably not suited for a long--or even short--term relationship, with all of its unexpected pitfalls and complications, compounded by nagging self-doubts. Somehow, however, she had formed a liking for this strange new man in her life--or more appropriately--at the edge of her life. They had made an odd pair strolling through town together. Yet, she could not erase him from her mind. She had always been attracted to strays that no one else wanted to be bothered with, or had any use for. Was Dominic such a case? She did not know and felt unqualified to judge her own motivations or actions. She felt this was something best left to professional analysts. In spite of her rationalizations, she held a hope he would call her again.

Theirs had been a case of two misfits fitting together, at least for a brief period of time.

The ringing of the telephone jarred her back to reality. She held her breath. She was not expecting anyone to call. Could it be . . . ? No, that would be too much of a coincidence. But what was coincidence but fate in disguise? Probably a wrong number or one of the Village's committee persons inviting her to a social function to which she had no interest in attending.

"Hello?"

"Hi, Aunt Em!" said the cheerful voice on the other end of the line.

"Oh, hi Chris! It's good to hear from you. How's everything at home? How's school going?"

"Everything at home is just fine. Mom and dad had a great trip to Egypt and brought me back a camel. I've named him Jojo."

"A camel?" Emmy's mind had not completely shifted from her previous thoughts to this conversation. A real camel?"

"No, silly. A stuffed camel. From a souvenir shop. It's on the bed with my other stuffed animals."

"Oh! Sorry. Guess my mind was on a different plane. But I'm back now."

"I hope so. Schools going well. I'm back on campus, living in the dorm again. The school opened up a class for a required subject I need that wasn't going to be taught this semester, which would have caused me to graduate late. But, now, with luck, and some heavy studying, I'll still be able to graduate next May."

Chris wanted to tell her aunt about her pregnancy scare, but thought better of it. She decided it was best to keep her private life to herself. Her gynecologist diagnosed the lateness of her period as probably being stress related.

"So, Aunt Em, what have you been up to?"

"Not much. It's been quiet around here since you left."

"Oh, you mean it was noisy when I was there?" Chris teased.

"You know what I mean," her aunt replied.

"So. Have you talked to Billy recently?"

"Only briefly, a couple times when I've passed him in the hall. Pop Bates has him on a fast track, catching up on projects."

"Oh, you mean I kept Billy from doing his job?" Chris asked, feeling a pang of guilt.

"No. Not at all. Pop's arthritis has been bothering him lately and he's walking funnier than I do. So, Billy's taken over some of his chores. "

"You don't walk Funny, Aunt Em. You're the only one who thinks you do," Chris replied, supportively.

"Have you heard from Billy lately?" Emmy replied, avoiding the sensitive subject of her leg.

"He calls me two or three times a week. He wanted to call everyday, but I told him he would have to get a second job if he did--just to pay his phone bill. And I'm hitting the books pretty heavy, so it's probably best we each have some time to ourselves."

"Spoken like a real grownup, Chris."

"I'm getting there. Who knows, in another five or ten years, I may be an adult." They both laughed at this prospect. "Billy's saving up his money and is going to try to come visit me over Thanksgiving. I'm looking forward to that. I miss him a lot."

"I'm sure he misses you, too."

"I hope so. Changing the subject, what's new in your life? Broken any hearts lately?"

"Funny you should mention that. Mr. X, uh, Dominic, rather, Dom and I went to see some old time movies in town over the weekend."

"Oh, so you've got three men on the line, huh? Do I sense a romance blooming?"

"I doubt it. You know how jinxed I am in that department. I haven't known many men, but the ones I have known haven't exactly been stellar examples of manhood. But, Dominic seems nice. In the brief time we've spent together, I've seen a side of him

I don't think he lets many people see. I thought when the phone rang that it might be him."

"Oh, waiting by the phone for your man to call, huh?"

Emmy was glad Chris couldn't see her blushing. "No. No. Nothing like that. But, he is good company--if you don't mind doing most of the talking. He's polite, considerate and I don't have to worry about any animal instincts emerging."

"His or yours?" Chris asked jokingly. "Maybe you two are just slow starters."

"I doubt if there'll ever be an occasion to find out. We had a good time--but I don't expect to hear from him again. He's a very private and introverted person."

"We'll see," Chris replied. "I need to go now. I have a class in ten minutes. I'll talk to you again soon." Chris gave her aunt her new phone number, and said, "Give me a call when you can. If the line's busy, it's probably Billy. Bye, Aunt Em. I love you!"

"I love you, too, Chris. Study hard and make us proud. Bye."

Emmy's phone did not ring again the rest of the day. However, the following morning at three minutes past nine, it did ring. Emmy was up, dressed and reading the morning paper. Why can't they print more good news, she wondered. Sometimes, reading about all the trouble in the world depressed her. She absentmindedly picked up the receiver and in a monotone said "Hello?"

"Uh, Emmy? This is Dominic. Uh, Dom. I hope I didn't call at a bad time."

"Oh, hello Dom." Her voice softened. "No, I'm just catching up on the news."

"Uh, that's good. What I was wondering. I mean if you aren't doing anything, if you would like to play some tennis this afternoon?" He held his breath, waiting for an answer.

"Actually, I don't play tennis, Dom. But, thanks for the thought."

"Uh, neither do I. But, it's never too late to learn, so they say. We can learn together. I hope I'm not too forward, but I reserved a court for two this afternoon--but I can cancel it," he quickly added.

Dominic's tone of voice sounded almost pleading. Emmy felt guilty turning down his offer. All of the reasons she did not want to play ran quickly through her mind, and she said, "What time did you say?"

"Uh, two this afternoon, court three."

"OK. But, I warn you, I'm not very athletic. So, you'll probably get a lot of exercise chasing balls."

"That's OK." Emmy could hear the relief in his voice. She could not turn down his plaintive pleas for her company. "I'll check out some rackets and balls," he volunteered.

"Good. I'll see you in court." Dominic did not acknowledge Emmy's bad pun, unaware she had made one.

Emmy slowly replaced the receiver in its cradle and tried to understand why she had agreed to meet Dominic for tennis. Somehow, it was becoming more difficult to tell him no. She began to rationalize the consequences of her behavior. Although she did not wear shorts, she had a pair of lightweight cotton sweat pants she could wear with a white polo shirt as a tennis outfit. And, she had a pair of seldom worn tennis shoes with a built up heel in the left one. Perhaps she could suffer through an hour of physical activity to avoid hurting the feelings of this lonely man. As an afterthought, she wondered if that was the only reason she had agreed to meet him. She was beginning to question her responses when it came to his interest in her.

At three minutes past two, Emmy arrived at the tennis courts. Dominic was casually and awkwardly hitting a ball against a wooden backboard. When he saw her, he hurried over to open the gate in the fence. There was a smile on his face. He had been concerned she would not come.

"Hi. You look nice," Dominic offered.

"Thank you," Emmy replied, smiling.

"Uh, here's your racket. I hope it's OK."

"It looks fine," she replied. Under her breath, she said, "What difference does it make? I won't be able to hit the ball anyway."

They each went to their side of the net and Dominic lobbed a ball into her court. She swung and missed it. He hit another one, which she also missed. On her third try, she connected, and watched the ball arc over the far end chain link fence.

"Oops!" she said, embarrassed.

"That's OK. You'll get the hang of it." Dominic's smooth movements belied his telling her that he had never played before. Or, maybe he was just naturally athletic, Emmy thought. After receiving a few more lobs, Emmy found herself returning most of them to Dom's side of the net. Her stroke was not pretty but it was functional. By the third game, they were having exchanges of several in bound hits. The lift in her shoe allowed her to move around the court swiftly and gracefully. She was surprised at herself. Maybe her mother hadn't wasted all that money on dance lessons for her, after all, she thought. Forgetting her initial embarrassment, she was beginning to enjoy herself. By the time their hour was up, they were playing more relaxed and easily. They gathered up the balls and toweled themselves off. Emmy had barely perspired. Dominic's T-shirt was soaked with sweat, and his thick hair was matted against his forehead. They left the court and sat on a bench facing some new arrivals and watched them warm up.

"Whew! That was fun," Emmy exclaimed.

"I'm glad you enjoyed it," Dominic replied. "It's a good game once you get the hang of it."

"And you told me you never played before," Emmy chided him playfully.

"Maybe once or twice. But, I always liked sports and seemed to do well at them, given a little practice. Would you like to go to the snack bar and get something cold to drink?"

"Good idea." Emmy was feeling good. This was the most physically active she had been in a long time. She realized that she did not get much exercise, other than Tai Chi, using her leg as an excuse not to do more. The pair lingered in the snack bar, enjoying their fruit drinks. They were the objects of a few surprised looks, smiles and whispered words. Emmy noticed, but apparently Dominic did not. His eyes were focused on her face, and he did not even see others passing by them or sitting at nearby tables. She had to admit they did make a strange looking pair--him being so big and lumbering and her being so slender and delicate looking. Dominic had kept to himself so much since moving into the Village that most of the other residents did not remember seeing him before, except for a few who recognized him from his dark corner in the dining room.

Others of the community who were surprised to see two such different looking individuals together soon became accustomed to seeing them frequently; in the window bright section of the dining room, walking to and from the lake, hitting golf balls on the putting green, and wherever else on the surrounding campus people walked or gathered. They were even seen in the fitness room exercising together. Emmy began doing leg strengthening exercises in addition to her stretching movements. Her legs were feeling stronger and firmer than they had since she was forced to stop dancing. The two of them even began attending the weekly dances together. Emmy surprised herself at how lithely she moved around the floor. It was almost like old times. With the lift in her shoe, and renewed strength in her legs, she experienced very little problem with dance steps or her balance. And the pain in her leg ranged from negligible to nonexistent. Dominic, by contrast, danced like the well muscled athlete he had been, albeit slightly awkward, with ramrod straight posture. But, he was improving. And he enjoyed it. It was an opportunity to hold Emmy in his arms. That was the best part. He marveled at how firm, yet yielding her slender body was. She was poised and moved gracefully and effortlessly. He felt proud to be her partner. After awhile, if others looked at them, it was only to notice how well they fit together on the dance floor.

Chapter 34

LIFE AFTER LIFE

AUTUMN WAS WANING and winter was beginning to show subtle signs of its impending approach. The distant mountains were beginning to adorn their pinnacles with caps of snow, glistening in the sunlight. Mornings and evenings were sweaters. Afternoons were shorts and T-shirts. Each change of weather prompted appreciation of Mother Nature's wide variety of offerings.

For the past two months, since their first excursion together into Braxton Falls, Emmy and Dominic were seeing each other regularly. In the eyes of the other residents, they had officially become a couple.

Emmy admired Dominic for his quiet strength and gentleness of spirit. He had been captivated by Emmy's graceful elegance and sensitivity--and her porcelain beauty. With patience and understanding of his lingering inner turmoil, she had softened his negativity, helping him realize that life was more about togetherness and belonging than it was about self and selfishness. Initially, they had been drawn together by their differences. They had remained together in spite of them. Since she and Dominic had begun seeing each other, Emmy seldom felt pain in her leg and had become less self consciousness about the way she walked. Dominic seldom felt a need to become depressed. Even an occasional rattle or squeak in his old car failed to unnerve him. For the first time in his life, he had someone to be with to share life's adventures. He and Emmy completed each other with their sharing, and in so doing, completed themselves. Although they had been seeing each other for some time, in terms of expressing their emotions, they had progressed slowly. They had not gone beyond a good night kiss before they parted to go to their separate apartments. Both were still burdened by memories of past relationships and the years of aloneness and absence of companionship. Both had been alone too long to overcome their fears and suspicions about opening themselves up too much too soon to another person. The closest they had become physically was when they attended Village dances and could feel comfortable holding each other close. Their desires were still dampened by the remnants of personal histories and their lingering after effects.

Billy was having second thoughts about his planned trip to Boston. He brought the subject up as he and Pop were having coffee during an afternoon break.

"Pop, you've been around and I'm just getting started living my life. It's very confusing to me. I'm having so many thoughts and doubts. I really care about Chris, but she's going to be graduating from college next year, and will probably go to graduate school. And me--I went to a trade school, and that's all I know. I have to admit that when she was here we enjoyed each other's company, and I have a lot of fond memories of that time. But, I'm just wondering if it's possible for me to live in her world--or her to live in mine. I have enough trouble just trying to figure out my life day to day, let alone long range."

Pop had listened to Billy patiently and quietly, looking at him understandingly with his wise, world weary eyes. He remained silent for what seemed to Billy like minutes--and then he said,

"Son, if there's one thing I've learned in this life, it's that you can't keep walkin' in your old shoes. Memories are fine, but you gotta keep goin' forward and live in the present, and prepare, best you can, for the future. Now, you take me for instance. I was a wild sixteen year old high school dropout when I lied about my age and education and joined the military. They sent me to some schools, gave me some trainin', taught me some skills and helped me grow up. After three or four hitches, I retired as a certified master mechanic. I worked on everything from Jeeps to aircraft engines, and lots of stuff in between. If you're so gol-durned concerned about the differences in Chris's and your education, Ashland's got a good Junior College--and it ain't that far away. You could take some night courses. Old Man Kimmerman might even be willin' to kick in some tuition money to help a young, ambitious fella like you better hisself. Him and Mrs. Kimmerman have sure helped me out of some deep water durin' my time here. Just remember, son, excuses for not doin' somethin' are easy to come by, but you can't hang your hat on 'em."

Billy respected Pop's common sense way of looking at things, and his frank way of expressing himself; although sometimes he didn't understand his peculiar sayings. But, this time, it was perfectly clear what Pop meant, and it made sense. He could take some college courses, and maybe in two or three years, earn an associate degree in technology or business. In Billy's mind, it was worth seriously thinking about.

Dominic lay in his favorite position, hands clasped behind his head, eyes staring unseeingly at the dark ceiling. Since he met Emmy, he felt reborn. He had never before had anyone treat him so good or be so nice to him. His philosophy of life had been get them before they get you. Don't depend on anybody, and keep others from becoming dependent on you. His viewpoint had, without his knowledge or intention, begun to change. The longer he knew Emmy, the more his attitude began to soften. He had never been by nature a mean man--bitter at times, thoughtless perhaps, but never cruel or uncaring. It was just that he had felt he needed to protect himself from the world outside and the heartless and uncaring people who inhabited it. From his viewpoint, if he did not look out for himself, no one else would. In spite of these beliefs, he had come to trust Emmy. But, he still had some suspicions about her. He could not understand why an attractive, educated woman like her would want anything to do with someone as rough around the edges as he considered himself. By having avoided others most of his life, he also had neglected learning how to interact with them. He felt like a caveman in a big city. He was way out of his element. He was grateful to Emmy for pretending not to notice his ugliness and lack of social graces.

Dominic had never danced before meeting Emmy. But, not only did he enjoy the dancing, but he enjoyed more feeling the warmth of her body close to his. His dancing was improving. The timing and movements came naturally to him and Emmy had taught him how to relax and not be so stiff. She had told him that he was a quick study. He was too embarrassed to ask her what that meant, but the way she had smiled at him when she said it, he was certain it was a good thing. He was aware that she had been a professional dancer on the New York stage, and was somewhat intimidated by her graceful dancing. But, the joy of holding her in his arms overrode any such feelings and made them bearable. When they were on the dance floor together, it was to Dominic as though no one else existed. They seemed to glide across its smooth surface as one body. In addition to holding her in his arms when they danced, he always looked forward to the bonus of their goodnight kiss. The first one had been a hesitant, puckered peck on the lips. Since then, their kisses, although still close mouthed, were becoming softer and more lingering. It was difficult to hold back his desire for more, but he did not want to become too forward and cause her to retreat from him. She had become an important part of his life and he did not want to lose her, so he made a special effort not to exceed the boundaries of their relationship. But, still . . . He forced a prurient thought from his mind.

Emmy and Dominic enjoyed the Saturday night dances. He had learned how to dip her, firmly yet gracefully. She had such a small waist, it was easy for his arm to encircle it. He had a strong desire to kiss her when she came back up from her dip position, but restrained himself. During intermission, they would sit at a table near the dance floor, sipping root beer, although there was an open bar for those who desired something stronger. For them, root beer and being together was all they needed. Their conversations had become more open and relaxed. Emmy learned about Dominic's growing up in the east, his years of hardship, and his accidental career path. She told him of her music and dancing education and career. Nothing was said about her accident or Dominic's lack of experience with the opposite sex. He felt that his one chaotic excursion into sex with the starlet was neither appropriate nor something he wanted her to know about. He was not proud of it, even though he had not initiated the brief tryst. He excused his actions as stemming from extreme loneliness--and youth. Nor did Dominic ever ask Emmy about her slight limp. She thought the omission was out of tactfulness. In truth, he had never even noticed it.

As had become their custom after the dances, Dominic saw Emmy to her door. This time, he bravely took her small hand in his as they walked down the hall. In response, she gave his hand a gentle squeeze. This simple gesture excited him. Arriving at her door, she unlocked it. Dominic leaned forward for his good night kiss. Instead Emmy said, "Would you like to come in for a cup of coffee?" Dominic's first impulse was to say no, that he didn't drink coffee this late--it kept him awake. But, instead he said, "I'd like that." He was not anxious to leave her company any sooner than he had to.

They entered the darkened room and Emmy snapped on a small table lamp.

"Sit down, Dom. I'll put the kettle on. Or, would you rather have tea?"

"Either's fine. What's your preference?"

"Well, since it's late, how would you like some decaffeinated tea?"

"That would be fine," he replied. He was not a tea drinker, but he felt this was not the time to reveal that fact.

"It'll just be a minute," she said, returning to the living room. She sat on the couch next to him. "I really enjoyed tonight, Dom. You're getting to be quite a ballroom dancer." Dominic blushed slightly. "You're a good teacher," he replied.

Without thinking, he reached over and took her hand in his. He had the sudden fear that she would withdraw it from his grasp in embarrassment. She did not.

Looking into Dominic's eyes, Emmy said, in a mock pouting tone, "You didn't give me my good night kiss yet." She surprised herself with her boldness.

Dominic released her hand, moved his face to hers and gently kissed her on the lips, his mouth lingering there. She put her arm around his neck as if to hold him to her. He slid his arm around her waist, pulling her closer to him. They remained locked in an embrace, neither one moving. Emmy's lips parted slightly, and Dominic accepted the invitation. One kiss followed another--each one longer and deeper than the previous one. Their pent up emotions found Emmy lying back on the deep couch, her head on a pillow, Dominic beside her. His hand began moving under and up the skirt of her long dress, along her bare leg--the injured one. She quickly placed her hand on top of his, outside of her skirt, just below her scars. Dominic mistook her hand stopping the path of his hand on her thigh as rejection, instead of what it was--Emmy not wanting Dominic to feel her scars. He sat up, obviously aroused, but embarrassed.

"I'm Sorry, Emmy. I didn't intend to be so forward." She enjoyed the feel of his hand on her, but was still too self conscious to tell him about her disfigured leg. But, she knew she had to say something in explanation.

"It's just me, Dom. I guess I'm just not ready yet. It's been a long time." She could not tell him there had only been one other man touch her, back when she was in college, and she had not wanted him to. Maybe another time, she thought.

"I think the kettle's whistling," Dom said. It had been doing so for several minutes, previously unnoticed by either of them. Emmy stood up, smoothed her skirt, and said, "I'll just be a jiffy." She quickly made tea, her hand shaking as she poured the water into the cups. She had not wanted Dominic to stop, but she felt even stronger about him not discovering her scarred leg.

Nothing more was said about their moment of passion. Both were embarrassed and neither knew what to say that would be appropriate, so they drank their tea in silence. Dominic looked at his watch and said, "It's getting late. I should probably leave and let you get to bed." Emmy just nodded. They were looking deeply into each other's eyes, neither wanting to let the other one go. With regret, Dominic arose. Emmy walked him to the door. Their good night kiss was their longest one yet. Their bodies were pressed together tightly, held there by each others arms. Emmy broke the silence.

"I owe you an explanation, Dom."

"No you don't. I was out of line. I apologize. I just got carried away."

"I owe you an explanation, Dom," she repeated. "But, can it wait until tomorrow, when my head's a little clearer?"

"Of course. But, it's not necessary."

"Yes it is. It really is. If we're going to continue seeing each other, it's very important. Tomorrow?"

Dominic nodded, a forced smile on his lips. "Tomorrow," he repeated, releasing her from his grasp. He kissed her lightly and then quickly left, returning forlornly to his lonely apartment.

Each of them lay in their bed, re-examining the events of the evening. Emmy had wanted Dominic more than she thought she could ever want any man. But, she was afraid that when he saw her scarred body, he would no longer want her. And she did not want to lose him. Perhaps in the cold light of day, she would have an answer to her dilemma.

Dominic tossed restlessly in his bed, entangling himself in the covers. He was unable to sleep, and lay there repeating, "Stupid, stupid, stupid!" for being so forward in his behavior toward Emmy and causing her to recoil from him. He told himself that he would behave more like a gentleman next time. He thought that maybe his ugliness repelled her, and that she did not want his clumsy advances toward her. He knew that his lack of any real experience with women did not make him attractive to them and that his ape-like body probably repulsed Emmy. He rationalized that she was just seeing him because she felt sorry for him, humoring him to be nice. He turned onto his side, pulled the sheet up over his head, and said, "Tomorrow." His mind soon clouded and he slept a restless sleep.

Chapter 35

THE UNVEILING

EMMY AWOKE EARLY. She had worried most of the night about Dominic's reaction to her apparent rejection of his advances. She had promised him an explanation tomorrow, which was now today. She had hoped that overnight something would come to mind to satisfy his concerns without telling him the real reason. She realized this was probably not possible--that the best course of action was just to tell him the truth, and accept whatever impact this might have on their relationship. If they should continue to see each other, sooner or later he would become aware of her physical imperfections. So, she decided that the only approach was to be completely honest with him and hope for the best. She continued to consider her decision during her shower and afterward, while dunking a piece of unbuttered toast in her morning tea. During this thinking process, she changed her mind several times. Tell the truth? Shade the truth? Lie? The truth won. She just hoped he would call today. Maybe he would not want to see her again, or think she was just leading him on. These and a variety of other thoughts crowded her mind.

The phone rang. Emmy looked at the clock--two minutes past nine. It must be Dom, she thought. For some reason, this seemed to be when he usually called.

"Hello?" she said, and held her breath, expectantly.

"Morning Emmy. How are you?"

"Fine, Dom. How are you?"

"OK. I hope I didn't call you too early--in the middle of breakfast or something."

"No. I just finished my breakfast."

"Good. I was just wondering if you would like to go in to Brewster. They're having their Oktoberfest this weekend."

"Sounds like fun. What time would you like to go?" She breathed a sigh of relief.

"We could have lunch here and go right afterwards, if that's OK?"

"That's fine with me. Why don't I meet you in the cafeteria about noon?"

"OK. I'll see you soon. And . . . . Oh, never mind. See you then. Bye."

"Bye."

It was still almost three hours before she would meet Dominic. This would give her some more time to plan what she was going to say to him--and how she would say it. In her preoccupation, she remembered she had forgotten to feed Stray. She fixed a bowl of wet loaf cat food with a side of dry food. He was waiting patiently outside the French doors. When she went out to him, he meowed and rubbed against her leg. She set the food on the patio and sat down beside it. Stray let Emmy know that she was late with breakfast by eagerly thrusting his face into the bowl and eating noisily. She petted him while he ate. She remembered she had not brushed his fur for several days and that she needed to do it before she went to lunch. While Stray ate, Emmy sat and talked to him, feeling his purring against her hand on his back.

"What am I going to do, Stray? There are some things I need to tell Dom, but I don't know if I'm brave enough to do it! I promised him I would explain my last night's reactions to him today. If I tell him the truth, he might not want to see me anymore. If I don't tell him the truth, he probably won't want to see me again either. What would you do?" she asked the cat rhetorically. She was answered by a guttural meow that she interpreted to mean, "Don't ask me silly questions while I'm busy eating." She continued to pet him. He finished, lapped at the water bowl, and then strode off indifferently toward the woods. A cool breeze blew across Emmy's bare arms. Another omen of a not too far off winter, she thought. She wondered how Stray would survive the season outdoors.

When Emmy arrived at the dining room, Dominic was already there, seated by the windows, sunlight creating an aura around his body. When he saw her, he stood up and hurried to meet her, greeting her with, "Are you hungry?"

"Not much. How about you?"

"Same."

They got in line, selected their food and returned to the table. They ate without words. There remained a sense of tension between them. After finishing a light lunch, Emmy said, "I need to stop by the apartment for a sweater. The weather seems to be cooler today."

Dominic nodded agreement.

Brewster was located seventeen miles northwest of Braxton Falls. Emmy had only ventured there once since moving to the Village. During the drive, both Emmy and Dominic remained deep in thought, each wondering what the other one was thinking. When they arrived at their destination, the parking area was filled. Dominic circled the area until a car left and then pulled into the vacated space. Emmy spoke first.

"It looks like a lot of other people decided to come today." Looking at the sky, she said, "Those clouds don't look good. It would be a shame if the town's biggest event of the year got rained out early on its last day." The sun continued to play hide and seek with the clouds. Emmy and Dominic soon became part of the throng of people milling about the fairgrounds. They explored the various exhibits and merchandise booths. Under a canvas, tent-like structure, a German Oompah band, dressed in lederhosen, played a lively selection of polkas, marches, waltzes and a smattering of contemporary music. The band leader asked audience members for requests. Emmy requested the waltz Beautiful Ohio, and to her surprise, they played it as well as had the skating rink organist of her youth.

The afternoon passed all too quickly, and they had, for the moment, both forgotten about their unfinished business. Dark gray rain clouds continued to gather and the sun silently retreated. Rain began to fall, softly and gently at first, then more heavy and insistent. Emmy and Dominic agreed it was probably a good time for them to leave for the Village before the weather became even worse. They ran across the parking area, pelted by large, stinging raindrops before reaching the protective shelter of Dominic's car.

By the time they arrived back at the Village, the rain had become a full blown thunderstorm, complete with jaggedly dancing lightning. They hurried into the building, collecting more raindrops on their hair and clothing. Arriving at Emmy's apartment, they went quickly inside. Emmy went into the bathroom and returned with two bath towels, tossing one to Dominic. They dried their faces and hair and made futile attempts at brushing the wetness from their clothing. Emmy turned on the gas fireplace. Dominic remained standing in front of it, dripping water into small puddles on the brick hearth, his clothes too wet to sit on the furniture. Emmy disappeared again. This time, she came back holding a short, pink terrycloth bathrobe decorated with small, embroidered red roses.

"Here, Dom. Get out of those wet clothes and see if you can get into this," she said, handing the robe to him. She again left, returning this time wearing a three-quarter length navy colored flannel robe, and continuing to dry her long, loose hair. When she saw Dominic in front of the fireplace in her too tight robe, holding his wet clothes uncertainly in front of him, a confused look on his face, she could not help but laugh.

"Where's my camera when I need it?" she said, trying unsuccessfully to stifle another laugh. Dominic just stood there, not quite sure what to do next, embarrassed by the appearance of his large frame barely wrapped in a too small woman's robe.

"Here. Give me your wet clothes," she ordered. He meekly complied. She took them into the bathroom and hung them over the shower rod. She noticed that he had even taken off his underwear, which was almost as wet as his outer clothing.

"I probably should go back to my apartment," he said weakly, after Emmy had come back to the living room for the third time.

"Like that? I have to agree you'd look cute walking barefoot down the hall in my pink robe, but can you imagine if anyone saw you, the rumors that would start? You coming out of my apartment, dressed only in a robe?" She was enjoying his obvious discomfort, and was unsuccessful in controlling her laughter.

"Easy for you to laugh. You sure look a lot better in your robe than I do in mine." He looked at himself in the wall mirror and couldn't help but laugh at his reflection. Their earlier tensions were forgotten.

Emmy suddenly realized both of them were wearing nothing under their robes. This created a strange, warm sensation in her. She thought perhaps this was a made to order opportunity for her to explain about the self-consciousness she felt about her body.

"Dom, do you remember that I said I would tell you today why I pushed your hand away last night?"

"Uh huh." Dominic was apprehensive about what she was going to say next and could not but worry that she was going to tell him she did not want to see him again.

"Well, there's no time like the present," she said bravely, pulling aside the robe to reveal the pale skin of her scarred leg contrasted against the darkness of the robe. "Now do you understand?"

"No," he said simply.

"Don't you see my leg?" she asked, somewhat frustrated by his lack of reaction.

"Uh huh. It's very nice. But what does that have to do with anything?"

"Do you see my scars?" she said.

"Where?" he asked.

"Right here!" she said impatiently, as she pointed to the two parallel lines on her mid thigh. Dom walked toward her. When he came within arms length, he leaned forward and undid her belt and peeled the robe from her shoulders, letting if fall silently to the floor. Then, he stepped back, looked at her, and exclaimed, "You're beautiful!"

He then attempted to remove the pink robe from around his still damp body, but had difficulty freeing his muscular arms from the tight sleeves. Even standing in front of Dominic in her nakedness, Emmy could not suppress a laugh at his efforts in trying to peel the garment from him. Finally, he succeeded. He put his arms around her waist, pulled her to him and kissed her lightly on the lips. Their naked bodies were pressed against each other. Holding her around the waist with one hand, he moved his other hand up her back, and under her unfettered hair. He kissed her again--longer. They both realized there was no turning back from this embrace. Dominic repeated, "You're beautiful!" Without a word, Emmy took his hand and led him into the bedroom. They made love silently, but urgently, unleashing a passion that had been pent up for too many years. This was the first truly meaningful lovemaking for both of them. This was what they each had yearned for, but which had eluded them their entire lives. Afterward, they fell asleep in each others arms--Dominic's face nestled in Emmy's hair, which smelled of outdoors freshness.

Dominic was the first to awaken. He raised himself on one elbow, and looked down at Emmy's sleeping face. "You're beautiful," he said, in a whisper. Emmy's eyes opened slightly. She was momentarily startled, seeing his smiling face and tousled hair above her. Lacking anything better to say, she said, "Good morning!" and stretched. Dominic slowly lifted the covers from Emmy's body and pulled them down to her feet, repeating "You're beautiful! What did I do to deserve someone like you?"

"You don't think I'm ugly?" she asked, somewhat embarrassed by his looking at her completely unclothed.

"There's nothing ugly about you. You're the loveliest woman I've ever seen."

"You're not so bad yourself," she said, putting her arms around his neck and raising her lips to his. "What about my scars? How can you stand looking at them?"

"What scars? You mean those two little lines on your leg? You can barely see them. I'd show you some real scars, except most of them are hidden by my hairy body." He gently kissed each of the two, faint parallel lines on her thigh. Her sensitivity about her scars ended at that moment.

They continued to lay next to each other, now totally relaxed and talkative. Emmy explained why she had not wanted Dominic to touch her scarred leg because she was so self conscious about it. Dominic, in turn, apologized for his lack of skill in lovemaking, explaining that he had only been with one other woman one time, during his entire life. Emmy thought to herself, that what he lacked in experience, he had more than made up for in enthusiasm. They exchanged intimate details about their earlier lives and the fateful events that had blown them in each others direction. Emmy told him about her short career as a dancer and her struggles to overcome the physical and emotional scars of her automobile accident. Dominic told Emmy about growing up in a poor New York neighborhood, his lack of formal education and how he became a stunt man because there was nothing else he could do or was suited for. They learned more about each other's pasts on this one morning than they had during the entire time they had known each other. It felt good to unburden the details of their lives to someone who sincerely cared about knowing them. The only thing Dominic did not tell Emmy was about the revolver he had bought and what his plans had been for it. He made a mental note to sell it back to the pawn shop the next day.

Two more people in the world had found each other and were experiencing the happiness that only those too long lonely could fully understand or appreciate.

Chapter 36

RESURRECTION AND REVELATION

A VEIL HAD BEEN lifted. Emmy and Dominic now saw each other, not in their previous image of who and what the other one was, but as they had come to be revealed to each other. They had settled into a mutual giving and accepting relationship. Emmy was happier than she thought she would ever again be. She was no longer sensitive about the scarring on her leg or her limp, which she had previously magnified in her mind, but which, generally, went unnoticed by others. Now, when weather permitted, she wore shorts in public. When she attended Aquacise classes, she wore a conventional one piece swimsuit instead of long pants. A member had complimented her on her figure and beautiful legs. Still another woman asked if she had been a model--as she seemed so poised and confident.

Dominic no longer harbored plans for self destruction. His 38 caliber revolver now lay in a glass cabinet of the pawn shop where he had purchased it, among several other similar objects. He had no desire to revisit thoughts of what he had once considered the purpose of his former "special friend." Now, he looked forward to each new day with anticipation instead of dread. He even spoke to other residents he passed with a cheery hello, freely exhibiting his toothy movie star smile, now framed by its well trimmed beard. He was happy. He had found a good woman, although he still could not understand what she saw in him. But, he did not question his good fortune in now having Emmy in his previously solitary and unhappy life. She had filled his emptiness. He even began attending Tai Chi classes with her, and became quite popular with the other members--being the only man. Although embarrassed at first, he came to enjoy the attention he received from others in the class. However, in his heart, Emmy was the only woman he wanted or needed. To please her, he had even traded in his Checker car for a newer and more comfortable and fashionable mid size Buick with only 54,000 miles on the odometer.

Emmy and Dominic had become regulars at the weekly community dances. They made a striking couple--Dominic, with his swarthy Italian complexion, dark eyes and distinguished gray black hair and beard--and Emmy, with her Scandinavian paleness, blonde hair and blue eyes. These physical differences gave other residents cause to sometimes refer to the pair lightheartedly as "the salt and pepper set."

Although now officially a couple, they continued to maintain separate residences. Having both come from conservative backgrounds, they did not feel comfortable flaunting their relationship. That, however, did not prevent them from occasional overnight visiting privileges in each others homes. By now, it was obvious to most residents of the Village who knew them or saw them together that they were more than merely friends.

Leaves were continuing to exhibit their rich fall colors, but autumn was beginning to act more and more like winter. Trips to Braxton Falls became less frequent, replaced by evenings in front of the fireplace, drinking hot chocolate and talking or watching television. They would cuddle on the couch, Dominic's arm around Emmy, her head nestled against his shoulder. The warmth of his body and the sound of his soft, even breathing gave Emmy a feeling of peace and contentment. Many nights they did not see the end of a program, having moved to the bedroom, occasionally without even bothering to turn off the set until much later. These were nights Dominic usually did not return to his quarters. These were nights when they did not get up the next morning for breakfast.

One Indian summer evening, Emmy and Dominic walked down the winding path to the lake to feed the Canada geese--which had made a brief stopover on their way to warmer climes. On the way back up the hill to their apartments, Dominic suggested they stop at the gazebo and rest a few minutes. This was unusual for him, as he seldom tired. After some small talk, he dropped to his knees in front of Emmy. Her first thought was that he was having another heart attack.

"Are you all right? You look paler than me," Emmy commented, her brow knit.

"I'm fine. I just want to ask you a favor--if that's OK." Emmy was puzzled. This behavior was not at all like him.

"What is it Dom?" she asked, concern in her voice.

"I was just wondering. Don't feel you have to. But it would mean a lot to me."

"Go on," Emmy said, fearful that something was wrong--with him, or with their relationship.

"I was just wondering," he repeated. "I was just wondering if you would do me the privilege of marrying me." Emmy was speechless. This was the last thing she expected to hear him say. Before she could speak, he reached into his pocket and removed a small, black box. Opening it and taking her hand, he placed a diamond ring on her finger. "Will you?" she thought she heard him say, his voice sounding far away. Tears began streaming down her cheeks.

"Of course, you silly man!" As he started to get up, Emmy threw her arms around his neck and pulled his face to hers, covering it with kisses.

"You will?" Dominic replied, as though a yes answer was too good to expect.

"I will!" she said, still holding him so tightly he had difficulty breathing.

"Thank you," he said, gasping for air, and not knowing what the proper response was to an answer of acceptance to a proposal of marriage.

"I'd be proud to be your wife, Dom," Emmy said.

"Me too," he said, somewhat flustered by her enthusiastic response to his proposal. "I mean, I'd be proud to be your husband," he clarified.

They continued to hold each other tightly, Dominic continuing to struggle to breathe. His face suddenly lit up in a smile, and he said, "This calls for a celebration. How about we go into town and have dinner at the most expensive restaurant we can find?"

"How about, instead, we go back to my place and I fix you a big spaghetti dinner?" Emmy countered.

"That's better yet," Dominic said with enthusiasm. The pair rapidly walked the rest of the way back up the pathway, arms around each other--the eyes of both of them now misty.

After dinner, Emmy said "We need to make some plans."

"OK," Dominic said. "Like what?"

"Like when and where."

"Oh, I hadn't thought about that."

"First things first, then. When do you want to get married?"

"Is tomorrow too soon?" Dominic asked, innocently.

"Probably," she said, smiling. "Next. Where do you want to get married, in a church or would you prefer a civil ceremony?"

"How about here?" Dominic replied.

"You mean in my apartment?"

"No. Here--in the Village. We could get a pastor, priest or rabbi--whatever you want--to marry us in the chapel." Then, as an afterthought, he said, "I never even thought to ask you what religion you were."

"I grew up Methodist," Emmy said. "But for too many years, I haven't been much of anything. How about you?"

"I was raised Catholic, but I can't remember the last time I went to Mass or Confession."

Emmy's eyes brightened. "Here's an idea. I don't know if we can do it but why don't we see if we can have an ecumenical ceremony--a priest and a minister?"

"That sounds good to me," Dominic agreed. "But, what will we raise our kids as?" Dominic occasionally surprised her with his dry wit, which usually showed itself when least expected.

"I don't think that's an issue, Dom," Emmy said, giving him a teasing, raised eyebrow look.

"Yeah. But, it's a nice thought," Dominic replied, grinning widely.

Then, looking down at her sparkling new ring, Emmy said, "You shouldn't have, Dom. This must have cost you a fortune."

"Nothing's too good for my lady," he replied. He would never tell her that the down payment was the money he received for selling his revolver back to the pawn shop owner.

"Your lady. I like that. And you're my gentle man." Emmy paused between the two words.

The next two weeks were busily occupied with wedding arrangements. They both agreed that, at their stage in life, there was no point in delaying any longer than necessary. Emmy made the arrangements. Dominic chauffeured her to town, where she found a St. Thomas parish priest and a Methodist minister who agreed to jointly officiate. Arrangements were made with the congratulating Village staff to reserve the chapel and order flowers.

Dominic asked Billy to be his best man. He agreed readily. Emmy called her sister Lorraine and Chris and to tell them the news. They were both surprised, but genuinely happy. They and her brother-in-law Philip would be attending. Billy was doubly pleased. He would get to see Chris again sooner than expected, and he was glad to finally see Dominic so happy and enthusiastic about something. He felt that Emmy had brought Dominic emotionally back to life and given him a reason to continue to live.

Chapter 37

THE BIG DAY

DOMINIC WAS NERVOUS. The suit he had bought for the wedding did not fit him properly. It was too tight across his broad shoulders-- and the shirt collar and tie felt confining around his neck. He had never had a real relationship with a woman before Emmy. The closest he had come to having a girlfriend was that awkward one time encounter with the bit player actress. And now, here he was, sixty years old and getting married for the first time, to a woman who, in his opinion, he was unworthy of. He had never been comfortable in the presence of large numbers of people. Now, he was going to be married in front of not only Emmy's family and his friend Billy, but surrounded by Village residents and staff members, most of whom he did not know and who did not recognize him, but were in attendance primarily for Emmy's benefit. On the movie set he had gotten used to dozens of people milling around during his stunts--from directors to script girls and all the in between cast and crew members. But, on the set he had usually been so focused on his stunt or his one or two lines of dialog that he did not even notice others being there until he had performed. Afterward, he would hurriedly retreat to the stunt performers' trailer, change clothes and quickly leave the studio, unnoticed. This, however, was real life, not a movie, and his only line did not need to be rehearsed or memorized. Nevertheless, he had practiced repeating "I do" over and over in front of a mirror. He was going to be a married man, something he never thought would happen to him. Since meeting Emmy, his life and attitude about living had changed in several ways, all for the better. His biggest fear about getting married was the possibility that Emmy would have last minute second thoughts and decide she did not want to marry him. He had failed to understand why a woman like her, who had everything, would want to spend the rest of her life with someone like him, who had nothing--not looks, charm, education, wealth, personality--or any of the other things women seem to admire in men. He was quick to admit that he was just a plain, ordinary man, nothing more, nothing less. He certainly was not anything special, that was for sure, he reckoned, examining himself closely in the mirror. He vowed that if Emmy did decide to go through with the wedding, he would spend the rest of his life making certain she never had any cause to regret her decision. He would dedicate his life to her and do everything he could to make her happy. Before Emmy, he lived more empty years than he cared to remember, years in which he felt he had nothing to live for. Now, since she had come into his life, he realized that he had everything to live for.

Dominic's thoughts were interrupted by organ music. He was standing stiffly at attention at the front of the chapel, a single bead of sweat running down the center of his back. Billy, his best man, stood reassuringly by his side. Next to Emmy was Chris, her maid of honor, a smile on her face and the possibility that at any moment she would burst into tears, which she fought valiantly not to let happen. Billy and Chris looked relaxed and at ease. But, then, why wouldn't they, Dominic thought. After all, they weren't getting married. Although, from the way they kept looking at each other, one had to wonder what was going through their minds at the moment.

While dressing and even during her short walk down the aisle, the occasion seemed surreal to Emmy. She had long ago given up any hope of marrying. Although an outgoing person by nature, she had lived alone and been lonely ever since her accident, after which she had considered herself a throwaway person. She felt it was a miracle that she had found such a good and caring man, whom she believed truly loved her. She promised herself that she would make him a good wife and do everything possible to make him happy--and keep him happy. To have a man like Dom come into her life was too good to believe. Although she had heard many times that there's someone for everyone, she had passed it off simply as a cliché--having given up on the possibility of it ever applying to her.

Dominic glanced over at Emmy to reassure himself that she was really there. He had not changed his mind about her from his first impression the day he helped her up from her fall. She was beautiful. Besides her outward beauty, she was beautiful inside--intelligent, thoughtful and caring.

Emmy was dressed in a simple, eggshell white dress. Her ponytail had been rearranged into a shorter, semi-pageboy hair style. Her blonde hair seemed to glow in the reflection of the chapel's lights. The pinkness of her cheeks dotted the otherwise porcelain paleness of her face.

The officiating clerics had agreed that Father Brighton would conduct the initial part of the ceremony--up to the exchanging of vows. At that point, Pastor Reynolds would finalize the ceremony. The wedding began with the priest saying, "Dearly Beloved, we are gathered here today in the sight of God and in the face of this company to join together this man and this woman in Holy matrimony, which is an honorable estate instituted of God, signifying unto us the mystical union that is between Christ and His Church."

Dominic could feel more rivulets of perspiration trickling down his back. The next words he heard were those of the minister, asking, "Do you, Dominic Xavier Graystone, take Mary Elizabeth Stratton to be your lawful wedded wife?"

Dominic heard himself reply, "I do!" in a loud and enthusiastic, yet somewhat hoarse voice.

The minister turned his gaze to Emmy and asked, "Do you Mary Elizabeth Stratton, take Dominic Xavier Graystone to be your lawful wedded husband?" Emmy, with her eyes moist, looked lovingly at Dominic and softly said "I do." Dominic audibly breathed a sigh of relief. He could feel the tension draining from his rigid body. Emmy had accepted him. They were actually being married. He was light headed and his legs felt as though they would not support him much longer.

"I now pronounce you husband and wife. You may now kiss the bride." However, the last three words were unnecessary, as Dominic and Emmy were already locked in an embrace, kissing.

They were married. It had not been a dream. Dominic felt numb with the realization that he had waited his whole life hoping to find someone like Emmy, but never expecting to. Now he had. He was happier at this moment than he could ever remembered being.

The reception following in the dining hall was filled with what appeared to be the entire Village community. Dominic bore up well, accepting congratulations from well wishers and firmly shaking the hands offered him. He and Emmy had their first dance together as husband and wife, gliding smoothly around the floor. Dominic still felt as though he would wake up in the morning and find it had all been just a dream.

It had been no dream. The morning after, Dominic awoke to see Emmy laying beside him, still asleep, her golden hair spread out across her pillow and partially covering the side of her face. He kissed her gently on the forehead, so as not to wake her. He lay there for several minutes, just looking at her, admiring her beauty and the innocence in her sleeping face. He marveled in the wonder that she was now his wife, "to have and to hold, in sickness and in health, until death do we part." Besides Emmy saying, "I do," that was the only part of the ceremony he could remember. What a heavy responsibility, he thought, and what a wonderful opportunity--to be able to spend the rest of his life with the woman he loved.

Chapter 38

NEWLYWEDS

THE DAY AFTER their wedding, Emmy and Dominic missed breakfast and lunch. However, they did manage to join Emmy's relatives and Billy for dinner in the dining room that evening. Emmy had requested there be no gifts. She was surprised to find two small packages and an envelope on the table when they arrived for dinner. Chris and Billy had given them matching wrist watches. Chris's comment when the newlyweds opened their gifts was that they probably needed them, since they had already failed to appear for two meals that day. Emmy blushed slightly. Dominic did not know how to react. The symbolism of the gifts had escaped him. Inside the envelope were a note and a check. The note said simply, "For tickets to Boston. Don't be strangers--love, Lorraine and Philip." Since Billy had planned to go to Boston over the holidays, the three of them could now make the trip together.

Chris's parents liked Billy from the time they first met him. Traditionally, fathers often take longer to warm to their daughter's boyfriends than do mothers. But, Billy and Chris's father chatted easily about the weather, the wedding, sports, politics, and life in general. When Chris had told her father that Billy was a maintenance man, Mr. Patric had pictured him in greasy overalls and a plaid shirt. He was pleasantly surprised at how clean cut Billy looked. In his wedding suit, and later in khaki trousers and golf shirt, he could easily have passed as a college student or young businessman. It did not take long for Chris's father to realize that Billy was a better match for his daughter than Brad, whom he had never liked, mainly because of his self centered and selfish ways. Mr. Patric had been relieved when Chris told him that she and Brad had ended their relationship. Although Billy barely had a high school education, he told Chris's father that he had begun taking night courses at the local junior college, and hoped to earn an associate degree in business management. Chris's mother was impressed with Billy on a different level--by his politeness, personality, warm smile--and his deep blue eyes.

The Patric's had planned to leave the day after the wedding, but decided to extend their trip another two days. They had comfortable lodgings in Braxton Falls and Chris had promised to take them on a tour of the town and the antique shops, for which Mrs. Patric had a weakness. Chris also had an ulterior motive. The longer her parents stayed, the more time she could have with Billy. Unknown to her, her parents were not unaware of this ploy. And, as Mrs. Patric had said to her husband, who had wanted to leave as originally scheduled, "Let the young people enjoy being young." Mr. Patric had learned early in their marriage that it was not wise to treat his wife's suggestions lightly. His decision to stay longer also was influenced considerably by Billy telling him that Braxton Falls had an excellent eighteen hole golf course. With a nearby golf course and a ready made partner, what more could a man on vacation ask for? This made for an ideal situation--the women could go antiquing, shopping and lunching while he and Billy played golf.

What with the wedding and socializing with the Patric's afterward, Billy and Chris were not able to spend any time alone together. The next day found the group in Braxton Falls. Mrs. Patric bought some "treasures" for their home, while Mr. Patric and Billy spent the day on the golf course. Chris's father won their match by five strokes. He was aware that Billy had intentionally missed some easy putts to allow him to win, but he said nothing about it. He accepted Billy's gift graciously and with silent appreciation. Billy's reasoning had been sound. It was not a good idea to outdo your possible future father-in-law during your first quality time together. Everyone had been satisfied with the day's activities and results, except possibly for the young couple, who were restlessly looking for an opportunity to spend some private time together. The group enjoyed dinner at Bernardi's, a restaurant well known locally for its scampi and lobster. After dinner and some conversation, the Patric's returned to their hotel room. Dominic drove Emmy, Billy and Chris back to the Village so they could continue their visiting.

After some refreshments and casual conversation, Emmy asked Billy if he would mind taking Chris back to her parent's hotel. It had been a long and busy day for the newlyweds and she and Dom were looking forward to an early bedtime.

"Sure. I'd be glad to," Billy replied enthusiastically. Emmy had a dual reason for her suggestion. She knew that Billy and her niece needed some time alone, plus she and Dom were emotionally and physically exhausted after the events of the past few days.

"We understand you newlyweds want to be alone," Chris said, winking at her aunt.

Emmy did not blush, but there was a hint of redness on Dominic's dark face. Good nights were exchanged and Billy and Chris left.

"Those are two good kids. I like that Billy. He always treated me like a real person," Dominic said.

Emmy gave him a wifely scowl. "You are a real person. You're my real person. Don't you ever forget it. I love you and I feel blessed to have you in my life."

"OK. Now can we go make love?" he asked playfully.

"Aren't you tired of that by now?" Emmy replied teasingly.

"With you as my wife, that's one thing I'll never get tired of."

"That's sweet," Emmy replied, understanding the underlying meaning of his words.

"Race you to the bedroom," she added quickly.

"Only if you give me a head start. After all, I'm older than you," he bargained.

After leaving the Graystone's apartment, Chris and Billy walked hand in hand down to the lake. The sun had been replaced by a ghostly first quarter moon, and the temperature was rapidly dropping. Winter was offering a fresh reminder of its not too distant arrival. They shortened their walk and headed back up the hill, briefly stopping at the gazebo for some hugging and kissing. Both were in short sleeve shirts and the wind was becoming uncomfortably cool.

"We need to get in out of the night air," Billy said.

"Your place or mine?" Chris asked.

"Let's make it mine," Billy replied. "It's closer, and, besides, your parents are in yours."

"Well, then. That's settled," Chris said.

The pair half-ran back to the warmth of the building complex and down to Billy's apartment. Once there, they warmed their bodies against each other. Soon, they had shed their clothing and were together under the covers in Billy's bed.

"Oh. I see you've got a new bed spread," Chris observed.

"Well, after our other time here, it seemed like a good idea."

"I like it. It's you."

"I like it too. It's even better with you sharing it with me."

Billy opened the drawer of the bedside table, taking out a length of six attached condoms.

"Aren't you being a little presumptuous?" Chris asked, grinning.

"I hope not," Billy replied.

"Do you think those will be enough?"

"You give me too much credit, young lady."

"I'll be the judge of that," she replied, laughing at their lighthearted exchange. After her previous scare, she was glad Billy was being so responsible and thoughtful.

Their lovemaking was slower and more relaxed, yet more fulfilling, than the last time they had shared a bed.

Afterward, they lay quietly in each others arms, savoring the memory of their oneness.

"I'm not cold any more," Chris said, finally.

"I hope not. You know how fragile the male ego is."

"I don't think I could ever be cold with you holding me like this."

"I'm glad. I feel the same way." He gently kissed her. Moving his face back from hers, Billy looked into Chris's eyes, shadowed by the light coming into the bedroom from the partially opened bathroom door.

"I love you," he said simply.

"I love you, too, Billy," Chris responded, her eyes beginning to moisten.

They held each other tightly, fearing that if one of them let go, the other would vanish. They would be separated all too soon as it was. They knew they needed to treasure each moment of their time together.

When Chris awoke, she looked at the bedside clock.

"Eleven fifteen! We need to go," she said, gently shaking Billy. These were words he was not prepared to hear.

They dressed hurriedly and shared a deep kiss that would have to last them until Boston.

At eleven thirty seven, Chris was knocking on her parent's hotel room door, Billy standing nervously beside her. They heard slow, plodding footsteps and a lock being turned. The door opened and Mrs. Patric's head appeared, her eyes half closed and her hair flat on one side.

"Hi mom," Chris said.

"What time is it?" Mrs. Patric asked sleepily, squinting into the light from the hallway.

"Later than it should be. We got so involved talking that the time just flew by. Sorry I woke you."

"I'll survive. Did you kids have a good time?"

Chris and Billy looked at each other, not quite certain of the best way to answer that question.

"Uh, yes. We visited with aunt Emmy and Dom for awhile, and then we walked down by the lake and gazebo, until it started getting colder. Then Billy went to his apartment and got me a jacket." That was the end of Chris's voluntary explanation. She hoped she would not be pressed for any further details. She did not like to lie. But, she would have liked even less to tell her mother how they had spent the evening.

"Well, you better come in and get to bed. We've got a busy day tomorrow. Be quiet. I think your father's still asleep."

This was unusual for her parents. In the past, whenever she would be out late, they would both wait up for her or lay in bed awake until she got home, routinely greeting her with, "How was your evening, Chris?" Chris thought that maybe the fresh country had had a tranquilizing effect on them plus the fact that, for the past three years she had lived on campus. Regardless, she was thankful no more explanations about her evening were required. She made a brief visit to the bathroom, changed into her night clothes and climbed into her mother's queen sized bed, thinking how it was not nearly as warm as Billy's.

Chapter 39

EPILOG

SEASONS COME AND go at Twilight Manor. The years pass quickly and quietly.

After their marriage, Dominic moved into Emmy's apartment. Monolith Pictures continues to pay his living expenses--giving the couple rent-free lodgings. Dominic has an occasional heart fibrillation, but nothing serious. Emmy watches over him like a mother hen. They continue to walk hand-in-hand the mile down to and around the lake most mornings before breakfast. Other residents still comment on how the two of them act more like honeymooners than a couple about to celebrate their fifth anniversary. Dominic still marvels at how fortunate he is to have Emmy as his mate--and he is not hesitant about mentioning it to her often. She never tires of hearing it. The one thing he has never mentioned is how, in his opinion, she had saved his life during his dark days. He continues to be a devoted and caring husband and Emmy treasures his love and gentle strength, and the wonder of having him to share her life. Having both spent most of their adult lives alone and lonely, with seemingly no prospect for change in the future, they still consider it a miracle that they found each other. Emmy once remarked to Dominic that he treated her like a princess. From that moment, Princess became his favorite name for her.

In view of their past physical problems, the pair has become more health conscious and exercise regularly in the fitness room, and play tennis whenever time and weather permit. Emmy's leg has become stronger and the fitting of a new corrective shoe gives her not only improved balance, but more self-confidence. Her limp is virtually non-existent. For their third anniversary, Dominic gave Emmy an upright piano, and she again became serious about music. She serves as the official pianist for the Village's chapel services and plays at most of the community's social events.

Dominic's long hidden desire was to write a movie script. When he mentioned this to Emmy, she encouraged him to do it. With a story line that had been simmering in his mind for years and Emmy's help with spelling, grammar and typing, he wrote a draft screen play for a semi-biographical action movie, "Streets of Doubt." When finished, he sent it to his old director, who, though retired, still had influential connections in the film industry. Several weeks later, to Dominic's surprise, he received a letter from Monolith studios offering to buy rights to the story--providing Dominic make some minor changes. Largely, because of his stunt performer career--which was more highly respected in the industry than he had realized--he was even offered a position as second unit assistant director for the project--which he readily accepted. The production company provided Dominic and Emmy a mobile home to live in while the film was being shot on location in Canada. Dominic even made a cameo appearance, as a villain of course, and got to reprise his favorite line, "You got me," followed by a slow, dramatic fall to the floor. As soon as production wrapped, the couple hurried back to the familiarity and comfort of Twilight Manor to resume their normal lives, and to once again enjoy being surrounded by their friends and neighbors.

As a result of the movie, Dominic has become somewhat of a local celebrity, even occasionally being asked for his autograph, to which he willingly obliges.

Pop retired and took as a full time job wooing, winning and wedding widow McGillicuddy, and moved into her house in town. Maybelle chooses to continue to work at the diner. She enjoys the banter and exchanging of gibes with the customers too much to give it up. And the tips are good, some weeks exceeding her salary. When Pop asks her when she plans to retire, her standard answer is "Next year--maybe." He has come to accept that "maybe" is the main part of her reply.

Pop does not actually consider himself retired. He claims to have a full time job just keeping the widow's house in repair and, in his words, "keeping Maybelle's boiler boiling." He continues to enjoy his Saturday nights out at Larry's Office Bar, where he now entertains a new generation of patrons with his tall tales and impresses them with his skill in dominoes. He no longer plays billiards, his explanation being that all that bending over the table aggravates his back. The real reason was his late-coming acceptance that he had never been, nor would he ever be, a winning pool player. Since Pop's marriage, he has scaled down to one beer during his Saturday night visits to Larry's and has adopted an earlier curfew--now that he has a wife to go home to. On the home front, he and Maybelle--both strong and vocal personalities--have periodic disagreements about various subjects, not the least of which is the color of her hair. He has told her that it reminds him of a bale of hay sitting on top of a pumpkin. Her response is that Pop is just jealous because he doesn't have enough hair to color. He seldom wins an argument and his ill timed and outspoken comments occasionally provide him an opportunity to spend a night on the parlor sofa.

On Occasion, while Maybelle is at work, Pop will venture back to the Village to visit with Billy and other staff members and residents, and check on his "babies," the boilers, to ensure they are receiving proper care and respect. Billy had been an apt student and keeps everything in the heating and cooling departments running smoothly. This fact has given Pop a sense of personal pride in his role of educating the young man.

When Pop retired, Billy inherited his title as Chief Building Engineer. The Kimmerman's hired two other maintenance workers to carry most of Billy's routine workload, to enable him to concentrate on tending the big silver boilers and continue attending evening classes at Pierpoint Junior College, where he would earn an associate degree in Business Management. The Kimmerman's, who provided Billy considerable tuition assistance, were in attendance when he graduated--with honors. Billy considers them his adopted parents. They had no children of their own and treat him more like a son than an employee. They even offered to finance his continuing education toward a bachelor's degree at a four year university, but Billy said he would rather remain at the Village. Since graduating, he has become the Village's operations manager. Recently, there's been a rumor circulating that he has been inquiring about admittance to Boston University.

The Kimmerman's moved to town, where they opened a real estate office. Mr. Kimmerman ran for and was elected Mayor of Braxton Falls, a position he still holds. Mrs. Kimmerman became active with the local school board and was later elected to its presidency, serving two terms.

Chris completed her master's degree program in psychology at Boston University and was accepted into their doctoral program. She has obtained a part time position in the school's clinical psychology laboratory, which helps finance her continuing education. She and Billy keep in touch by telephone and enjoy an occasional visit together during summers and holidays. Their future together is still not a certainty, although neither of them seems to be interested in dating others. There remains a strong bond between them and they appear satisfied to occupy themselves with their current relationship and with their continuing educational and career pursuits.

Bradley van Hooten flunked out of medical school during his first year. At last report, he was selling used cars in Trenton, New Jersey. He is still single.

Mrs. Murtenson passed quietly and peacefully on to that Great Library in the Sky. She was found with her favorite book of the moment open on her petite chest, its pages covering bits of broken potato chips.

Nathan and Sadie Schultz's toilet problems ended with the passing of Mr. Schultz at age ninety two. Mrs. Schultz continues to miss him and their toilet lid arguments.

Mrs. Barquette finally gave up in her attempts to find the perfect color for her apartment walls, and resignedly settled on the original Sahara Sand beige she started with.

Mrs. Leighton reluctantly accepted the fact that it was her, and not the oven, that was the major cause of her cooking problems. She just had no talent for the culinary arts.

Mrs. Murphy passed on prematurely at eighty five from the after-effects of a fall suffered when she tripped over a throw rug on her way to the bathroom. Her funeral was said to have been well attended.

Mildred O'Neill Mitchell, "Mom," recently turned ninety seven. She was given an early one hundred year birthday party—just in case. Her friends presented her a century plant with a hundred one dollar bills attached to its branches. She shows only minor signs of slowing down and still attends an occasional Tai Chi and Aquacise class.

Stray, the orphan cat, wandered away to the woods one spring day, never to return. Emmy cried for a week. Dominic consoled her as best he could.

An archaeologist from St. Louis University became interested in the history of the former convent and the mysterious disappearance of the members of its order. The Kimmerman's granted them permission to conduct limited digs on the grounds surrounding the building. During one such dig, the archaeological team uncovered, in a section of ground near the wooded area, twenty three unmarked graves containing badly deteriorated wooden coffins containing human remains. Religious relics were discovered in several of them. In another dig, a small group of grapevine roots were uncovered. Unfortunately, during renovation of the convent during its conversion to a retirement residence, many findings from the property may have been lost to a landfill. The history of the Order once it left its original site continues to be pursued--with no other significant success as yet. The only information verified about the building itself was that it had originally been constructed circa 1890. Subject to funding availability, there are tentative plans to remove a section of the earthen floor of the wine cellar to investigate the ground beneath it, and to do some limited digging and electronic sounding device testing in the courtyard area.

Otherwise, life at Twilight Manor continues on as usual, uninterrupted by outside influences. The occupancy waiting list continues to grow longer. With only rare exceptions, it seems as though the Village's residents just do not want to leave--and refuse to die.